WHO I BELIEVE

JAMEY MOODY

Who I Believe

©2022 by Jamey Moody

All rights reserved

Edited: Kat Jackson

This is a work of fiction. Names, characters, places, and incidents are the product of the author's imagination or are used fictitiously. Any resemblance to an actual person, living or dead, business establishments, events, or locales is entirely coincidental. This book, or part thereof, may not be reproduced in any form without permission.

Thank you for purchasing my book. I hope you enjoy the story.

If you'd like to stay updated on future releases, you can visit my website or sign up for my mailing list here: www.jameymoodyauthor.com.

I'd love to hear from you! Email me at jameymoodyauthor@gmail.com.

As an independent author, reviews are greatly appreciated.

❦ Created with Vellum

CONTENTS

Also by Jamey Moody	v
Chapter 1	1
Chapter 2	9
Chapter 3	16
Chapter 4	24
Chapter 5	32
Chapter 6	39
Chapter 7	46
Chapter 8	54
Chapter 9	62
Chapter 10	68
Chapter 11	76
Chapter 12	82
Chapter 13	90
Chapter 14	99
Chapter 15	106
Chapter 16	113
Chapter 17	120
Chapter 18	127
Chapter 19	134
Chapter 20	142
Chapter 21	149
Chapter 22	157
Chapter 23	165
Chapter 24	173
Chapter 25	181
Chapter 26	188
Chapter 27	195
Chapter 28	202
Chapter 29	211
Chapter 30	219

Chapter 31	227
Chapter 32	236
Chapter 33	245
Chapter 34	253
Chapter 35	259
Chapter 36	268
Chapter 37	276
Chapter 38	286
Chapter 39	296
Chapter 40	305
Twelve Years Later	313
About the Author	317
Also by Jamey Moody	319
Chapter 1	320
Chapter 2	328
Chapter 3	336

ALSO BY JAMEY MOODY

Live This Love

The Your Way Series:
*Finding Home
*Finding Family
*Finding Forever

The Lovers Landing Series
*Where Secrets Are Safe
*No More Secrets
*And The Truth Is ...
*Instead Of Happy

*It Takes A Miracle
One Little Yes
The Great Christmas Tree Mystery
Who I Believe

*Also available as an audiobook

Colossians 3:14
Love is more important than anything else.
It is what ties everything completely together.

1

"I could use a little help," Rebekah Taylor said to herself as she looked to the sky. Wondering what else could go wrong that morning, she sighed as she entered the school and hurried down the hall to her daughter's classroom. When she reached the doorway she stopped and looked inside. The teacher smiled and joined her in the hall.

"Are you Anna's mom?"

"Hi, yes. I'm Rebekah Taylor. I didn't get to meet you when I enrolled Anna last week."

"I met your mother then," the teacher said.

"Yes, that was my mother. I teach at the middle school and unfortunately couldn't be here for her first day."

"Yes, your mother explained. I'm Diane Cody. It's nice to meet you."

"Is Anna okay?"

"Yes, but she was a bit withdrawn today in class." Ms. Cody paused. "I know that she is dealing with a lot. There is a program that I thought might help."

"Oh, okay." Rebekah shifted from one foot to the other.

"It's an after school art program that has helped several of our students. They use art as a type of therapy. It's quite innovative and run by licensed counselors. It might be worth a try." Ms. Cody looked at Rebekah with compassion.

Rebekah looked past the teacher and could see Anna mindlessly moving a crayon over a paper on her desk. Tears stung the back of her eyes. She knew how much her daughter was hurting because she was too.

"Okay, Ms. Cody. What do I need to do to sign her up?" Rebekah gave the teacher a grateful smile.

"I'll take care of it. I'll send them the information in the morning, and they'll email you the details. They pick the kids up and take them to the studio after school. You can pick her up there. If you have any questions please don't hesitate to call me or them."

Rebekah nodded. "Thank you."

She walked into the room towards her daughter's desk. "Anna?"

"Mommy!" The little girl got up and walked into her mother's arms. Rebekah held her close and stroked her back.

"Let's go home, baby."

Rebekah picked up her backpack, took her hand and walked towards the door.

"Bye Ms. Cody," Anna said softly.

"Goodbye, Anna. I'll see you tomorrow." Ms. Cody nodded at Rebekah and smiled.

As they walked down the hall Rebekah asked, "Did you have a good day?"

"Am I in trouble?" Anna replied softly.

"No, honey. Why do you think you're in trouble?"

"Because the teacher called you to school."

Rebekah squeezed Anna's hand in reassurance. "She

wanted to tell me about an after-school program she thought you might like."

"What kind of program?"

"It's an art program. You love to color pictures for me."

Anna nodded and Rebekah could tell she was thinking about what she'd said.

"Why don't you try it tomorrow and if you don't like it then you don't have to go back," Rebekah said gently.

"Okay. As long as I don't have to talk to more doctors."

"No doctors," Rebekah assured her. "Would you like to go to the park and play for a while before we go home?"

"Not really. Can I watch *Barbie* on Netflix instead?"

Rebekah sighed. "You don't want to play? It's a beautiful day, honey."

"You like being outside, Mommy. I don't."

Rebekah unlocked her car and opened the back door for Anna. She watched her buckle her seat belt and said, "I'll make a deal with you. When we get home you can watch two episodes of *Barbie* while I pack. Then you have to walk around the block with me before dinner."

Anna eyed her mother and hesitated before speaking. "When are we moving out of Grandma and Grandpa's?"

"This weekend."

"Okay, two *Barbies* and a walk."

Rebekah smiled and closed the door. She went around and got in the driver's seat and turned to look at Anna. "You know, Grandma and Grandpa are really going to miss you."

"We're only moving down the street."

"Yes, but you brighten up their house. They'll miss you."

"I want to have my things in my own room again, Mommy."

"I know you do and you will."

"It won't be like my room at home though."

"No sweetie, it won't. But you like your room in our new house."

"I like my old room better."

Rebekah looked in the rearview mirror and saw Anna cross her arms over her chest and look down. She thought this move would help Anna and hoped to get her little girl back. Everyone kept telling her to be patient, but she missed the happy, carefree eight-year-old that Anna had been. Maybe this art program that Ms. Cody recommended would help.

She pulled into her parents' driveway and had to agree with Anna. It would be nice to have their own place again. She never dreamed that at thirty-one she would be living with her parents again, let alone with her daughter in tow.

Anna went in and walked straight back to Rebekah's room. She found the remote and turned on the TV.

"Hey, can't you say hello to your Grandma?" Rebekah said, following her into the room.

"Sorry." Anna walked back into the kitchen. "Hi Grandma." She gave the woman a hug and started back to Rebekah's room.

"Hold on, sweetheart," Helen Mathews said. "I made your favorite cookies today." She held out a plate loaded with cookies. Anna smiled at her grandmother and took one.

"You can have two," her grandmother bent down and whispered.

"Thanks Grandma." Anna took another and hurried back to watch TV.

Rebekah smiled at her mom. "Thanks Mom."

"We got a smile out of her. That was worth it."

"Her teacher has recommended her for an after-school

art therapy program. They pick the kids up and take them to the studio."

"I've heard about it. They seem to be doing good things for troubled kids."

"I don't know what else to do for her. This has got to work."

"She will come out of this. It hasn't been that long since her dad died. She's just sad. Kids always bounce back."

Rebekah looked at her mom and sighed. "She's not going to bounce back from this, Mom. Neither of us are." She reached down and picked up a cat that had been rubbing between her legs. "Come here, big guy." She nuzzled the cat and it began to purr.

"I know it's hard, honey. You did the right thing moving back here with us."

"At least I lucked into the position at the middle school. They don't usually need teachers in the middle of the semester."

"It's a blessing. The church and the community will embrace you both. You'll see."

"Hello family," Daniel Mathews exclaimed as he walked in the back door.

"Hi Dad." She put the cat back down and her father reached down to pet it on the head.

Helen walked over and kissed Daniel on the cheek. "How was your day, honey?"

"Blessed." He smiled. "Where's my favorite granddaughter?"

"She's in my room watching *Barbie*. I'm sure she'd love for you to watch with her," Rebekah teased.

He chuckled. "Is it a good idea to let her watch TV after school?"

"She's going for a walk with me after two short episodes."

Daniel nodded. "The church secretary wanted to put you both on the prayer list."

Rebekah bit her lip. "I'm not sure that's a good idea, Dad."

"I'm the pastor, honey. I approve the list before it's published in the newsletter or church bulletin. If you'd rather not be on it, I'll have you removed. But you might get comfort knowing our congregation is praying for you."

"Dad, I know you mean well, but you also know how I feel about God right now."

Daniel looked at her sternly and then his face softened. "God loves you, Rebekah, and so do we. I think I'll go check on *Barbie* and Anna."

"Tell her she has five more minutes."

He nodded and left the kitchen.

"Honey—"

"Mom, don't, please. I cannot handle a discussion about religion and God right now." She didn't wait for a reply. "When we get back from our walk I'll help with supper."

"Okay, honey."

Rebekah walked into her bedroom and found her dad sitting on her bed watching *Barbie* with Anna. She smiled and shook her head. "I wonder what your parishioners would think if they knew their pastor watched *Barbie*."

"They would think I'm a wonderful grandfather," he said, grinning at her.

Rebekah glanced at the TV and saw the credits begin to play. "It's time for our walk, Anna."

"Just one more?"

Rebekah narrowed her eyes.

"Okay. A deal is a deal," Anna said, getting up.

"Enjoy, girls. It's a beautiful day," Daniel said.

"Do you want to ride your scooter while I walk?"

"No, I'll walk with you," Anna said, taking her mom's hand.

They walked along in silence and Rebekah swung their arms.

Anna looked up at her and smiled. "Can you see our new house from here?"

"We might be able to see it when we get to the corner."

"Mommy, do you like your new school?"

Rebekah chose her words carefully. "So far, so good. I'm still learning my students and the teachers. How about you?"

"So far."

Rebekah chuckled.

"I like Ms. Cody. She's nice." Anna paused for a moment and then continued. "A couple of girls were talking about going camping with their dads. It made me miss Daddy. I never got to go camping with him."

Rebekah's heart dropped. "You know, your daddy didn't really like camping. Maybe you and I can go sometime."

"What if I don't like camping?"

"If you don't like it then we'll find something else to do."

Anna nodded and Rebekah could see she was thinking about something.

"Look," Rebekah pointed down the street they just crossed. "You can just see our house."

Anna looked and smiled. "I see it." She looked up at Rebekah. "Mommy, when we move can I get a dog?"

"Oh," Rebekah said as they began to walk again. "I'll have to see if the landlord will let us have pets. I'm not sure we can."

"What's a landlord?"

"We are just renting this house, honey. It's kind of like borrowing it, and the landlord is the person we're borrowing it from."

"But I still have a room, right?"

"Yes you do. It's our house, but since we don't own it there are some things we may not get to do, like have a dog. I'll find out, maybe we can."

"Can we turn around now?"

"Yes. We need to help Grandma with supper. I think she might be making mac and cheese especially for you."

"Yummy!"

Rebekah laughed. "Thank you for walking with me, Anna. I missed you today."

"Why?"

"Because I haven't gotten to see you. We had to hurry through breakfast and then we were both at school all day. You are my favorite person and I missed you."

"I am?"

"You are."

"You're my favorite person too, Mommy," she said, squeezing her hand.

The cracks in Rebekah's heart had scabbed over and left her numb. Anna's love was the only thing she actually felt anymore. Sometimes it made her sad and other times, like now, it soothed her.

2

"Baby, please don't do that."

"What did I do?"

"Very funny," Megan Neal said to her best friend.

Crystal laughed. "What has this little bundle of love done now?" She bent down and rubbed the wiggly little puppy.

"Oh nothing, she just chewed up another shoe this morning while I was in the shower. And now she likes to give little bites with her needle teeth when you try to pet her," Megan explained. She scooped the puppy up and cuddled her in her arms while she rubbed her belly. "That's my sweet little Wanda wonder."

"I know you named her after a superhero, so have you figured out her superpower yet?"

"I think it's chewing or general destruction," Megan said, rubbing her belly again. She put her down and the puppy ran from one end of the room to the other.

"Her superpower is cuteness. Just look at her go!" They both laughed.

"We have a new student coming in with the after school group," Crystal commented as she watched the puppy.

"I saw that. We have her parental consent form and I'll set up the prelim session with her mother when she picks her up today. I know she's a single mom, but I don't know the circumstances. Diane didn't elaborate in her email."

"Okay. If you'll set up the easels and supplies for today's session I'll go get the kids."

"I'll be glad to so I can keep an eye on this little terror," Megan said as Wanda curled into a ball and settled on a blanket next to Megan's feet.

"Aww, she's not so terrible right now."

Megan chuckled. "And she's out. Thanks for agreeing to let me bring her to work. I think she'll help the kids as much as art does."

"Whatever it takes, right?"

Megan sighed. "I'm so glad we did this. I loved being a school counselor, but I feel like we're doing so much more here."

"We are as far as the kids that we get. I know how overwhelmed the school counselors are. I wish we could come up with a way to make sure none fall through the cracks."

Megan nodded and looked down at her puppy.

"Okay, I'm off. See you shortly with our Van Goghs."

Their therapy center was a large, open, inviting room. The area to the right of the front door was for group therapy sessions. There were bean bag chairs and comfy couches where the kids could relax. To the left was an area with small tables where games could be played or sometimes the kids did their homework. In the back right area, long tables were set up. Today they had easels on them because the kids were going to paint. Sometimes they did other art projects with different mediums.

In the back left corner of the room Megan and Crystal both had offices for private sessions. There was also a little kitchen area where they had snacks and drinks for their clients and their parents.

Megan planned to keep Wanda in her office with a baby gate across the door so the puppy could see her, but not disturb the kids while they painted. She set canvases on the easels and made sure each station had brushes and paints for today's project.

It had been twelve years since Crystal convinced her to move from her native California to Georgia. They were college roommates and Megan had stayed in California and began her counseling career while Crystal went to Georgia. When she left, she told Megan it was time for them to be brave and adventurous. Megan thought she was crazy and would be back within a year.

To her surprise Crystal thrived and it took her eight more years to persuade Megan she would love Georgia too. So under the premise that she would come for the summer and see what Crystal was raving on about, at thirty-one she moved to Georgia. Twelve years later they now had their own therapy practice and were still best friends.

Megan put Wanda in her office and placed the baby gate in the doorway. She gave her a treat and looked up as she heard the door open.

Six elementary school kids came through the door and she waved at them. "Back here. We're painting today."

"Hi Megan, hi Megan, hi," the kids greeted her and each took their place behind an easel. One little girl trailed behind the others and she looked at Megan guardedly.

"Hi. You must be Anna. I'm Megan." She beamed at the little girl. "We are so happy you joined us today. I have an easel right here for you. Have you ever painted before?"

"I did a class with my Mommy one time. We painted snowmen."

"That sounds like fun. Did you like it?"

Anna nodded.

"Oh good. Let's get an apron on you and we'll get started," Megan said. She tied the strings in the back while Crystal went to the front of the table and started the class.

Megan went around and talked to the kids as they painted. They were working with colors today. They wanted the students to paint what they were feeling inside. Some painted in circles, others painted lines, and some did swirls or shapes.

Crystal instructed them to paint what they felt inside when they were happy, when they did a kind deed, when someone did something nice for them; then when they were afraid, when they were ashamed, when they were hurt; and finally when they were sad.

The colors varied from bright to dark as was expected. But when Megan stopped behind Anna's painting she noticed most of the colors were the same. There was nothing dark or bright; the colors were subdued in between.

"Which color is your happy color, Anna?" Megan asked.

"This one," Anna said, pointing to a medium blue.

"I love that color. Is it your favorite?"

Anna tilted her head, gazing at the canvas. "I guess. Blue is my mommy's favorite color."

"Which color is your sad color?"

Anna pointed to another shade of blue that was nearly the same as the happy blue.

Megan noted the lack of change in her color choices, but didn't question her because she didn't know why Diane had recommended her for the program. She didn't want to cause Anna any added anxiety. After she completed her session with Anna's mother, she and Crystal would be able to come up with a plan to help her.

The class was almost over when Wanda, trying to get Megan's attention, barked quietly from the office. The puppy had napped through most of the class.

"What was that?" Anna asked, looking in the direction from where the bark had come.

"That's my new puppy, Wanda."

"Can I meet her?" Anna asked excitedly.

That was more emotion than the little girl had shown since coming into the therapy center.

"Sure."

They walked over to Megan's office and Wanda began to wiggle her tail and whine.

"She's so cute!" Anna exclaimed as she bent down to pet her through the doggie gate.

Megan let her pet the puppy as she licked at her through the holes.

"Anna, would you do something for me?"

The little girl looked up at her briefly and nodded, but continued to touch the puppy.

"Come over here and paint what color you're feeling inside right now with Wanda licking your fingers."

"Can I come back and play with her?"

Megan nodded.

Anna got up and went back to her canvas and began to paint again. Megan noticed she had a small smile on her face as she painted the strokes of a lighter blue next to the other shades of blue. It was as if she had painted a vertical rainbow using shades of blue.

"I think I like that blue better than the others. How about you?"

Anna stopped and looked at Megan and smiled. "I do too."

Neither of them noticed that Rebekah had walked up and had been watching them.

"Meg?" she said, shocked.

"Hi Mommy," Anna said, turning around. "Look what I painted."

Megan turned around when she heard her name and looked into clear blue eyes that immediately made her heart race. She couldn't believe it. Those eyes were unforgettable and ones she thought she'd never see again. Then she saw the light auburn hair that framed the face she often saw in her dreams.

"Rebekah," she said, obviously just as surprised. Megan couldn't stop the smile that grew on her face.

Rebekah returned her smile and then shook her head. "What..."

"I..." Megan stammered.

"Mommy, are you okay?" Anna said.

They both shook themselves out of the daze.

"Hey baby," Rebekah said, tearing her eyes away from Megan. "That's beautiful."

"It's your favorite colors," Anna said proudly.

"It is."

"This is wild," Megan said softly. "I'm Anna's—"

"Teacher," Rebekah interrupted and widened her eyes.

Megan nodded. "Yes," she said slowly.

Rebekah leaned in and said softly, "I try not to use doctor or counselor around her. She's been to several."

Megan nodded her understanding. "Anna has created a beautiful painting that you are welcome to take home."

"Megan, can I go play with Wanda now?" Anna asked her with a wide grin.

"Yes, go ahead. I'm going to visit with your mom."

"Okay," Anna said, quickly going back to Megan's office.

When she was gone Rebekah turned to Megan. "You're her counselor?"

"I am." Megan looked into Rebekah's eyes and her heart pounded once again.

"I don't know where to start..."

Megan nodded. "I hoped to have a visit with Anna's mother after class to do what we call a preliminary session. We need to get background information and then come up with a plan going forward."

Rebekah nodded. "Okay, just one question first. Who is Wanda?"

3

Megan chuckled. "Come with me and I'll introduce you."

Rebekah followed Megan to her office and they found Anna sitting in front of the doggie gate playing with the puppy.

"This is Wanda," she said to Rebekah. "Anna, let's take the gate down. She can come out now that class is over." Megan slid the gate to the side and Wanda began jumping on Megan's legs, then she ran out of the office and back to lick Anna's face.

The little girl giggled then laughed when Wanda ran around the room.

Rebekah watched Anna chase behind the puppy. The room was empty of other children, allowing Anna and the puppy plenty of space.

Crystal walked up and smiled at Rebekah. "I see you've met our newest addition."

"This is Anna's mother, Rebekah..." Megan started.

"Taylor," Rebekah said, smiling at Megan.

"Crystal and I are the counselors. We both work with the students. Let me show you around," Megan said.

She gave Rebekah a quick tour as Anna played with Wanda.

"Do you have time to chat about Anna now?" Megan asked.

"Sure," Rebekah replied.

"Oh good. Hey Anna, I need to chat with your mom about the program. Would it be okay with you if we go to the park right behind our building? You could help me out by walking Wanda while we talk."

"I'd love to walk her," Anna said, her excitement obvious.

"Would that be okay?" Megan asked Rebekah.

"Lead the way." Rebekah could feel butterflies in her stomach and quickly took a deep breath to chase them away.

"I'll lock the front door and leave you to it. See you tomorrow. It was nice meeting you, Rebekah." Crystal gave Megan a confused look, but didn't say anything.

"You too."

Megan got the puppy's leash and put it on her and they went out the back door, walking the short distance to the park.

"Wanda is an unusual name for a dog," Rebekah commented, her tone light and teasing. "Is there a story?"

"She is named after Wanda Maximoff," Megan began.

"She's the Scarlet Witch in the comics," Anna said.

"That's right. She has a shield that protects her and the ones she loves."

"She can also change things in time," Anna added.

"I think she changes time for me because most of the time she makes me happy," Megan said.

"Most of the time?" Rebekah asked.

"I was not very happy this morning when I found a hole in one of my favorite shoes," Megan replied. "That's the third pair she's destroyed."

Anna laughed.

"We're going to sit on this bench," Megan told her. "You can take Wanda around this path in front of us. It goes in a circle and will lead you back here. We'll be able to see you the whole time. Okay?"

Anna looked to where Megan pointed and nodded. "Okay. Don't worry, I'll take good care of her."

"I know you will." Megan smiled at her.

"She asked me just yesterday if she could have a dog," Rebekah said as they sat down.

"She can play with Wanda anytime."

Rebekah met Megan's eyes and for a moment they simply looked at each other.

"I can't believe it's you. It's been, what, twelve years?" Rebekah remembered those warm brown eyes and Megan's chocolate brown hair like it was yesterday.

"It has. I came here twelve years ago this summer," Megan said.

Rebekah continued to look at Megan and finally sighed. "What do you need to know about Anna? Let's start there."

"Okay. Uh, well, she obviously has something going on."

"When she laughed at Wanda outside your office I almost cried. She hasn't sounded that happy and carefree since her dad died," Rebekah began.

"What happened?"

"We lived in Miami."

Megan looked down and smiled. "So that's why I haven't seen you since that summer."

"You weren't sure if you were staying, remember?"

"I stayed," Megan said, meeting her eyes.

Rebekah nodded. "Ben had a car wreck and didn't make it. There's no elaborate story. It was an accident. He and Anna were inseparable. His death has been really hard on her. We have been to several different doctors and counselors. That's why I hesitated when you were about to tell me you were her counselor. I watched you with her for several minutes and could see that she likes you. I didn't want to thwart your efforts simply by using the word counselor."

"I get that. I'm sorry, Bekah. That has to be hard for you, too."

Rebekah looked up when she heard Megan shorten her name. She smiled as a sweet flashback ran through her head. "The accident happened last summer and Anna hasn't gotten any better. I decided that maybe moving home would help. She loves my parents and she's their only grandchild."

"I remember you didn't have any brothers or sisters," Megan said softly.

"There just happened to be an opening at the middle school. My father would say I was blessed, but I call it lucky. I hurriedly packed us up and moved home."

"I'll do everything I can to help your little girl, Bekah," Megan promised.

Maybe her dad was right. Megan Neal might just be a blessing after all.

"Have you been back here long?" Megan asked.

"No. We both started school last week."

"Does she have trouble sleeping?"

"Sometimes she wakes up at night and she looks so sad. She doesn't cry, but I can tell she misses Ben."

"Has she had any problems at school?"

"No. She withdrew into herself yesterday and that's when Ms. Cody suggested your program."

"We asked the kids to paint different emotions today and you noticed that Anna's painting was all different shades of blue. The brightest color she painted was right after she met Wanda. I think she's having trouble feeling anything."

Rebekah nodded. "That sounds right. After school yesterday I wanted us to go to the park and play before we went home, but she didn't want to. Look at her now."

Both women looked over at Anna and laughed as she talked to Wanda. There was energy in her steps, a lightness Rebekah hadn't seen in what felt like a very long time.

"Does she talk about her dad?"

"Not really. I don't *not* talk about him. She did mention that two girls in her class were talking about going camping with their dads. She feels like she missed out. We've never been camping, but I told her we'd give it a try."

Megan nodded as Anna and Wanda came closer.

"Is Crystal your friend that talked you into coming to Georgia?"

Megan looked over at her surprised. "You remember that?"

"I remember you were here teaching at the college for your friend. She wanted you to stay, but you weren't sure."

"I was teaching a summer class for counselors. She spent that summer in Europe and when she came back I decided to stay."

"What made you stay?"

Megan looked at Rebekah and those brown eyes looked right into her soul. She could feel her cheeks reddening.

"We're back!" Anna exclaimed, ending the moment.

"There's my sweet girl. Did you have fun with Anna?" Megan asked, scooping the puppy into her lap.

"What kind of dog is she?" Anna asked.

"She's a pound puppy. I got her at the shelter. I'm not sure what she is. I think she has some Pomeranian or Chow Chow in her because she is so fluffy. But mostly she's full of love. Don't you think so?" Megan grinned at Anna.

"Yes. Maybe she can come over and play with me. Mommy, do we have a fence at our new house? If we can't get a dog, maybe Wanda can come visit."

"Uh, we do have a fence," Rebekah answered.

"We're moving this weekend. I get to have my own room again," Anna said, petting the puppy's head while Megan held her.

"That's nice." She looked at Rebekah. "You're moving? Do you need help?"

"No, but thank you. There's a house for rent not too far from my folks. We're moving Saturday."

Megan nodded. "Did you have fun today, Anna?"

Anna smiled at her and nodded.

"Would you like to come do art with us again next week?"

"Can I?"

"You sure can. I know Wanda would love to see you again."

"Is it okay, Mommy?"

Rebekah nodded. "We'd better go honey. I'm sure Megan has things to do."

They started to walk back to the therapy center. Megan handed Anna the leash and she and Wanda ran along in front of them.

"Thank you," Rebekah said softly. "This is the happiest I've seen her in—I don't know how long."

"I don't think it's me. I think it's Wanda. I'm glad she could give her a little happiness today."

They walked back inside the counseling center and Megan said, "Why don't you let me keep your painting until next week? That way it will be dry and you can put it in your new house."

"That would be nice. One less thing to move." Rebekah chuckled.

"Okay," Anna agreed.

"Anna, can I take your picture with Wanda?"

Anna nodded eagerly. Megan took her phone out of her pocket and snapped a couple of pictures.

"I'll send this to your Mom's phone and when you look at it you'll be light blue inside."

Anna giggled.

"Is that your way to get my phone number?" Rebekah teased.

Megan scoffed. "It's on your consent form."

Rebekah laughed and held out her hand for Megan's phone. She handed it to her and Rebekah entered her number.

Megan grinned and sent the picture to Rebekah's phone.

Her phone pinged with the incoming text and Anna jumped up to see.

"There you go," said Megan.

Anna smiled at the photo and nodded. "Thank you, Megan."

"You're welcome." She walked them to the front door and unlocked it.

"Let us know if you have any questions," Megan said, opening the door.

"Thanks again."

Megan nodded. "Bye Anna."

"Bye Megan."

"It was really nice to see you again." Rebekah said, lingering in the doorway for a moment.

"Maybe it's my lucky day," Megan said, looking warmly into Rebekah's eyes.

"Maybe."

4

On the way home Rebekah looked into the rearview mirror and could see Anna smiling as she looked out the window.

"Did you have fun at art today?"

"Uh-huh."

"Do you want to go back again next week?"

"Can I?"

"You sure can. I thought your painting was beautiful."

"Thank you."

"Megan and Crystal are really nice, aren't they?"

"I like them."

"You know who liked you?" Rebekah asked her.

"Megan?"

"Yes, I'm sure Megan liked you, but I think Wanda liked you very much."

Anna giggled. "I think so too. She's so cute. Her name needs to be Wanda Wiggly. You should see her when she gets excited, Mommy. She wiggles her little butt."

Rebekah chuckled. "She does?"

"Yes, it's so cute."

"Maybe you can play with her again next week."

"I hope so."

Rebekah pulled into her parents' driveway and they went inside.

"Hi girls," Helen said. "How was your art class, Anna?"

"It was fun, Grandma. I made a painting of my feelings. I get to bring it home next time I go."

"I can't wait to see it."

"Then Megan let me play with her puppy. Her name is Wanda."

"Megan?" Helen asked.

"Megan and Crystal are her instructors. Wanda is Megan's puppy. She let Anna play with her after class," Rebekah explained.

"And then she let me walk her at the park!" Anna exclaimed.

Helen looked at Rebekah, seeming confused.

"Honey, why don't you go wash your hands and then you can tell Grandma all about it."

When Anna left the room Rebekah said, "The counselors needed to know Anna's background. We went to the park outside the therapy center so we could talk. She walked the puppy while I explained the situation to Megan. Mom, you should've seen her. She laughed and giggled and really smiled. I haven't seen her that happy in such a long time."

"That's wonderful. Maybe this is what she needed."

"Oh, I hope so."

"You're getting a dog?" Daniel asked, walking into the kitchen.

Rebekah shook her head. "Did Anna tell you that?"

"She said she played with a puppy today and she might get a dog when you move."

"I told her I didn't know if we could have pets. She played with a puppy at art therapy today," Rebekah explained.

"She was very excited," Daniel said.

"I was just telling Mom that I haven't seen her that happy in a very long time."

"That's wonderful news. It's what we've all been praying for," he commented.

Rebekah helped Helen finish making dinner and Anna told them all about her painting. She talked about how nice Megan was and how much she liked playing with Wanda.

Later that evening after a bath, Rebekah read to Anna until she fell asleep. She got ready for bed and couldn't stop thinking about Megan Neal.

She couldn't believe her eyes when she walked into the therapy center and saw Megan working with Anna. Even after twelve years she would've known Megan anywhere.

She remembered those soft brown eyes and when Megan looked at her it felt like she saw into her soul. Sometimes she had to look away for fear of falling and losing herself completely. She closed her eyes and could feel Megan's silky dark brown hair gliding between her fingers.

Rebekah abruptly sat up and opened her eyes. *What are you doing?* That was a long time ago. They had both lived another life since then. The important thing right now was Anna. Megan just happened to be her counselor. A very good counselor because she had already reached Anna and made a difference.

She lay back against her pillows and sighed. Over the years she had thought about Megan from time to time and wondered what she was doing. How ironic that she was right here the whole time.

* * *

Megan rolled over and moaned. She opened her eyes and that's when she realized she'd been having a vivid dream starring Rebekah. "Oh, God." She sighed. Bekah Mathews or now Bekah Taylor had been in her thoughts since she'd left the counseling center.

She couldn't believe it when she heard Rebekah say her name. It was as if she was dreaming. When she turned and saw those striking blue eyes she couldn't think for a moment. It was like they had been whisked back in time and Rebekah was meeting her as she'd done so many times.

She still considered that the best summer of her life. Crystal had been in Athens since they'd finished their masters degrees, and she'd wanted Megan to move there and open a counseling center. After being a school counselor for eight years, Megan had finally agreed to come spend the summer with Crystal. They planned to co-teach a graduate counseling class at the university. At the last minute Crystal got the opportunity to spend most of the summer in Europe, leaving Megan to teach the class, living in Crystal's apartment and knowing no one in Athens.

Then she'd met Rebekah. She was young and beautiful and intense. They had many conversations of religion, truth, and loyalty. Then there were times they debated movies and TV shows. Megan smiled, remembering how passionate Rebekah could be about favorite characters and shows.

"Rebekah Mathews Taylor," she said aloud. "And sweet aggrieved little Anna." Megan once heard someone say that grief was love with no place to go. She believed that was what Anna suffered. Her dad was still very loved, but she couldn't express it because he was no longer here.

As happy as she was to see Rebekah again, Anna had to be her focus right now. She knew she could help the little girl and that's exactly what she planned to do.

But that didn't mean she couldn't relive some very happy memories of her and Bekah tonight. Then she would put them back in her heart where they'd lived all this time.

Over the years she'd wondered about Bekah and hoped she was happy and living a good life somewhere, even though she'd wished it was with her. She sighed, rolled over and tried to go back to sleep.

* * *

When she got to her office the next morning Crystal was already there.

"Hey," she said with concern in her voice. "Bad night?"

Megan yawned. "Sorry, I didn't sleep well last night."

"Is everything all right?"

"Sure. Why wouldn't it be?" Megan said, putting her bag down.

"No reason." Crystal chuckled. "Defensive much?"

Megan looked up at her best friend and smiled. "I don't mean to be."

"So tell me about Rebekah Taylor."

"She's Anna's mom and told me a little about her yesterday afternoon."

"I know *who* she is, Megan. Who is she to *you*? It was obvious that you two knew one another."

Megan sighed. She looked at Crystal, trying to determine how much to tell her and then she decided honesty was the best way to go.

"Do you remember the summer you finally talked me into coming to Georgia and then abandoned me for Europe?"

"Abandoned is a harsh way of putting it. That was a great opportunity. You would've jumped at the chance too. If you hadn't been here I wouldn't have been able to go. I thought I had paid you back all these years."

Megan narrowed her eyes. "I'm not sure you have yet."

Crystal scoffed. "What does that have to do with Rebekah Taylor?"

"I met her that summer."

Crystal studied Megan for a few moments. Megan could tell she was thinking back in time and then she seemed to remember.

"Oh my God, Megan! Is she the woman you spent the summer with? The one that left and took your heart with her?"

"That's a little much, don't you think?"

"Not at all! I remember you moping around here for months. I don't think you even went on a date for a couple of years. Then you finally met Emily."

Megan leaned back in her chair, letting the comment about Emily go for now. "I can't tell you how surprised I was to see her."

"I'm sure! So, what now?"

"Anna, her little girl. That's what's important."

Crystal nodded. "I get that, but maybe it's a second chance for the two of you."

"I haven't heard from her in twelve years, Crystal. I don't think she's interested in second chances."

"You don't know that."

"Can we concentrate on Anna, please?" Megan told Crystal about Anna's father and that they had recently moved back to Athens. They discussed what they had observed in art therapy with Anna yesterday and created a plan going forward.

By the end of the day Megan was glad it was Friday because she had run out of energy. When she got home she took Wanda into the back yard and played with her for a while. She had taken her for a walk at the park during lunch and that would have to be enough for today.

Later that night she was half asleep on the couch when her phone pinged. It was a text from Rebekah along with a picture of Anna. She was waving and smiling into the camera.

Anna wanted to tell Wanda goodnight.

Megan chuckled. That smile went straight to her heart. She wanted so much to ease the hurt Anna felt inside.

Wanda was curled up at her side, asleep. If Megan got up to take her picture she knew she'd wake up and move. So she stretched out her hand and grinned, taking a selfie of her and the sleeping puppy.

Wanda is happily asleep, but missed Anna playing with her today. Did she have a good day at school?

Megan often texted with parents to check in on their clients during the week, but Anna was already special to her.

She did; no problems. Have a nice weekend.

Megan remembered they were moving and quickly texted back.

Hope your move goes well. Are you sure I can't help?

Megan could see the ellipses as Rebekah texted back.

That's so sweet of you to offer, but I have help. Sleep well.

Megan scoffed and said aloud, "I might sleep well if I could keep from dreaming of you."

Thanks, sweet dreams.

Megan looked at the picture of Anna and then pulled the one up she took yesterday of Anna, Wanda and Rebekah. She sighed and a smile played at the corners of her mouth. "Oh Wanda, wouldn't it be nice..."

5

"Honey, I've got to sit down for a minute," Rebekah said, plopping down on the couch.

"But we still have to put my bed up and hook up the TV, Mommy!"

"Come sit beside me for just a minute," she said, patting the couch next to her.

Anna sat down next to her mom and Rebekah took her hand.

"Look around this room," she said. Anna did as she asked and surveyed the room.

"I think it will be fine, don't you? We still have lots of boxes to unpack, but I think the couch, chair and TV look just right like this."

"Me too." Anna nodded. "I like my little area to read in the corner."

"It will look even better when we get your books in the bookshelf."

"Who's that?" Anna said, looking out the window. "It's Megan!" She jumped up and ran out the front door. "Megan!" she exclaimed, hugging her around the waist.

"Hi Anna." Megan grinned at the warm welcome. "Careful. I brought you and your mom dinner." Megan balanced two pizza boxes and had a bag over her shoulder.

"Hey!" Rebekah smiled from the front porch. "What in the world?" Megan Neal had always been thoughtful and Rebekah could see that hadn't changed.

"I thought you might be too tired to worry with dinner after moving all day." Megan shrugged, giving Rebekah one of her best smiles.

Rebekah remembered that sexy little dimple on Megan's left cheek. There it was in that smile she'd always felt was only for her. How quickly those memories had come back.

"That is so nice of you. Come in," she said, holding the door for her.

Megan stopped and smiled at Rebekah before going inside. "I hope it's okay."

"Get in here. Can't you tell we're hungry and happy to see you?"

Megan walked in with Anna right behind her.

"Sorry, but everything is a mess," Rebekah said, clearing a spot on the dining room table that was at the back of the living room.

"Of course it's going to be a mess." Megan laughed. "Anna, are you hungry?"

Anna nodded. "Where's Wanda?"

Megan chuckled. "She's at home. I didn't want her to be in the way." She looked up at Rebekah and continued. "I'm just dropping this off and then I'll get out of your way."

"Don't go! You haven't seen my room yet," Anna protested.

Megan looked at Rebekah.

"Please stay," she said softly.

Megan nodded then turned to Anna. "I even brought

paper plates in case you couldn't find your dishes." She began to unpack the bag and inside were napkins, paper plates, and several bottles of water.

Rebekah chuckled. "You thought of everything. I'm not surprised."

She put a piece of pizza on a plate for Anna and handed it to her. "You can sit in the living room, honey, but be careful."

Anna carefully carried her plate to the couch and sat down.

Megan handed Rebekah a plate. "Aren't you eating?"

"No, I brought this for you and Anna."

"Come on. You can have one piece."

They filled their plates and went to sit by Anna.

"I see you didn't forget my favorite kind of pizza," Rebekah said, taking a bite of the pepperoni and pineapple slice.

"How could I? You drilled it into my head." Megan chuckled.

Rebekah looked at her and she could see the same Megan from twelve years ago. There may be a wrinkle or two around her eyes, but she was still the smart, beautiful woman that captivated her heart so long ago.

"Do you like your new house, Anna?"

She nodded. "I'll like it better when the TV works and I can watch *Barbie*."

Megan laughed. "Maybe I can help. Is your internet working?"

Rebekah nodded as she chewed. After she swallowed she pointed to the bookshelf in the corner. "The router is there with the password on the back. I have YouTube TV. Do you know how to set it up?"

"I do. Where's the remote?"

Rebekah grabbed it from the end table next to the couch and handed it to her.

Megan went to work and had the TV going in a matter of minutes.

"Look at you!" Rebekah said, impressed.

"I'm here to help."

"Come see my room!" Anna exclaimed.

Rebekah watched as Megan followed Anna into the small room. The mattress to her bed was leaning against the wall along with the bed frame. In the corner was a small desk and chair. There was also a toy box and several boxes of unpacked toys.

"Wow, you have some cool stuff, Anna," Megan said, looking at her toys.

"We're going to set my bed up," Anna said.

"Mommy sure is tired, Anna. You may have to sleep with me tonight," Rebekah said from the doorway.

Megan looked around then said, "You know, Anna, you could lay your mattress on the floor and sleep there. It would be kind of like camping."

Anna's eyes lit up. "It would! Have you ever been camping? I never have."

"I've gone a few times. Maybe we could go sometime." Megan looked at Rebekah with her eyebrows raised.

Rebekah knew Megan was trying to make Anna feel better. "Maybe."

Megan laid the mattress on the floor. "What do you think?"

"Can I, Mommy? I like it!"

"Let me see if I can find your sheets or a sleeping bag." Rebekah left and came back with a *Barbie* sleeping bag. She spread it out on the bed and Anna jumped in the middle of it.

"Thank you, Mommy."

"You're welcome." She chuckled. "Megan, would you like to see the rest of the house?"

"Sure."

"It's just a two bedroom, one bath. But that's all we need right now."

They walked through the house and ended up in the kitchen. Rebekah opened the back door and they walked out onto the porch.

"Oh, there's a swing set," Megan said. "Anna will love that."

"Yeah," Rebekah murmured. Tears stung the back of her eyes as the weight of the entire situation suddenly settled on her shoulders.

"Hey, what's wrong?" Megan asked, gently placing her hands on Rebekah's shoulders. The familiarity of the motion wasn't lost on Rebekah.

"Sometimes it's overwhelming. It's me and Anna now and I've moved her from everything she knows. I hope I'm doing the right thing."

"You're doing the best thing you can for her right now. That's all you can do, Bekah."

A tear rolled down her cheek and she could see tears pooling in Megan's eyes. She was always so sensitive.

"I feel like I've found a friend again."

Megan smiled. "I'm right here for you. I've been here."

Rebekah leaned in and let Megan hold her. For a moment she felt like everything was going to be all right.

"Mommy, I can't get the TV to work," Anna yelled from the living room.

They pulled apart and Megan said, "Let me."

Rebekah nodded and Megan went in to help Anna.

She took a minute to gather herself and enjoy feeling

Megan's arms around her again. When she went back into the living room, Megan was sitting next to Anna as she watched an episode of *Barbie*.

She smiled down at them and then closed the pizza boxes and took the trash to the kitchen. When she turned around Megan was in the doorway.

"I want you to know that Anna is going to get better. Crystal and I have a plan and we'll help her navigate this new world along with you. You're not doing this alone, Bekah."

Rebekah sighed. "I can't believe this. Can we sit down one day and catch up on the last twelve years? Of all the people I need right now and here you are."

The corners of Megan's mouth curved into a smile. "I can't believe it either. Do you have any idea how many times I've wondered about you?"

Rebekah pressed her hand against the fluttering in her stomach. "Can we talk soon?"

Megan nodded. "But now, I'm going to go. I know you're tired."

"Thanks for the pizza. Anna will love camping tonight, too. You are something else, you know?"

Megan shrugged then walked back into the living room.

"Anna, I've got to go. I'll see you Tuesday for art."

"Bye Megan. Thank you for fixing my bed and the TV. Tell Wanda hi for me."

"I will."

"I can't wait to play with her again."

Megan chuckled. "She can't either."

Rebekah walked Megan to her car. "Thanks for catching me as I fell apart."

"You didn't fall apart. Just breathe."

"I remember you telling me that so long ago."

Megan shrugged. "It still works."

Rebekah nodded. "Good night, Meg."

"Night, Bekah."

Megan got in her car and drove away.

Rebekah stood there a minute, remembering back when she felt anxious and Megan would say, "Breathe, baby. Just breathe." Rebekah took a couple of deep breaths and let them out slowly.

"You're right, Meg. It still works," she said as Megan's car turned the corner and then was gone.

6

"Good job today everyone. Don't forget to take your paintings from last week home with you," Crystal said to the group. Today they had a group session after a movement lesson. The kids were led through controlled movements and breathing exercises which calmed them in preparation for a group discussion about emotions.

"Megan, may I play with Wanda?" Anna asked politely.

"Yes, Anna. Would you let her out of the office so she can run around?" Megan said, smiling at her.

"Yes ma'am."

Rebekah walked in and waved at Megan as Anna ran to her office. "Let me guess, she's going to play with Wanda."

"You are so smart, Ms. Taylor."

Rebekah chuckled.

"Anna has been very polite today. Is there something I should know?"

"She is learning that she gets her way more often when she is polite."

"Ah, that makes sense." Megan grinned at Rebekah. "How's the unpacking going?"

"The only boxes left to unpack are things we rarely use. I need to find a place to store them."

"Hi Mommy," Anna said, Wanda prancing next to her.

"Hi sweetie. I see your new best friend has found you."

Anna giggled as Wanda hopped on Megan's legs and wagged her tail. Megan held up her hand and firmly said, "Wanda, down."

The little puppy obeyed and sat at Megan's feet. "Good girl," she said, patting her head. Megan looked at Rebekah and Anna. "I have to stop her from jumping on people now or when she gets bigger it will be a problem."

"I'll remember that when she jumps on me," Anna said.

"Come here you little bundle of love," Rebekah said, bending down and picking up the puppy.

"Megan, thank you for sharing your food with us the other night," Anna said.

With a raised eyebrow, Megan looked at her. "You're welcome?"

"And thank you for sharing Wanda with me. I like playing with her."

"You're welcome, Anna. She likes playing with you." Megan looked at Rebekah for clarity on what was happening.

"Why don't you explain to Megan why you're thanking her, honey."

"The other day in Sunday School we learned about sharing. People share food with others and other things, too. It made me think of how you brought pizza the other night and you always let me play with Wanda. It's like you're sharing her. We're supposed to thank people when they share with us."

Rebekah smiled at Anna and then at Megan.

"You are very welcome, Anna. I know you don't have to come to art, but I'm glad you do because it makes me happy to see you. Would that be like sharing your time?" Megan asked.

"Yep," Anna said with a smile. "I like sharing with you."

"I like it, too."

"Hey, Anna and I were hoping you could have dinner with us Saturday night. We should have everything unpacked and I'll cook for you," Rebekah said, putting the squirmy puppy down.

Megan raised her eyebrows. "Cook?"

Rebekah laughed. "Anna, do I know how to cook?"

"Yes ma'am! Mommy is a chef." Anna took off when Wanda decided to run around the room.

"So you learned to cook." Megan grinned.

"I did. We want to pay back your kindness. Are you busy Saturday? Maybe we could catch up a little?"

Megan chuckled. "I'd love that."

"Oh, uh, I'm not sure how to ask this." Rebekah winced. "I mean, it is Saturday night. Is there someone you want to bring or…"

Megan smiled at Rebekah's awkwardness. "There's no one, Bekah. It's okay. I don't have a hot date on Saturday night or a girlfriend."

"I wasn't—" Rebekah's face began to turn red.

"I know. It's okay." Megan chuckled.

"Can we take Wanda for a walk around the park?" Anna asked, holding Wanda's leash in her hand.

"Do you have time?" Megan asked Rebekah.

"Sure. Those boxes can wait a little longer."

Megan told Crystal they were leaving and they went out

the back door to the park. Anna went on ahead and let Wanda run.

"They both have little legs yet there they go." Megan laughed.

"Why is it that kids like to run instead of walk?" Rebekah mused.

"So much energy. She's helping me though. Wanda will be ready to sleep when we get home."

"How was Anna today?"

Megan took the change of subject in stride. "We had a group session where we encouraged them to talk about their emotions. I asked her how it felt to have her own room in her new house and she said 'happy.'" She paused and looked at Rebekah. "There is one thing we do with all of them that you should do too."

"What's that?"

"When we ask kids how they're doing or how their day was, their automatic response is 'good.' We want them to be more specific or tell us why they are good because sometimes they're not."

"Oh. You're right. I see that in my students and Anna does it too. I usually follow up with more questions, but I'll watch for that and encourage her."

"How are things going with you? With your class?"

Rebekah looked at Megan sideways.

"Oh, sorry. It's not a trick question. I genuinely want to know. Do you like your school?" Megan asked.

"Yes. My classes are getting used to me. We're getting to know one another."

"Oh good, I'm glad. Anna seemed more at ease when she came in today, so I'm hoping she's less anxious or withdrawn in class. Of course, knowing she would get to play with Wanda may have added to her mood."

"She does love that puppy."

"She is obviously paying attention in Sunday school," Megan commented.

"That sharing lesson resonated with her. She told me about it when we were waiting for the service to start and she used you and Wanda as examples."

"I'm not sure what to think about that."

"She noticed your kindness, Meg. What's there to think about?"

Megan nodded and smiled at the way Rebekah said her name. They continued along the path and Megan said, "I saw your dad is the head pastor of your church now."

"Mmm, it's his church, not mine."

"I remember our discussions on religion."

"Do you?" Rebekah said, looking over at Megan. "I was young and trying to figure it all out."

"Have you? Figured it out?"

"I think I have for me. That would be a fun discussion, wouldn't it?. Maybe it'll come up Saturday night."

"I'm looking forward to it."

"You know, I'm the same age now that you were when we met."

"That's right, you are. I think you've seen a lot more than I had at thirty-one."

"I don't know about that. What I do know is that I appreciate our conversations and how you respected my ideas back then. When I hear nineteen-year-olds today I wonder if I sounded so naive and full of myself."

"You didn't. You were thoughtful and questioning."

Rebekah chuckled. "I can't wait until Saturday."

Megan smiled at her and before she could say anything Anna came running up with Wanda.

"What's her superpower today, Anna?"

"Making me happy," she answered.

"I thought you were happy when you came into the center today," Megan said.

"I knew I was seeing you and Wanda. That makes me happy."

"Then we need to work on what will make you feel happier at school. That sounds like a good project, doesn't it?"

"If you say so."

Megan chuckled. "I say so. How about you, Mommy?"

"I think it's a fine project. Maybe I'll help."

"Can our next project be to make Mommy happy?" Anna asked.

"What? I'm happy, honey," Rebekah replied, her brow furrowed.

"I saw you crying the other night and Megan hugged you and made it better. I know sometimes you cry at night, Mommy. You don't have to hide it from me. I'll hug you and make it better. Just like playing with Wanda and talking to Megan makes me feel better."

Rebekah opened and closed her mouth several times.

"Anna, did you know that when I see you and your Mommy, I feel happy?" Megan asked, covering Rebekah's silence.

Anna nodded. "That's why we like sharing time. It makes us happy."

"How did you get so smart?" Rebekah said, finally finding words.

Anna smiled and shrugged.

Wanda began to bark, obviously wanting to join the conversation.

"Wanda says she's happy to be with us, too, but it's time for her to go home," Megan said.

"Come on, Wanda Wiggly," Anna said, leading her back to the counseling center.

"She amazes me sometimes," Rebekah said softly.

"Yeah, she's very perceptive."

"I had no idea she heard me at night and saw us the other night."

"The next time you feel sad and she's gone to bed, call me, Rebekah. I know sometimes we need to cry, but I'm always here. Always," Megan said earnestly.

Rebekah sighed. "I know you are." She slapped Megan's arm and added, "And you were here the whole time!"

Megan chuckled and held up her hands. "I decided to stay."

Rebekah shook her head and followed Anna into the building.

7

Megan walked back into the counseling center with a big smile on her face and saw Crystal putting the art supplies away. She hurried over to help her.

"Did you get them to their car okay?" Crystal asked.

Megan stopped and looked at her best friend. "What do you mean by that?"

Crystal chuckled. "I'm trying to count how many times you've walked clients and their parents to their cars," she said, looking up and pretending to count on her fingers. "Oh, I know. None!"

"Ha ha, very funny."

"Of course, none of the other parents happen to be women you've slept with... Or have you?" Crystal teased.

"What the fuck, Crystal!"

"I'm kidding, Megan! Come on!"

Megan stopped and felt a small smile creep onto her face.

"I wish you could see how you light up when Anna comes in. And when Rebekah comes in? I need sunglasses to stand the brightness when you see her," Crystal said. "Before you say anything, it's a good thing, Megan. I'm not teasing or getting on you."

"For the record, I have not slept with any of our clients' parents and it was a long time ago with Rebekah."

Crystal chuckled. "Is there some reason you haven't asked her out yet?"

"I'm her daughter's counselor!"

"Technically, I'm her daughter's counselor. And in just three sessions I've seen a marked difference in Anna."

"I know. She opens up more every time she comes in."

"You never did tell me the whole story of that fateful summer," Crystal said.

"You make that sound ominous."

"Wasn't it? You lost your heart."

Megan sighed. "It was rather clandestine. We didn't necessarily hide, but it was like we were in our own little bubble."

"So you were at my apartment fucking your brains out when you weren't in class?"

"Really? And you wonder why I don't talk about it with you!"

"Am I wrong?" Crystal protested.

"Yes, you're wrong. We didn't want to be around other people. We talked about so many things and it was interesting and exciting and intense."

"You will not make me believe all you did was talk," Crystal deadpanned.

Megan dropped her head and rolled her eyes. "I didn't say that. I'm trying to explain how it was. I've never been that captivated by another person and she was too."

"It must have been hard when she left."

"It was hard on both of us, but we agreed. I hadn't

decided if I was staying here and she was going back to school. Come on, Crystal, she was only nineteen and I was the first woman she'd ever been with. She was discovering her inner self and in a way I was too. We were at very different places in our lives, but in some ways the same. Does that make any sense?"

"Sure it does. You were leaving all you knew and coming out here to take a huge risk."

"And you ran off to Europe."

"Are you ever going to let that go? Imagine if I had been here. You and Rebekah may never have met."

"But we did and now I wonder if we've been given a second chance."

"You're a licensed counselor, you know what to do. Communicate with the woman!"

"I'm having dinner with them Saturday night. Rebekah wants to catch up on the last twelve years."

"What are you going to tell her?"

Megan shrugged. "There's not a lot to tell."

"Are you going to tell her that you had a girlfriend, but she lived in Atlanta and you wouldn't move or let her move here?"

Megan sighed. "Rebekah was married and would be still if her husband hadn't died."

"That doesn't mean you can't be together now. Think about it."

"Sorry, it's after 5:00. The counseling center is closed."

"I'm asking as a friend, Megan."

"I don't want to think about it, Crystal. Okay?"

"You can't fool me. I know you've thought about it. But that's a conversation for another day. Why don't you come home with me and have a beer? Kim will be home soon."

"Thanks, but Wanda and I have a date with a squirrel at the park by our house."

"You know, Wanda sure seems to like that little girl, too."

"Wanda likes everybody," Megan said, clipping the leash to her collar.

"Yeah, but not like she does Anna." Crystal squeezed Megan's shoulder. "See you tomorrow."

"Bye." Megan looked down at Wanda. "You do like Anna, but I think Rebekah is your favorite."

The puppy looked up at her, wiggling her tail.

"That's what I thought."

* * *

"Hi Daddy," Rebekah said, standing in the doorway to Daniel's office.

"Well, hi there. This is a treat," Daniel said, smiling.

"Anna has handbell practice so I thought I'd visit with you if you aren't busy."

"I'm never too busy for you."

Rebekah walked in and sat in the chair opposite his desk.

"How is Anna?"

"You know, she's better. This therapy is helping."

"Maybe she's beginning to settle in," he said.

"She really likes her counselors and I can see her opening up a little more each day."

"Oh good. Hey, why don't you two come over for dinner Saturday night? Your mom would love that and we can watch a movie. I miss our movie nights since you moved out."

"Dad, we've only been gone a week," Rebekah chuckled.

"Besides we're having Anna's counselor over for dinner Saturday night. She brought pizza by the night we moved."

"That was kind of her."

"It was. You'll be glad to know Anna is using what she learned in Sunday school."

"What did she do?"

"After her Sunday school lesson she thanked Megan, her counselor, for sharing her food with us. She's the one that brought the pizza when we moved."

Daniel chuckled. "Good for her."

"She also has the puppy that Anna loves. I think the puppy has helped with her therapy as much as the art sessions."

"That program must be good if you can already see a difference."

"I actually knew Megan several years ago. I didn't realize she was still in Athens."

"Oh?"

"I met her one summer when I was home from school."

"Hmm, it was the summer you questioned everything."

Rebekah tilted her head. "You remember that?"

"Of course I do. That was the last summer you came home. You were finding your independence and didn't want to go to church. Remember?"

"I remember," Rebekah said softly. She had so many questions back then. After meeting Megan she'd had even more. The feelings that grew between them that summer went against everything the church taught which went against everything her parents believed. Rebekah knew the difference between right and wrong and the feelings she had for Megan couldn't be wrong because they felt so right. She remembered talking about that with Megan many times.

"You worried us," her dad continued. "It felt like you were rebelling against the church and us."

"I don't know if rebelling is the right word, Dad. I began to realize that everything the church teaches isn't necessarily true for me."

"What do you mean by that?"

"I don't agree with everything the church teaches and that's okay with God."

Her dad furrowed his brow and narrowed his eyes.

"I've done a lot of talking with God and we're okay," Rebekah said, meeting his gaze.

"I'm glad to hear that. Does that mean you'll come to Sunday school?"

Rebekah smiled. "That means God and I have an understanding. It does not include Sunday school for me at this time. I will come to hear you preach and bring Anna to Sunday school for now."

Her dad nodded. "Okay, but I reserve the right to revisit this later."

Rebekah chuckled. "We can talk about God anytime you want, Daddy. Isn't that what you do?"

"It is. It might surprise you to know that over the years some of my views regarding the church have changed."

Rebekah nodded. "Over the years the church's views have needed to change. Their eyes needed to open, don't you think?"

Daniel nodded and before he could say anything Anna walked in.

"Hi Mommy, hi Grandpa," she said, climbing into Rebekah's lap.

"Did you ring that bell?" Daniel teased.

"Grandpa, you know it isn't like that." She rolled her eyes.

He laughed. "Give me a hug. I miss you at the house. It's too quiet."

Anna got up and hugged him as Rebekah looked on and smiled.

"Come on, kiddo. We'd better get home. I have homework to do tonight," Rebekah said.

"Teachers have homework too?" Anna looked at her with surprise.

"Sometimes. We have to get things ready for you each day. I'm glad tomorrow is Friday."

"Has it been a long week?" her dad asked.

"Not necessarily long, we're just busy. Aren't we, Anna?"

"I like doing things after school."

"I know you do, but sometimes it'd be nice to go home and not do anything."

"Are you girls still walking in the evenings?"

"Sometimes," Rebekah said.

"Then you need to walk by and say hi. Grandma misses you too," he said to Anna.

"Okay. We will," Anna said, walking over to Rebekah and taking her hand.

"See ya, Dad."

"Bye Grandpa."

They walked to the car and Anna said, "We can invite people to come watch us when we play our bells in church. I want to invite Megan."

"You do? Well, you can ask her Saturday night when she comes to dinner."

"Do you think she'll come?"

"I don't know." Rebekah thought Megan would probably do anything Anna asked and vice versa. Twelve years was a long time and she wondered how Megan felt about some things that they had talked about back then.

The connection they had was still there. She knew Megan felt it because she could see it in her eyes. Those eyes. They were like warm chocolate and could make her melt with one look.

What do you want, Rebekah? She'd asked herself that so many times since seeing Megan again. Maybe the question should be: what do you want, Megan?

8

Megan turned onto Rebekah's street and the butterflies intensified in her stomach. She remembered this same feeling when she knew Rebekah was coming to her apartment all those years ago. A deep breath followed by a slow exhale helped to calm her beating heart.

"You've got to calm the fuck down," she said aloud. Rebekah had been questioning her sexuality twelve years ago. She obviously answered that question by marrying Ben and then having Anna. That made her smile. What a sweet little girl. Being with Anna made her wonder about her decision not to have kids.

When she was with them it felt so easy and natural. It was how she imagined her life would have been if she and Rebekah had found a way to be together. But alas, here they were twelve years down the road and somehow they'd reconnected. Megan was determined to control her emotions and not let her heart get carried away.

This was a chance to at least have Rebekah as a friend and Anna was a bonus. The last thing she wanted to do was mess this up by falling in love. She scoffed. "Falling in love? You never stopped loving Bekah." She sighed and shook her head. Wanda looked at her, tilted her head one way and then the other.

She pulled into Rebekah's driveway and pushed all those feelings down into her heart.

"Come on, Wanda, my love. You have to be on your best behavior. We want them to invite us back or come to our house. Okay?" she said, stroking the puppy's head.

Before she could knock, the door swung open and there stood a smiling Anna. "Hi!" she said excitedly. Then she bent down to pet Wanda. "Hi girl. I'm so happy you came to play with me."

"Hey," Rebekah said, wiping her hands on a towel. "Anna, don't you think we should let Megan come inside?"

"Sorry." Anna stepped back and let them walk into the living room.

"Hi," Megan said to Rebekah with a smile.

Wanda jumped up on Rebekah's legs and looked up at her.

"No Wanda," Megan said, reaching for the pup.

"It's okay, Meg. She's just saying hi." Rebekah looked down at the puppy and held out her hand just like she saw Megan do. Then she said, "Down." The puppy obeyed and Rebekah rewarded her with a pat on the head. "Good girl."

"Something smells wonderful," Megan said.

"Mommy and I made an apple pie for dessert," Anna said proudly.

"Can we have dessert first?" Megan asked with a grin.

"No ma'am," Rebekah said firmly. "Come on back and I'll show you why. I thought we could play outside with Wanda before dinner."

"I brought this," Megan said, handing Rebekah a bottle

of wine. She had texted her earlier to see if she could bring anything and Rebekah had suggested something to drink.

"Oh good. I haven't had a glass of wine in ages." She smiled at Megan and then started to the kitchen.

Wanda followed close behind her with Anna and Megan next.

"I'm making chicken fried steak. That's why you can't have dessert first," Rebekah said when they walked into the kitchen. "Is it still your favorite?"

"Yes! I can't believe you remember," Megan exclaimed.

"Oh, I remember lots of things. Do you still only have it occasionally as a treat?"

Megan grinned and nodded. "Yes, but I do love it."

"Great. Now let's go play. You and Anna can keep me company in the kitchen while I cook the steak later."

"Come on, Wanda," Anna said, opening the back door.

Megan followed them out and looked around. "You've been busy. This looks great, Bekah."

"Thanks. I got my patio furniture out of storage and cleaned up the porch. It's amazing what sweeping and a little water can do."

"Do you like it here so far?"

"Yeah, the neighborhood seems okay and the house is just what we need right now."

They both watched Anna and Wanda run around the yard. When the puppy got tired she simply stopped and lay down. Anna giggled and let the puppy rest.

"Megan, would you push me?" Anna asked, walking over to the swing set.

"Sure."

She pushed Anna and Wanda joined them, running under her feet before running to where Rebekah sat on the porch.

They all played for a while before Rebekah suggested they go in and open the wine.

She handed the opener along with the bottle to Megan. "Anna, I'm sure Megan would help you put a puzzle together while I cook the steak."

"I'll try," Megan said, pouring each of them a glass of wine.

Rebekah looked into Megan's eyes and said, "To old memories and making new ones."

Megan clinked her glass to Rebekah's and smiled.

"Oh this is good," Rebekah hummed.

"We never did drink much before, did we?"

"I was a baby. Besides, we had other things to do," Rebekah said, raising an eyebrow.

Megan's mouth went dry. Before she could respond, Anna came back in with a puzzle. She dumped the pieces out onto the small kitchen table.

"What do we have here?" Megan said, sitting in one of the two chairs.

"It's a unicorn."

"Oh I see on the box. What's your favorite color?" Megan asked.

"I like this purple," Anna said, pointing to the unicorn's striped horn on the box.

"That's pretty. I like this bright blue right here." Megan pointed.

"That's Mommy's favorite too."

"It is?"

"Hey Anna," Rebekah said, preparing the steak to fry. "Did you know that I met Megan many years ago when I was in college?"

Anna looked up at her mother and then at Megan. "You know each other?"

"Sort of," Rebekah continued. "We haven't seen each other in a very long time, but we had a lot of fun."

"I didn't know your mommy had moved back here until she came into the center to pick you up that first day. What a surprise!"

"Yeah it was. A happy surprise, right Anna?"

She nodded as she snapped a piece of the puzzle together. "How did you meet?"

Megan smiled. "I was teaching a summer class at the college and one day after class I walked out of the building and saw this woman talking to a bush."

"What?" Anna said, interested.

"Yep, that part is true. Except I wasn't talking to a bush. I was talking to a scared little kitten. I was trying to coax it out from under the bush."

"I walked over and together we were able to get the kitten to come out," Megan explained. She looked at Rebekah. "How is Neal?"

"Neal!" Anna exclaimed. "That's Grandma and Grandpa's cat."

Rebekah laughed. "That's the cat. Neal is living his best life."

"When we got the kitten out I took it home with me because your mom didn't think your grandparents would let her keep it," Megan said.

"But it turns out that Megan is allergic to cats!" Rebekah chuckled.

"What happened then?" Anna asked anxiously.

"Well, Megan tried, but she sneezed and her eyes swelled up, so it was evident that Megan couldn't keep him." Rebekah gazed at Megan and said affectionately, "You tried so hard."

"I think today there are medicines I could take and I could probably have a cat," Megan said.

"I never was sure if you were so upset that you couldn't keep the cat or because you were afraid it would disappoint me," Rebekah said, pinning Megan with a look.

Megan shrugged.

"What happened?" Anna interjected.

"I explained to Grandma and Grandpa and they let me bring the kitten home. I named him Neal after Megan."

"Your name isn't Neal," Anna said.

Megan chuckled.

Rebekah walked over and put her hand on Megan's shoulder. "Anna, let me introduce you to Megan Neal."

"Ohhhhh!" Anna exclaimed, laughing. "That's a great story."

Megan liked the feel of Rebekah's hand on her shoulder. She looked up and said, "I can still see you with your butt in the air halfway under that bush."

Rebekah giggled. "I knew that's what made you come help me." She smacked her playfully on the arm.

"I didn't mean it that way!" Megan protested.

Rebekah laughed and went to put the steak in the frying pan.

"Why didn't you stay friends?" Anna asked.

"Well, your mommy had to go back to school," Megan said.

"At the time Megan wasn't sure she was staying in Athens. She thought she might go back to California."

"Is that where you lived?"

"Yep, I grew up in Cali, but I decided to stay here in Athens. You know Crystal?" Megan asked Anna. She nodded. "Crystal is my best friend. She wanted me to move here so we could open the center and do art with kids."

"So you decided to stay here then."

"I decided to stay here." Megan snapped a piece of the puzzle into place.

Anna looked at her mom then at Megan. "That's sad that you weren't friends."

Rebekah stopped and looked over at Anna and Megan. "I wish I would've known you stayed."

Megan looked up and met Rebekah's gaze. "I don't know how we didn't run into each other somewhere. You came home to visit, didn't you?"

Rebekah gave her a sad smile. "I didn't very often. Holidays mostly. Did you go home for the holidays?"

Megan nodded. "Yeah, I did. But still, you'd think we'd have seen each other sometime."

"I guess the time wasn't right." Rebekah broke her gaze and put biscuits in the oven.

"It sure does smell good, doesn't it, Anna?" Megan turned back to the puzzle, wondering if this was the right time.

"I even made homemade biscuits," Rebekah said.

Megan couldn't believe Rebekah was cooking her favorites. That had to mean something.

"Before you say anything, Anna and I wanted this to be a special dinner because we're so happy you're our friend."

Anna reached over and put her hand on top of Megan's and squeezed. "Wanda too."

Megan smiled and could feel tears sting the back of her eyes. All the feelings she'd pushed down in her heart were now in her throat. She squeezed Anna's hand back and then frantically looked around. "Oh no, where is Wanda?"

"She's right here," Rebekah said calmly.

Megan saw that Rebekah had put a towel on the floor

next to the door and Wanda was snoozing peacefully. She sighed in relief.

"Why don't you two go set the table? We'll be ready to eat in a few minutes."

"Yes ma'am," Megan said, getting up and winking at Anna.

9

Rebekah had been nervous when Anna ran to the door to let Megan and Wanda in, but she was also excited. Megan and Wanda easily fit right in and her jitters had quieted as soon as Megan smiled at her.

It was fun telling Anna how they met. She had chuckled to herself during the story, knowing Megan had been checking her out that day. The first time Megan's hand brushed against hers was like lightning pulsing through her body. She felt it again when she put her hand on Megan's shoulder earlier this evening.

"Mommy, we should say a prayer before we eat," Anna said as they all sat at the dining room table.

"Okay, but you have to say it," Rebekah instructed her.

"Join hands," Anna said, holding out her hands to Rebekah and Megan.

They reached across the table and Rebekah gently put her hand in Megan's. She felt Megan immediately run her thumb over the back of her hand just as she'd done many times before.

Anna said a simple prayer and then smiled at both of them. "Let's eat!"

They filled their plates and ate and talked and laughed.

"I know I keep saying this, but it's so good," Megan said between bites.

"I'm glad you like it. I learned how to cook chicken fried steak and couldn't help but think of you. I only dreamed I'd get to make it for you someday."

Megan stilled and gazed across the table at her. "I wonder what other dreams might come true."

Rebekah almost looked away because Megan was doing that thing where she looked right into her soul, but then Anna got their attention.

"Megan, I'm playing the handbells at church next Sunday. Would you like to come hear me play?"

A huge smile grew on Megan's face. "I'd love to, Anna. Just tell me when and where."

"You're welcome to go with me," Rebekah added.

"Thanks. I'll have to leave Wanda at home. Okay?" she teased Anna.

The little girl giggled. "I don't think Grandpa would mind."

"Oh yes he would." Rebekah laughed.

They finished the meal and Rebekah brought out the apple pie. She cut it and dished out the pieces and said, "You know, a little ice cream on top would make this even better. What do you think, Anna?"

"Yes ma'am!"

Rebekah went back in the kitchen and brought out the ice cream. She put a scoop on a piece of pie and handed it to Anna.

"Ice cream?" she asked, looking at Megan.

"No thank you. Not this time. I don't want to hide one bit of flavor from the pie."

"Meg," Rebekah said, shaking her head. "You always say the best things." She handed her the pie and added, "There's a lot of love baked into that pie, isn't there, Anna?"

Anna nodded as she ate a spoonful of ice cream.

Megan took a bite and nodded. "I can taste it."

"Maybe I'll see if you know what you're talking about," Rebekah said, taking the ice cream back to the kitchen. When she came back, she took a bite of her pie and moaned. "This is delicious. I'm not bragging; it must have been my helper."

Anna grinned and kept eating. When she swallowed she looked at Megan. "We get to watch a movie after this."

"You do?"

"Can you stay? We hoped you'd have movie night with us."

"I'd like that." Megan smiled. "Very much."

"Yay!" Anna exclaimed. "Have you seen *Luca*? That's what we're watching. It's supposed to be really good!"

"I haven't seen it yet. I've heard it's great!" Megan eyed Anna and grinned. "But first I have to help with the dishes."

"You don't have to do that," Rebekah protested.

"Oh yes I do, Bekah."

Anna giggled. "I like how you call Mommy Bekah."

Megan chuckled. "Sorry, that's what I called her a long time ago."

"It's okay, Meg," Rebekah said, stressing her name.

Anna giggled again. "Can I call you Meg?"

Megan gave her a stern look then laughed. "Come on, let's do the dishes so we can watch *Luca*."

They cleared the table and Megan put the dishes in the dishwasher as Rebekah put the food away. Anna took

Wanda outside so she could go to the bathroom and run around before the movie.

"She's so funny," Anna said, coming in with Wanda on her heels. "She runs around in circles and then just stops. We've got to teach her to play fetch."

"Hey Anna, I saw your bicycle in the garage and I was wondering if you'd like to come ride bikes with me. I have a good place to ride at a park near my house."

"Can I, Mommy? I'd like that."

"Your mom can come too." Megan chuckled.

"I don't have a bike," Rebekah replied.

"I have two."

"You do! I'd like that, too. We used to love riding bikes, didn't we, Anna."

"Yeah, we rode with Daddy," she said quietly, rubbing Wanda's head. "Can we do it tomorrow?"

"We sure can," Megan answered cheerily.

Anna went to the couch with Wanda, both ready for the movie.

Rebekah looked at her and held up her hands.

"It's okay," Megan said to her softly. "I wouldn't have asked if I didn't want to do it."

"Okay. I'm glad you're here. I don't know what to do or say sometimes when she talks about her dad."

"You're doing fine." Megan smiled compassionately. "Let's watch the movie."

Rebekah nodded and they joined them on the couch.

When they'd settled in Megan watched Wanda crawl over and snuggle up against Rebekah.

"I knew it," she said, staring down at the puppy.

"What?" Rebekah said, petting the puppy's head.

"I think you're her favorite," Megan said with a smile.

Rebekah chuckled. "It's only fair since you were Neal's favorite even though he made you sneeze your head off."

"I can't believe Neal used to be your cat," Anna said.

"Not really. He didn't live with me very long."

"Shh," Anna said. "The movie's starting."

Rebekah looked over Anna's head at Megan and laughed quietly. Megan widened her eyes and laughed with her.

At one point during the movie Anna hid her face behind Rebekah's shoulder. She raised her arm and put it over the back of the couch. "It's okay, he made it."

Anna looked back at the TV, clearly relieved.

Towards the end of the movie Anna was getting tired and rested her head against Megan's arm. Rebekah smoothed her hand over Anna's head and then rested it for a moment on Megan's shoulder. She looked over at Rebekah and smiled.

Megan looked back at the TV and Rebekah took the opportunity to study Megan's profile. All these years she'd been right here in Athens wondering about her. So many what-if's were running through her head—or were they God things? She'd always loved Megan; she was sure of that. Was this their second chance? Was this their time? Had God led them back to one another? Of all the counselors in Athens, Anna ended up in Megan's program.

"You're missing the end of the movie," Megan whispered, quickly glancing at her.

"Right," Rebekah replied and turned to the TV.

When the movie was over Anna stretched and a big yawn escaped her mouth.

"I think it's someone's bedtime," Rebekah said.

"But it's Saturday," she weakly objected before yawning again.

Megan chuckled. "Sounds to me like you're tired."

"Come on, sweetie," Rebekah said, getting up. "I'll be back in a few minutes."

"Can Megan tuck me into bed too?" Anna asked, following her mom.

"Sure she can. You go brush your teeth and I'll get your pajamas."

Megan smiled. "Are you sure?"

"Of course. Come on."

Anna brushed her teeth and changed into her pajamas.

"Your room looks awesome, Anna," Megan said when Anna came into the room and crawled into bed.

"Hey, are we still going camping sometime?" she asked.

Megan nodded. "Yes ma'am. Thank you for everything, Anna. This has been one of the best nights I've had in a long time."

"You're welcome. I'll see you tomorrow."

Rebekah sat down on the side of her bed and smoothed back her hair. "Thanks for helping me with the pie. I know that's why it tasted so good." She bent down and kissed her on the forehead. "I love you, baby. Sweet dreams."

"I love you too, Mommy."

10

Rebekah pulled Anna's bedroom door almost shut. "How about another glass of wine?" she asked as they walked back into the living room.

"Am I going to need it?"

She chuckled. "Twelve years is a long time; it may take a few."

"This has been such a nice evening, Bekah," Megan said, taking the glass she offered.

"It has." She sat down on the couch and looked at Megan. "Well, twelve years?"

"It's kind of obvious what you've been doing. I think Anna is amazing."

Rebekah smiled. "She is incredible. But there's more to the story. You go first. What made you stay?"

"Oh, uh..." Megan took a sip of her wine and moved nervously on her end of the couch.

"Hey, you were always open and honest with me. That's one reason I was able to wrestle with what I'd been taught and find my way."

"What do you mean?"

"I remember what you told me about struggling with God and being gay growing up. You know what that did for me. You were always honest and didn't hold anything back. Please don't think you have to now."

"You know, Crystal says that when you left you took my heart with you." Megan paused for a moment and stared into Rebekah's vivid blue eyes. Then she took a deep breath. "One reason I stayed is because I hoped you would come back."

"Did you pray about it?"

Megan looked at her and narrowed her eyes.

"I know you did. Would it make you feel better to know that I did come back to find you? It was two or three weeks later. I went to your apartment but no one was there. I came by several times but never did see your car in the parking lot."

Megan sighed. "I moved! That was Crystal's apartment and I got my own place right after she got back." Megan shook her head and couldn't believe her ears. Rebekah had come back.

"Before you get too upset, just imagine how that may have turned out. I was a teenager in love. How volatile would that have been?"

"You may have been nineteen in age, but you weren't in how you thought and felt."

Rebekah shrugged. "What happened after that?"

"Crystal and I opened the counseling center. I had a girlfriend for a few years. She lived in Atlanta."

"It didn't work out?" Rebekah asked, tension in her voice.

"No. I didn't want to move."

"I can understand that with your job and all, but she wouldn't move here?"

"That wasn't an option. I didn't ask her."

"Oh," Rebekah said with a smile. Then she chuckled. "I can't believe how jealous that just made me."

"Jealous?"

"Yes." Rebekah released a big breath.

Megan looked at her skeptically and continued. "That's all until this little girl came in for counseling and I immediately felt a bond to her. When you walked up behind us that day and said my name, I thought I was hearing things."

Rebekah smiled. "I couldn't believe it was you. I had to stand there for a moment and take a breath."

"Crystal always wondered why I didn't simply call you, but we made an agreement and I knew how hard it was for you and how much you were struggling."

"Oh I knew exactly what I wanted when I went back to school, but I didn't know how to get it."

Megan nodded. "I'm glad you came back. We can help Anna, but I'm also happy to know that you're all right and somewhat happy."

Rebekah smiled and took a sip of her wine. "Ben knew all about you."

"What?"

"I met him at school. We were friends first and then dated my senior year. When I said, I knew what I wanted when I went back to school but I didn't know how to get it, I meant you."

"But—"

Rebekah held up her hand. "I wanted you and kids and a family, but I also wanted to go to school. I thought about that when I went back to school and couldn't figure out how to get it all. That's when I came back. I decided that I would tell you all of this and maybe together we could figure it out."

"Oh, Bekah."

"I know. For a minute, I took it as a sign from God that this wasn't the path for me."

Megan shook her head.

"I said for a minute. You have no idea how much your honesty helped me all these years."

"What do you mean?"

"I remember you told me that you struggled growing up with being gay and your belief in God. This is how I remember it," Rebekah said.

Megan leaned back on the couch and let her continue.

"You said that at first you thought you were a bad person and that you were going against God. But the more you prayed on it and the more you tried to be that good person, the clearer it became. You dated guys and convinced yourself that your first love—what was her name again? Valerie, wasn't it?"

Megan nodded.

"You convinced yourself that you didn't love women, you only loved her. And that it was the person you loved, not the sex or gender. When you realized that wasn't true and you were fooling yourself, you talked to God."

"That's right. I talked to God."

"I remember you didn't say you prayed, but that you talked to God. I loved that. My dad is always preaching that God listens, so just talk to Him."

"I believe that's true."

Rebekah took a deep breath. "You told me that you can believe in God and still be gay. That you talked to God and He—"

"Or She," Megan interrupted.

"Or She." Rebekah nodded. "That He loved you, He made you, and He was okay with who you are."

"That's right. I still believe that. The church isn't God. The church was telling me that I was going to hell and that I was a bad person. God wasn't."

"I have taken that with me all these years and have had several talks with God along the way."

"After you left did you doubt us? I mean—" Megan sighed. "What I'm trying to say is, did your feelings change for me and about us?"

"No! I have never doubted our feelings and I have never thought loving you was wrong. If anything I wanted to feel that again, but no one, Meg, makes me feel like you do."

"Oh God," Megan murmured. Her eyes widened as she realized what she'd said.

Rebekah giggled. "I never tried to date any other women. I won't say I wasn't attracted to women, but they weren't you. You know, I had a lifetime of being the preacher's daughter to go along with the teachings of the church to get past. And then there was the idea that I had lost you. Needless to say my sophomore year was a lot. But something in my heart kept telling me it would all work out. I thought about you all the time, but I knew I had to finish my degree. I wanted to finish my degree."

Megan smiled. "You did and I know you're a great teacher."

"I remember that summer, I was home one afternoon and Ellen's talk show was on. I asked my mom if she liked her. She said that she liked her show but that she didn't agree with her 'being with a woman' is how she said it. I took that as a positive because at least she didn't hate her or say she was going to hell."

"Have you talked to your parents about gay people?"

"Yes. We have talked about the church's views on homosexuality." Rebekah sipped her wine.

"Let's see, does your church say they love them and it's okay if they are a member and they will certainly take their money? But they won't let them get married in your church and your dad can't perform a gay marriage."

"That's right. Are you keeping up with my daddy's church?"

"Not necessarily. I was raised in the same denomination. When I go home to visit my parents I usually go to church with them. It's nice to see their friends. I've told my parents that it amazes me that the church feels that way." Megan rubbed the back of her neck. "If I were to get married, I would invite many of those people and they would want to come to my wedding. But it would have to be in another place. Sometimes it makes me so hurt and angry."

"I hope eventually that might change, but it is frustrating. I think about it every time I go to church. I grew up going to church and it's a part of my life, but I don't know that I can stay at that church if they don't change. How can they say everyone is welcome, but then put conditions on it and say they can't be included in all the church offers."

Megan nodded. "Some people don't believe in God because of the way the church treats gay people. I'm not saying my views are right. Everyone is on their own journey."

"Wouldn't it be nice if the church considered that? I believe in God. I don't believe all the church says because I know that anyone can manipulate what the Bible says to their own agenda."

Megan took a drink of her wine and then sighed. She looked at Rebekah and felt such compassion. She had gone through some of the same struggles that she had. How she wished she could've been there for her.

"I met Ben right after Christmas of my junior year,"

Rebekah said suddenly, seeming to want to finish her story. "We were fast friends and eventually began dating. I hadn't given up hope that I would find you again someday, but I told myself that it would happen at the right time for both of us. I don't think it was our time that summer, Megan. Anyway, Ben and I had fun and my parents liked him. I started my senior year excited and ready to get my degree. Everything was going along great until I ended up pregnant with Anna."

Megan couldn't hide her surprise.

"Yeah, I was surprised too. Ben wanted us to get married, but I wasn't so sure. Then I thought about how my parents would react and the church. I prayed. I talked to God and couldn't find a solution. So I married Ben, never told my parents I was already pregnant and we moved to Miami."

"Did you get married here? I can't believe I didn't know about it."

"We got married at school right before graduation, then we moved to Miami that summer. Anna was born in November and we've been in Miami ever since. When Ben died I didn't know what to do." Rebekah lowered her eyes. "Anna was withdrawn and so sad. We went to doctors and counselors. You know how I don't use those words around her. She loves my parents and I thought maybe that would help her, so I decided to move home."

"Wow, Bekah. You've been through so much."

"Yeah, but there was one constant through it all. I never forgot you, Megan. I kept thinking God has a plan, I just can't see it. I have to hang in there because everything is going to be all right. When I walked into the counseling center and saw you, it was like an answered prayer."

Megan had tears in her eyes. She scooted over and gently moved the sleeping Wanda to the other end of the couch. Then she wrapped her arms around Bekah. "I'm so sorry you had to go through all of this. We'll help Anna. I promise you."

Rebekah pulled back and smiled. "I know you will. Thank you."

Megan held one of Rebekah's hands and squeezed it.

"I'm not saying I expect anything from you, Megan. But I'm so grateful we found you and that you're helping Anna. I'm through living my life wondering what my parents or the church would think. I know who I am and who I believe."

11

Megan looked at Rebekah and smiled. "Do you know how long I've dreamed of this moment? How many times I thought about the moment when we would see each other again? You're not the only one that thought it would all work out somehow."

"But?"

"Anna isn't the only one that has had sorrow, Bekah. You have too. And just because you're an adult doesn't mean you don't have to heal and come to terms with it too."

Rebekah smiled. "Oh, my smart, compassionate Megan. If I've learned anything from this tragedy it's that we are not guaranteed time. I am not going to waste what we've been given. When we first met, I still had a lot to work out inside me, but you let me know it was okay to listen to myself. Even when I was conflicted I knew I had a good heart and could figure it out."

"What is your heart telling you now?"

Rebekah took Megan's hand and pressed it against her heart. "It's telling me that Anna comes first. There is no way

I'll jeopardize her emotional health or healing. But I can tell she trusts you and she knows she's special to you."

"She is and so are you." Megan laughed nervously. "This is all a bit surreal."

"Not to me. Don't get me wrong, Megan. I loved Ben, still do, always will. But you are who I'm *in love* with and always will be. And I know you still love me. You look at me and see inside my soul. No one else does that!"

Megan gently put her hand on Rebekah's cheek.

She leaned into the touch and closed her eyes for a moment. When she opened them she said, "Look at me, Meg. What do you see?"

Megan dropped her hand and grabbed Rebekah's. She stared into her eyes and Rebekah could feel the heat rising inside her. It was like Megan's love flowed into her and wrapped her in warmth and comfort, but it also excited her and made her heart hammer in her chest. She wanted to feel Megan's touch. She wanted to touch her again, but she also knew they had to go slow. The fire inside them was hot and intense and she had no doubt it was still there. They had to be careful not to let it consume them because she had Anna now and she needed them both.

"I see that questioning nineteen-year-old who was trying so hard to figure everything out. I also see a strong beautiful woman who knows who she is, but has suffered right along with her little girl. We have time, Bekah. I'm here. Anna's not the only one that has had to navigate big changes. You're back where people don't know or see the Rebekah I do."

"You're right. I am the preacher's daughter, but my views are very different from my parents' and they are beginning to see that."

"All I'm saying is that you don't have to change everything all at once. I know that your mind is going one hundred miles an hour and you want Anna to be the little girl she was before. You want your parents to accept the person that you've become, including your sexuality. You want to be able to go to the church you love and be welcomed for who you are just like anyone else."

"I do want those things, Meg, but I know I may not get them. I know Anna isn't the same little girl and won't be, but we'll help her grow into who she wants to be. What I really want is *you*."

Megan sighed. "You have me, Bekah. You always have."

Rebekah smiled and was leaning in to kiss Megan when she heard a noise.

"Mommy, I had a sad dream," Anna said from the doorway.

"Oh honey, do you want to come sit with Megan and me?"

Anna nodded and padded over to the couch and crawled up to sit between them. Rebekah put her arm around her and Megan took one of her hands and held it between hers. Wanda stirred and crawled over Megan, landing in Anna's lap. She stroked the soft fur on the puppy's head and sighed.

"What happened in your dream?" Megan asked quietly.

"Mommy, Daddy, and I were riding bikes. Then Daddy started going down the path to the lake, but I'm not supposed to ride down there so I couldn't follow him. Mommy and I waited but Daddy didn't come back."

"What happened then?" Rebekah prompted her.

"I don't know. I woke up."

"Were you scared?" Megan asked.

She shook her head. "No. Mommy was with me so I wasn't scared. I was just sad because I tried to go back to sleep and see where Daddy was, but I couldn't."

"I'm glad you weren't scared," Megan said.

"I know Daddy is in heaven, but I miss him," she sniffled.

Wanda looked up at Anna and gently licked her cheek.

"Aw, Wanda wants to help," Rebekah said. "I miss Daddy too, sweetie."

"You're supposed to miss your daddy, Anna. It's okay to miss him and it's okay to be sad. Maybe you were thinking about riding bikes tomorrow and that's what made you dream about it."

"Maybe," she said, stroking Wanda's head.

"You know, it's okay to be sad, but it's also okay to be happy," Megan said. "Does riding bikes make you happy?"

"Yeah, I like to ride bikes."

"Maybe your daddy was showing you that there's a new place to ride bikes. You couldn't ride to the lake at your old house," Megan said, looking at Rebekah for confirmation. When she nodded Megan continued. "But there's a new path for you to explore near my house."

Megan paused to let Anna digest this, then she asked, "Do you still want to ride bikes tomorrow?"

"Yes." She nodded.

Megan smiled. "Okay, only if you want to."

"I want to. I want to see the new path," she said, looking up at Megan.

Megan continued smiling down at her. "I can't wait to show you. While we're riding I want you to tell me all about the path you rode with your mommy and daddy."

"Okay, I will." Anna smiled at Megan and then looked at Rebekah. "Mommy, can I sleep with you tonight?"

Rebekah looked down at her daughter and wished she could take this sadness and pain from her little heart. "Yes honey, you can sleep with me."

"Do you want to spend the night with us, Megan? Mommy's bed is big enough for you and Wanda too."

"Aww, you are too sweet, Anna. I'd better take Wanda home. Maybe another time. Okay?'

"Okay." She smiled.

Rebekah looked at Megan and hoped she could feel the love she was sending to her.

"We'd better go so you can get back to sleep." Megan got up and Wanda raised her head. "Time to go, little sweetie. I think her superpower tonight is sleeping," she said.

"No, her superpower tonight is making me feel happy," Anna said.

"Honey, why don't you get the stuffed animal you're sleeping with tonight while I walk Megan and Wanda to their car."

"Okay. Bye Wanda," she said, petting the puppy's head. Then she wrapped her arms around Megan and hugged her. "Bye Megan, I'm glad you were here."

Megan patted Anna's back. "I had a really fun time with you and your mommy."

Anna left the room and Megan said, "You don't have to walk us out."

"I want to," she said, taking Megan's hand and weaving their fingers together.

Megan carried Wanda in her other arm.

"I'm glad you were here for that. I'm not sure what I would've said."

"You would've said the right things; don't doubt yourself, Bekah. You are her rock."

"Just like you used to be mine."

Megan opened her car door and put Wanda on the seat. She turned to Rebekah and said, "Call me tomorrow when you get through with church. Will Anna's bike fit in the back of your car?"

"Yeah, it will fit."

"Okay. I'll be ready when you call. Thank you for tonight," she said softly.

Rebekah leaned in and kissed Megan's cheek. She desperately wanted to kiss her lips but she knew Anna was waiting. "I can't wait to see you tomorrow."

"Me too." She was about to get in her car but turned and took Rebekah in her arms. She held her tight for a moment.

Rebekah sank into the hug and let Megan soothe her worries away.

Megan pulled away. "Good night."

"Text me when you get home," Rebekah said quickly.

Megan furrowed her brow and then softened. "I'm always here for you."

"I know. Text me." She smiled and held the door open for Megan.

She nodded and waited for Rebekah to walk back to the house before she drove off.

"We're going to be all right, Anna," Rebekah said as she watched Megan drive away.

12

Rebekah dropped Anna off at Sunday school and then made the short drive to the cemetery. She stopped in front of her grandmother's grave and got out of the car.

Since moving back to Athens she had not gone to Sunday school and had no plans to start. It was okay for Anna to attend for now and she hoped maybe she would make some new friends. Most Sundays she either drove to the park or came by here to place a flower on her grandparents grave.

"Hey Ma-maw," she said softly while placing a single rose at the base of the grave marker. She had a rose bush at the side of her house that was blooming with the most beautiful peach colored roses.

Her grandmother was a force. She once told her that women who say they are 'God-fearing' have it all wrong. *Why would you be afraid of God*, she said. *God is good and only wants the best for you. There's no reason to be afraid.* Rebekah remembered when she was in middle school her Ma-maw said to her, "Follow your heart, child. You won't be wrong as long as you do that because I know you have a good heart."

Rebekah could hear her grandmother saying those words like she was standing next to her. "Well, I'm following my heart, Ma-maw, just like you said. I'm not so sure the church is going to like it, but it's the right thing for me."

She had died before Anna was born and Rebekah knew she would have spoiled her. It made her sad that Anna didn't get to spend time with her, but she told her stories of things she and Ma-maw used to do when she was a girl, like bake apple pies.

Rebekah smiled at the thought of that. Her grandmother would have loved baking with them. Who knows, she may have been in the kitchen with them yesterday. She would've loved Megan, too. Ma-maw said that you shouldn't do things for others because God tells you to; you should do them because you want to help. She said you never knew when you might be the one that needed help. Megan was compassionate and passionate about helping others. That's what her grandmother would love.

Rebekah smiled at her grandmother's name on the footstone and said, "You'd love her because Anna and I do, Ma-maw, wouldn't you?" A bright red cardinal landed on the top of the grave marker. Rebekah quietly gasped. She had heard someone say that cardinals are like spiritual messengers from someone you've lost.

"Are you telling me it's okay, Ma-maw? I think you approve," Rebekah said with a smile.

The bird spread its wings for a moment then flew away.

"How about that!" Rebekah chuckled as she walked back to the car. She'd have to share that with Megan later.

Anna was excited to ride bikes that afternoon. All she'd talked about that morning was Megan and Wanda. Rebekah couldn't blame her, she was excited too. She knew that Anna would tell her parents all about last night and what they had planned for today. It would be interesting to see their reactions.

When she got back to the church, Sunday school was already out and the service was about to start. She saw Anna sitting with her mother in their regular spot. Rebekah always got a chuckle out of how people sat in the same pew, in the same seat every service. Beware the visitor that sat in a regular parishioner's spot.

"Hey sweetie," Rebekah said, sliding in next to Anna. "Hi Mom."

"I thought you were going to be late," her mother said, narrowing her eyes.

"Right on time," Rebekah replied, grinning at Anna and wrinkling her nose. Anna giggled.

The service began and her dad had chosen to preach about God's love.

"It's easy to love people who are our friends or family," he said. "But what about those that we don't like? Or those who choose lifestyles or politics that we don't approve of? Or maybe those we don't know at all?" He paused and looked around at the congregation.

"Jesus loved the ones that were considered the dregs of society, the unloveable. To love like God tells us to love everyone, you have to love the hard ones. We all have people that we don't particularly care for, but God says we have to love them."

Rebekah wondered if his congregation was listening and who they were thinking of when her dad said 'the hard ones.' Would they love her when they found out she loved a woman? More importantly, did it matter if they didn't?

As she pondered these questions, her dad wrapped

things up and they began to sing the closing hymn. On her way out she politely spoke to a few people she knew and then drove Anna to her parents' house for their usual Sunday lunch.

"I can't believe Neal was Megan's kitten first," Anna said, bending down to pet the cat as he greeted them at her parent's house.

"He wasn't for very long," Rebekah said.

"She should come over and see if he remembers her. Wouldn't that be something if he did?"

"Did what?" her mother asked as they walked into the kitchen.

"I found out that Neal belonged to Megan first," Anna exclaimed to her grandmother.

"What?"

"Do you remember when I brought Neal home?" Rebekah asked her.

"Of course I do. You said you found a kitten and didn't think we'd let you have it, so you gave it to a friend. That friend was allergic so you asked us if you could keep it. I don't know why you thought we wouldn't let you keep it," Helen told Rebekah.

"You would have if I'd brought it home?"

"Yes, we would have. Besides, Neal is a great cat," Helen added.

"Yeah he is," Rebekah agreed.

"Megan had dinner with us last night and brought Wanda over," Anna said excitedly. "And we get to go to her house and ride bikes this afternoon."

Helen nodded. "Oh is that so?"

"Yep. It's going to be so much fun."

"Honey, why don't you tell Grandma what you helped me do yesterday."

Anna smiled. "We baked an apple pie for dessert!"

"You did?" Helen smiled.

"We should've brought it with us today, Anna." Rebekah looked at her mom. "I don't know why I didn't think about it."

"We can take it to Megan's with us," Anna said.

"Isn't Megan your couns— uh art teacher?" Helen asked, stopping before saying counselor.

"Yes," Rebekah said. "She's also the friend that helped me rescue the kitten all those years ago."

"I thought she moved?" Helen said.

"I did too. Turns out, she ended up staying here. We were both very surprised that first day I picked Anna up from art."

"Hmm," Helen said, looking at Rebekah skeptically. "It's a small world."

"Thank goodness we found each other again," Rebekah mumbled to herself.

She helped her mom get lunch on the table as they waited for her dad to get home from church. Oftentimes parishioners would stop him after church for a word or two.

When they had all sat down and her dad prayed, they began to pass the bowls of food.

"I wonder why pot roast is a Sunday lunch favorite," Rebekah mused as she put a piece of meat on Anna's plate.

"It's easy to make. You can start it before church, cook it slowly and it's ready when you get home," her mom explained.

"I get that, but have you noticed we don't have it unless it's Sunday?"

"I don't like cooked carrots, Mommy," Anna said.

"I know that, honey. That's why I'm giving you a potato and how about green beans?"

Who I Believe

"Yes please and a roll. I love Grandma's rolls."

"Me too!" Rebekah grinned at her.

"Tell me about this biking adventure you're going on this afternoon," Daniel said.

"My friend Megan came over for dinner last night and invited us to ride bikes today," Anna said.

Rebekah chuckled to herself hearing Anna call Megan her friend. Honestly she wasn't wrong; she was both their friends.

"I have found out that Megan is also Anna's art teacher," Helen said to Daniel, stressing the last two words. "And she's also the friend who was allergic to Neal all those years ago."

Daniel looked at his wife and then at Rebekah. "How's that?"

"Megan was teaching a class at the college that summer I found Neal under that bush. She helped me coax him out."

"I thought she was a friend of yours?"

"She was and is. I thought she'd moved after the class was over, but turns out she and her best friend opened the center where she teaches art."

"We do other fun things there. That's where I get to play with Wanda, too," Anna added.

"Oh the superpowered puppy," Daniel said. "Well, I think we need to meet Megan." Daniel pinned Rebekah with a look.

"I want her to come see if Neal remembers her," Anna said excitedly.

Rebekah chuckled and looked down at her before looking back at her father. She couldn't quite read his expression, but she had a feeling he knew something that he hadn't shared with her.

"I saw you come into church right before it started,"

Daniel said to Rebekah. "I don't suppose you went to Sunday school?"

"No Dad, I didn't. I went out to the cemetery and left a rose on Ma-maw and Grandad's grave."

"That was nice of you," he said.

"Anna and I have a beautiful rose bush at the side of the house. I'll bring you one, Mom."

"They smell so good," Anna added.

During the rest of the meal, Rebekah's parents caught her up on church news and asked about her school and Anna's school as well.

"We'd better go, sweetie," Rebekah said, finishing up the dishes.

"Oh that's right. You've got a bicycle date," Daniel said.

"Anna, would you like to spend Friday night with us? We've missed movie night and YOU!" Helen said, wrapping Anna in a hug.

"Can I, Mommy?"

"I don't see why not."

"Great. We'll give Mommy a night to herself," Helen said. "We'll talk later in the week."

"Thanks, Mom. Give your Grandpa a hug," Rebekah said.

"I love you, honey," Daniel said, hugging Anna. He looked at Rebekah and held out his arms.

Rebekah smiled and walked into his embrace. "I love you, Daddy."

"I love you, too."

Rebekah gave her mom a hug and they went home to change for the afternoon.

She called Megan while they were in the car. "Hey Meg."

"Hi Bekah."

"We're on our way home from my parents' house. When do you want us?"

"Right now!"

Rebekah chuckled. "You're on speaker. Are you excited to see us?"

"Wanda and I both can't wait until you get here. Are you ready to ride bikes, Anna?"

"Yes and play with Wanda!"

"Come on over, girls. We'll be waiting."

Rebekah smiled as she ended the call and soon pulled into their driveway. "Let's take the pie with us," she said to Anna.

"Okay."

"You go in and change, then get your bike out of the garage."

"Okay, Mommy," Anna said, hurrying out of the car.

Rebekah went in to get the scissors and came back out to cut a rose for Megan. She remembered how Megan oftentimes had flowers or little gifts for her when she'd come to her apartment that summer. Maybe it was her turn to romance Megan and now that she knew Anna wouldn't be home Friday night, they could have a real date.

Just the thought made her heart rate speed up in her chest.

13

"Okay Anna, help me find her house. Do you see 1401?" Rebekah said as they slowly drove down Megan's street.

"There it is! I see it!" she exclaimed, pointing out the window.

"Oh, what a pretty house! It looks like Megan," Rebekah said, pulling into the driveway.

"What? It looks like a house," Anna said.

"I mean it fits her. It's the kind of house I would imagine her living in."

Anna tilted her head. "I kind of see what you mean. It's happy like she is."

"Yeah, it's a happy house."

The house was white brick with black trim and accents. It had a yellow front door that made the house welcoming. The yard was well kept and there were a couple of trees in the front. Rebekah saw Megan's car in the opened two-car garage. She noticed two bikes ready and waiting for them to ride.

Before Anna could run up to the front door it opened and a smiling Megan stepped onto the front porch.

"You found it." She grinned.

"Hi Megan," Anna said, smiling up at her.

"Hi Anna," Megan said cheerily, bending down. "Welcome to my home."

Rebekah joined them on the porch. "I love your house!"

"Thanks, I haven't been here long."

"Mommy said it looked like you. I said it looked happy," Anna announced proudly.

"Well, if a house can be happy then it is because both of you are here."

"Where's Wanda?"

"Look right through there and you'll see her in the window of the back door. She's waiting on you."

Anna walked in and went to the back of the living room.

"I'm so glad to see you," Rebekah said softly, squeezing Megan's hand.

"I'm glad you're both here," Megan said, her heartbeat picking up.

"Can I let her in?" Anna asked from across the room.

"*May* I let her in," Rebekah corrected her.

"May I let her in?" she parroted.

"Yes you may," Megan said, grinning at Rebekah.

Wanda came bounding in and stopped to lick Anna's face as she bent down. Then she ran straight for Rebekah and stopped at her feet, wiggling her tail.

"Look at this good girl not jumping up," Rebekah said, bending down and scooping the puppy into her arms. Wanda tried to lick her nose, but just missed. "Oh you are a feisty one, full of kisses."

Megan's chest swelled with happiness as she looked

from Rebekah holding Wanda to Anna grinning at them both.

"We want you to come over to Grandma and Grandpa's to see if Neal remembers you," Anna told Megan.

"Do you think he will?"

"I don't know. That's why you have to come over." Anna giggled then put her hand in Megan's.

"Would you like to play in the backyard with Wanda for a few minutes before we go ride bikes? She can't go with us and if you play with her now then she can nap while we're gone."

"Okay. Come on, Wanda." Anna took the puppy from Rebekah while Megan held open the back door.

Anna found Wanda's toys on the back patio and began to play with the pup.

"Show me your home," Rebekah urged Megan.

Megan held out her arms and said, "This is the great room." The living room was open to a dining area where a table with six chairs stood. Over to the other side, the kitchen separated the room with a large island.

Rebekah walked into the middle of the room and turned around. "I love it. What a beautiful fireplace and mantle."

"Thank you. I haven't done much decorating yet. Maybe you could help me?"

Rebekah spun around. "You know I'd love that."

"I thought so." Megan chuckled.

Rebekah moved into the kitchen and ran her hand over the top of the island. "Oh Megan, the things you could cook in this kitchen."

"*You* could cook. I'm not nearly as talented as you."

"I'm sure you could persuade me to make you dinner sometime." She grinned.

"You look like you belong there," Megan said from the other side of the island.

"What are you trying to say?" Rebekah raised an eyebrow.

"I didn't mean it like that. You look at home standing there."

Rebekah smiled and closed her eyes for a moment.

Megan wondered if she was imagining herself and Anna here because she already had.

"Come on, I'll show you the rest." Megan led them into the hall where two bedrooms looked out to the front yard. Across the hall was a bathroom and the laundry room.

"Oh, this is great having the laundry room right here. Mine was next to the garage in Miami. I had to walk through the entire house to put our clothes away in the bedrooms."

"I use this first room as a guest room and the other as an office. You can see I haven't done much to them."

"That's okay."

They walked to the end of the hall and through the primary bedroom door.

"Oh Meg," Rebekah said as she walked into the large bedroom. "This is wonderful."

"Wait until you see the bathroom. I think I bought the house because of this master suite."

Rebekah looked out the french doors into the backyard where Anna was playing with Wanda.

She turned to Megan and said, "That reminds me, would you like to go out with me Friday night?"

Megan's eyes widened. "Are you asking me on a date?"

"I certainly am. We didn't go out much before."

"We were kind of busy with other things," Megan said in a low voice.

"Oh, I remember. But you knew I was hesitant to go out

because I'd want to hold your hand or kiss you in public and I was too afraid."

"How could I complain about that!"

Rebekah giggled. "My mom invited Anna to spend the night with them Friday night. I'd love for us to do something together." She glanced at the bed before walking towards the bathroom.

"I'd love that too," Megan said, following her.

"Good God! I see what you mean. This bathroom is amazing," Rebekah exclaimed.

There was a huge shower and two sinks with a large tub. On the other side was a doorway that led to a large walk-in closet.

"And this closet. How fun would it be to fill this up!"

Megan watched Rebekah and couldn't help but hope someday that would happen.

When Rebekah spun around she wrapped her arms around Megan's shoulders and Megan's hands went directly to Rebekah's hips as they had done so many times before.

They were so close that Megan could feel Rebekah's breath on her face. She looked into Rebekah's eyes and saw her look down and lick her lips. She could feel her closing the distance between them just when they heard, "Mom! Megan! Where are you?"

Rebekah leaned away and smiled. "Soon," she whispered. Then she stepped out of the closet and called to Anna. "We're back here. Come see Megan's room."

While Megan calmed her heart as it slammed against her chest, Anna found them, Wanda hurrying behind her. "Wow! That's a big shower!"

Megan chuckled. "Are you ready to ride bikes?"

"Yes ma'am!" Anna exclaimed.

"Well then, let's go." Megan winked at Rebekah and they all went outside.

Megan grabbed a small backpack and put it on while Rebekah got Anna's bike out of her car.

"This is for you," she said, handing Rebekah a helmet.

"Thank you." Rebekah put it on and made sure Anna had hers on too.

"Okay, let's ride," Megan said in a tough voice.

Anna laughed and Rebekah looked at Megan and shook her head. "Yeah, we look like a biker gang all right."

Megan led them around the neighborhood and into a park that had dirt paths as well as paved ones. She and Anna raced a few times and laughter filled the air. She couldn't remember when she'd had such a good time and then realized that's exactly what she'd felt last night.

"Let's stop here," Megan said, pulling over and leaning her bike against a tree. She waited for Anna to put her kick stand down and handed her a bottle of water.

Rebekah found the water bottle that Megan had put on her bike and took a long drink. "What a perfect day for a bike ride. Let's sit in the shade for a minute."

They sat down beneath a tree and watched a couple of people play frisbee out in the field across from them.

"Isn't this a good place to ride?" Megan asked.

Anna nodded but didn't say anything.

Megan looked at Rebekah and furrowed her brow.

"Are you okay, Anna?" Megan asked.

"Yeah, I was just thinking about my daddy," she said in a sad voice.

"Oh good," Megan said warmly. "Would you tell me about him?"

Anna looked up at her, unsure at first and then when she started to talk, a smile grew on her face. "He used to say we had to stop so Mommy could rest when we rode bikes, but I knew he thought I needed to. He would race me sometimes, but he always let me win."

"What else?" Megan encouraged her.

"Sometimes I would ride to the store with him when he was getting beer for the football game. He'd always let me get a treat and then he'd say, 'Shh, don't tell Mommy. It's our secret.'" She looked at her mother and giggled.

Rebekah reached over and tickled her around the middle. "You two were always keeping secrets from me."

Anna laughed. "No we weren't. Stop!"

Rebekah stopped so Anna could catch her breath and watched as her face fell.

"Sometimes I forget what Daddy sounded like," she said softly.

"Do you have a video of him?" Megan asked Rebekah quietly.

"I do!" Rebekah reached into her back pocket for her phone and pulled up a video of Anna and Ben putting a puzzle together at their house in Miami.

Anna watched and smiled.

"I can show this to you anytime you want, honey. I have others, too."

"Daddy used to tickle me all the time," she said, leaning back against Rebekah.

"Hey Anna, I want to try something. Would you sit up and close your eyes?" Megan asked her.

Anna paused and looked at her and then sat up.

"Okay, your mom is going to put her hands around your middle," Megan said. She looked at Rebekah and nodded.

Rebekah placed her hands around Anna and squeezed gently.

"Now, I want you to close your eyes and feel your mom's

hands around you but I want you to imagine a time that your daddy tickled you," Megan guided her. She paused. "Can you feel it?"

Anna nodded.

Megan looked at Rebekah and wiggled her fingers, nodding at Rebekah to do the same.

Anna began to smile.

"Can you feel your daddy tickling you?" Megan asked softly.

Anna nodded again.

Megan waited for several moments to let Anna enjoy the feeling. She looked at Rebekah and could see gratitude in her eyes.

"Okay, will you open your eyes and look at me?" Megan asked.

Anna opened her eyes and looked at Megan with a small smile on her face.

"Whenever you're missing your daddy you can close your eyes, take a deep breath and imagine his hands on your middle, just like your mommy did. Then maybe you won't feel so sad."

Anna leaned back against Rebekah again and nodded. "Okay. I'll try that." She looked up at Rebekah and said, "I felt Daddy when my eyes were closed."

"Did it make you happy?"

Anna nodded.

"Anytime you want to see those videos all you have to do is ask, okay?" Rebekah told her.

"Okay."

Rebekah looked up at Megan. "Thank you, Megan, for helping us feel happy about Daddy."

Megan smiled at them both and took Anna's hand in hers.

"Daddy used to call me Anna Banana," she told Megan.

"He did? You are never going to believe this, Anna!" Megan grabbed her backpack and pulled out three bananas. She handed one to each of them. "I think your daddy knew we were riding bikes today!"

Anna happily ate her banana and grinned. "If we were at the center painting," she said to Megan, "I would be painting the brightest blue because that's how I feel inside!"

Megan grinned and glanced quickly at Rebekah and saw tears in her eyes. "My happy color is yellow. I would be painting a bright yellow."

"Like your front door?" Anna asked.

Megan laughed. "Like my front door."

Anna got up and hugged Megan. "Thank you for making me happy about Daddy."

Megan hugged her back with tears in her own eyes.

14

After a ride down a different trail and around Megan's neighborhood they pedaled back to her house.

"Wanda will be happy to see us," Anna said, getting off her bike.

"Yes she will," Megan agreed.

They went into the house and Wanda's tail wagged like the rotor on a helicopter.

"What a greeting! Is she always this excited when you get home?" Rebekah asked, petting the rambunctious puppy.

"Yes. She immediately cheers me up if I'm having a bad day."

"Aw, I hope that doesn't happen often." Rebekah rubbed her hand across Megan's back.

"My days have gotten much better recently," she replied.

"Is it okay if we go outside?" Anna asked.

"Yes, she'll be happy to have a playmate."

They followed her outside. Megan and Rebekah sat on the porch and watched Anna and Wanda play.

"I'll be right back," Megan said, going inside to get them all a drink. When she came back out she said, "Does Anna banana need another snack?"

Anna giggled. "No."

"Is it okay if I call you that?"

"Yes, it's okay if you call me that, Megan, but no one else."

Megan smiled as she threw the ball for Wanda and they both chased after it.

"You are amazing with her," Rebekah said, reaching her hand out.

Megan took it and smiled. "I want her to feel better."

"She does when she's with you. Let me correct that, *we* feel better when we're with you."

"This doesn't have anything to do with therapy, Rebekah, because I feel better when I'm with both of you."

They watched Anna and Wanda play and simply enjoyed being together.

Anna came back to the patio and sat in one of the chairs and took a long drink.

"You didn't tell me what you talked about in Sunday School today," Rebekah said.

"We're supposed to love one another," she replied.

"Oh, that's what Grandpa preached about. Do you remember what he said?"

"Yes, it's easy to love some people but not others."

"Isn't that the truth!" Megan said.

Rebekah chuckled. "Anna, can you give me an example of that?"

Anna thought for a moment. "Well, it's easy to love Megan and Wanda," she said, smiling at Megan and rubbing the puppy's head. "But it's hard to love Gavin sometimes because he can be mean."

Rebekah looked at Megan and said, "Gavin is a boy in her class." She noticed Megan's eyes glistening and saw her swallow and then look at Anna.

"I know what you mean, Anna. You and your mommy are very easy to love, but there are a couple of kids that come to the center ..." She didn't finish.

Anna looked up at her. "Really?"

"Yep."

"Honey, I think it's time for us to go."

"Do we have to?"

"Please stay," Megan pleaded. "We're having such a good time."

Rebekah looked at Anna's hopeful face and then at Megan. Those warm brown eyes begged her not to go. "Ugh, I can't say no to both of you."

"Yeah!" Anna clapped. "Megan, do you get the Food Network?"

"Yes," she answered, drawing the word out suspiciously.

"Mommy and I like to watch the *Kids Baking Championship*. Have you seen it?"

"I have. Those kids are incredible."

"Can, oops, may we watch it?"

Megan looked at Rebekah and she shrugged.

"Will you stay for dinner?"

"Oh no, we can't do that," Rebekah protested.

"Yes you can. How about we have breakfast for dinner?"

"Yes!" Anna exclaimed.

"Are you sure?"

"It would make me so happy," Megan said.

"Okay."

"Yes!" Megan said, holding up her hand to Anna for a high five.

They went inside and settled in to watch the show. Anna

sat between them and Rebekah put her arm across the back of the couch. She rested her hand on Megan's shoulder and couldn't help gently squeezing it occasionally. It had been such a nice afternoon.

Halfway through the show Megan said softly, "I'm going to start the pancakes. We can eat when this episode is over."

"I'll help," Rebekah said.

"No, stay and watch for a little longer. I'm just going to make the batter and get things going."

Rebekah watched Megan walk to the kitchen. *What a beautiful woman.* She had been in love with Megan for such a long time. Even when it didn't seem like she'd ever see her again that love was in her heart.

She put her arm around Anna and pulled her close. These were the people she loved most in the world. For the first time she felt like she and Anna were going to be okay. When Ben died she knew they would find a way to make it through, but at times it was hard to keep believing, especially when Anna was so withdrawn and sad. But since finding Megan again she believed a little more each day and now she could feel it.

Rebekah got up to help Megan. She walked up behind her and gently slipped her arms around her middle. Megan leaned back into her for a moment.

"Thank you for today," Rebekah said softly.

"I should be thanking you."

"What can I do?" Rebekah asked, slowly pulling away.

"Let's eat here on the island. The plates are in that cabinet and the silverware is in there." Megan indicated with her head.

"They're about to send someone home," Anna said from the couch.

"Okay," they answered in unison.

Megan had pancakes in the skillet and flipped them quickly before sidling up next to Rebekah, who was standing behind where Anna sat on the couch.

"Who will it be, Anna?" Rebekah asked.

"I'm not sure."

"I think Carson has to go," Megan said.

"Me too!" Anna agreed.

When the judges sent Carson home Anna turned around and held her hand up to Megan.

She high-fived her and said, "Let's eat!"

Rebekah and Anna sat on one side of the island and Megan flipped a pancake onto Anna's plate. She laughed when she tried to do the same for Rebekah and she missed. "Oops!"

They all laughed and Megan put the rest of the pancakes on their plates. There was fruit, butter and syrup to top the pancakes.

"I like breakfast for dinner," Anna said, putting a big bite of pancake in her mouth.

Megan chuckled and Rebekah winked at her.

When they were finished Anna went back to the couch to watch another episode while Rebekah and Megan cleaned up.

"The dishes are in the dishwasher. Do you want me to start it?"

"I will later," Megan said, putting the leftovers away.

Rebekah started towards the couch and stopped. "Megan," she said quietly. "Come see."

Megan walked over to her and followed her gaze. Wanda was curled up next to Anna where she lay on the couch. Both of them were fast asleep.

"If that isn't the cutest," Megan whispered.

Rebekah smiled, took Megan's hand and pulled her back

into the kitchen. She put her arms around Megan's neck and looked into her eyes. Megan had her hands on Rebekah's hips and pulled her closer.

"I can't wait until Friday," Rebekah whispered. She brought her lips to Megan's and when they touched she felt like she was home. These were the same soft but firm lips that changed her life. When she sank into the kiss Megan pulled her even closer. Their lips parted in perfect harmony and their tongues touched in the sweetest caress. This kiss was familiar and new. It began as a long awaited reconnection and then their hearts took over.

Rebekah could feel Megan's love as their tongues tangled and tasted and then the passion woke in both their hearts. Their breathing was short and quick, but they didn't pull away. They kissed with hope and possibility and most powerfully with promise.

When they had to breathe Rebekah pulled back but still held Megan close. She touched her lips to Megan's one more time before a smile crept on her face.

"You're all mine Friday," she said softly.

Megan nodded.

"Can we stay here?"

"Yes," she replied hoarsely.

"I'm going to show you all the love I've been saving all these years."

It was Megan's turn to smile. "I want it all."

Rebekah released a deep breath and closed her eyes. All she wanted was to keep kissing Megan, but she knew she had to get Anna home. She loosened her hold on Megan. "I've got to wake her up or she won't sleep tonight. That will make for a long tomorrow."

Megan nodded. "I'll carry her to the car."

Rebekah cupped the side of Megan's face. "I love you, Meg."

"I love you, Bekah."

"This won't be easy, but nothing with us ever was."

Megan shrugged. "Who wants easy when they can have this?" She grabbed Rebekah and kissed her with such passion and then she softened the kiss and pulled away.

"Good God, woman," Rebekah panted.

Megan winked and went over to move the sleeping Wanda from Anna's side.

"Sweetie," Rebekah said, rousing the sleeping Anna. "We've got to go home."

Anna moaned and her eyelids fluttered open. "I fell asleep."

"Come on, Anna banana. I'll carry you to the car," Megan said.

She let Megan pick her up and carry her outside. "Night Wanda," she mumbled as they went through the door.

When Anna was buckled into the seat, Megan walked around to Rebekah's side of the car.

"Text me when you get home."

"I will. Thank you for such a wonderful afternoon and night."

"Thank you, Megan," Anna said sleepily.

"You're welcome. I'll see you Tuesday."

"Okay," she said, yawning.

Megan reached in and gently ran the back of her fingers down Rebekah's cheek.

Rebekah put the car in gear and backed out of the driveway. The old familiar feeling of longing hit her like a brick. She remembered hating leaving Megan's apartment all those years ago. Maybe someday she wouldn't have to leave at all.

15

Megan looked down at her phone and smiled.

"I bet I know who's making you smile like that," Crystal said, walking into Megan's office and sitting down.

"How was your session with Easton?" Megan asked, putting her phone on the desk.

"You can read my notes in the file. Now, what did Rebekah say to put that smile on your face?"

"She doesn't have to say anything to make me smile."

"You speak the truth!" Crystal teased.

"I can't wait until tomorrow night. We have so much fun with Anna, but it will be nice to be alone and have a conversation of more than a sentence or two."

"Are you kidding me? How much talking do you really think you'll be doing? You haven't been together in twelve years!"

"Sex isn't everything, Crystal!"

"I'll ask you again Monday and we'll see what your answer is."

Megan sighed. "Of course I want to be alone with her, but I worry that it may be too fast."

"Her husband has been gone for a year. You are not some random person she met. She knows you; she's in love with you and has been for years. Trust her, Megan."

"I do trust her, but there's also Anna to think about."

"I couldn't believe the difference in Anna on Tuesday. It's because she was with you and Rebekah most of the weekend."

"Maybe. She's beginning to talk about her dad and remember happy times."

"I know. She's talked to me too. That's big, Megan."

She smiled and nodded. "I love that kid, Crystal."

"I know you do. I also know that you only want what's best for them. Did you ever think that maybe they need you?"

Megan locked eyes with Crystal.

"And you need them. Take a fucking chance for once in your life, Megan!"

"I did, Crystal, when I fell in love with Rebekah even though she was only nineteen. And then she left me."

Crystal tilted her head and gave Megan a compassionate smile. "She didn't leave you. Besides, she came back. Remember?"

"Yes, but she still has a lot to lose by being with me."

"A lot to lose? Like what?"

"Her parents, her church. We don't know how Anna will react."

"Anna will be fine. She loves you. I think there is a kid in her class that has two dads, come to think of it."

"What about her parents? And the church is important to her, Crystal."

"Do you really think they wouldn't come around? She's

their only kid and Anna is their only grandkid."

"I don't know. Her dad is a preacher. Remember?"

"Yeah, I remember. It will be a perfect opportunity for him to live what he preaches. Oh wait? What does he preach?"

Megan chuckled. "He's not one of those that preaches you're going to hell for being gay."

"I couldn't imagine he would be, but you never know. Look, you are getting so far ahead of yourself. Give this a chance. You and Rebekah have found each other again. This is a second chance for both of you and you're obviously madly in love with one another. Most people don't get that."

"I know."

"Rebekah knows Anna better than anyone and trusts you with her, right?"

"Yes."

"Rebekah has told you that she's in love with you, right?"

"Yes."

"You can't keep from smiling when you think about her, Megan."

"I want her to have it all," Megan said.

"Why don't you ask Rebekah what she wants because I think you are going to be right behind Anna on that list. *You* are the one to give her everything."

"But there are obstacles, Crystal. Rebekah said nothing is easy with us."

"And you'll get through them together. Who do you believe, Megan?"

"What?"

"Who do you believe? Do you believe the preachers out there that don't want to marry us? Do you believe that part of society that says we're evil? Or do you believe Rebekah when she tells you she loves you?"

Megan scoffed then nodded. "I believe Rebekah. I believed her back then when she was struggling with her sexuality and what she'd been taught. I believe her now because I can see it in her eyes and feel it in my heart."

"Then love her back, Megan. Don't let anything get in the way. Don't you believe in your love? It's powerful if it's lasted this long and you were together for such a short time."

Megan smiled. "It is powerful. It began that way and still is. We'll make it through anything now that we're together again."

"There's the Megan I know. Now go get Anna and those kids. It's your turn to drive."

Megan chuckled and got up.

"Is Rebekah picking her up after our session? Don't answer that. What a dumb question. Of course she is." Crystal laughed.

She got in the SUV and drove to the school. Crystal was right about everything. Megan knew everything she said, but sometimes you had to hear it from someone else. There would always be bumps in the road for them, but she knew they could overcome anything together.

Anna was excited to see her and it warmed Megan's heart.

"Are we painting today?" Anna asked.

"We are. Crystal will have everything ready when we get there."

"You're still coming to church on Sunday to hear me play handbells, aren't you?"

"I wouldn't miss it."

Anna grinned.

When the rest of the kids were buckled into the SUV Megan took them to the counseling center.

Crystal was ready to lead the session when the kids came in. They all started with her instructions and Megan stood back to observe.

"There's something for you in your office. I've got this," Crystal said to her. When Megan looked at her, clearly confused, Crystal laughed. "Just go."

She went into her office and there sat Rebekah. "What are you doing here?"

"Hey," she said, getting up. She closed Megan's door and then wrapped her arms around her and kissed her deeply.

"Wow," Megan said, breathless.

"I couldn't wait until tomorrow." Rebekah grinned and kissed her again lightly.

"I was going to make up some excuse to come by and see you after class."

Rebekah chuckled. "We've got it bad; just like the good old days. I've always wanted to say that."

Megan smiled. "We've got lots of good days to look forward to."

"Would you come to Sunday lunch with us after church?"

"Anna asked me earlier if I was still coming to hear her play."

"I want you to meet my parents. They have heard us talk about you often enough; don't you think it's time for you to meet?"

Megan's heart sped up and it wasn't just because Rebekah was in her arms. "Yes. I'd love to meet them. If they don't like me at least Neal will be there. Hopefully he'll remember me."

Rebekah tilted her head. "Anna and I love you. We'll protect you." Megan smiled and Rebekah continued. "They'll love you! How can they not when Anna and I do?"

"Oh it could happen."

"It'll be fine. I hope you like roast. We have it most Sundays."

"I love roast. I haven't had it since the last time I went to see my parents."

Rebekah gazed into Megan's eyes and had the sweetest smile on her face.

"So you love me, huh?" Megan said in a low voice.

"You'll find out how much tomorrow." Rebekah pressed her lips to Megan's.

"You haven't told me what we're doing," Megan said when they pulled apart.

"Dress casually. We'll be outside and then we're going to your place. I can't seem to get that huge shower and tub out of my head." She gave Megan a wicked smile.

Megan could feel her cheeks reddening and her heart speed up because that's what Rebekah did to her.

"You'd better get back to the kids. I told Crystal I only needed you for a few minutes. I'll wait here. I don't want to make Anna nervous."

"I needed this," Megan said, releasing a deep breath.

"Oh babe. I always need you. Don't ever forget that." Rebekah gave her another deep kiss then let her go.

* * *

After class Rebekah and Anna went by her parents' house.

"What a nice surprise," Helen said.

"Hi Mom," Rebekah said as Anna gave her grandmother a hug.

"I came by because I wanted to invite Megan to lunch on Sunday. She's coming to church to hear Anna play and I want you and Dad to meet her."

"She can see Neal then, too!" Anna said excitedly.

"Yes she can. We'll find out if he remembers her."

"That's fine, honey. We'd love to meet her."

"Don't do anything special. It's simply Sunday lunch with another place set at the table. Okay?"

Helen nodded.

"She likes roast," Rebekah added.

"Maybe we can ride bikes again," Anna said.

"We'll see." Rebekah turned to her mom. "When do you want Anna tomorrow?"

"Whenever."

"After school we'll pack a bag and I'll bring her over."

"Do you want to stay for dinner?"

"No thanks." Rebekah smiled.

Helen studied her daughter and asked, "Do you have plans?"

Rebekah gave her a measured smile. "Maybe."

"Have fun. You deserve it, honey."

Rebekah was surprised at her mother's words. "Thanks Mom."

"We're going to have so much fun tomorrow night, aren't we, Anna?'

"Yes ma'am!"

"Maybe we can do this every Friday night," Helen said.

Rebekah raised her eyebrows. "Let's see how tomorrow goes."

Helen smiled and nodded.

"Come on sweetie, we'd better get home."

"See you tomorrow."

On the way home Rebekah couldn't help but feel hopeful. She'd found Megan again, Anna was getting better and she was bringing Megan to meet her parents. *One step at a time*, she told herself.

16

Rebekah picked Anna up from school. "How was your day?"

"It was good," Anna replied.

"Just good?"

Anna looked over at her. "We played outside at recess and I got to swing. Ms. Cody said I did a good job reading out loud and I got an A on my math paper."

"That does sound good. Are you excited to spend the night with Grandma and Grandpa?"

"Yes. I know they miss me, so it will be good for them."

Rebekah stifled a laugh.

When they got home she went into Anna's room to help her pack. "Do you want to take anything to sleep with? You left a couple of your stuffed animals there."

"No. I can sleep with them. They've probably been lonely."

Rebekah chuckled. "They probably have."

"Mommy, are you sure you'll be okay? If you get lonely you can come over."

"I'll be fine, but that's good to know."

"What are you going to do?"

"I'm going out to dinner with Megan."

"Oh good, that way you won't be by yourself. Can we go see her and Wanda tomorrow? I didn't get to play with her yesterday since she had to stay home."

"I'll ask her." Rebekah looked around the room. "I think that's everything. Are you ready to go?"

"Yes ma'am."

Rebekah dropped Anna off at her parents' and then went back home to get ready for her date. She wondered if Megan was nervous. In a way *she* was nervous, but she was also excited. Rebekah loved the conversations they got into and she never had to be guarded with her opinions. It was obvious what was going to happen tonight since she was staying over at Megan's. She had thought about making love to Megan many times over the years.

Ben knew Megan was her first love and he had never seemed to feel threatened. It didn't bother him that she was bisexual. He knew that Rebekah loved him and that she was committed to their family. When she thought about it she could see Ben and Megan being friends. There were similarities between them. Maybe that's why she loved them both so much.

She looked in the mirror one more time and checked her makeup. A smile grew on her face. "You're going to your girl's," she said to her reflection. She locked up the house and drove to Megan's.

Before she could ring the doorbell Megan opened the door.

"I'm so glad you're here."

"Hi," Rebekah chuckled. "Are you anxious?"

"I'm happy to see you. Come in," she said, stepping aside so Rebekah could walk in.

Rebekah squeezed Megan's hand as she walked by.

"Was Anna okay at your folks?"

"Yes. She made me laugh. She thinks she's doing them a favor because she knows they miss her."

Megan chuckled. "Do you want a glass of wine before we go?"

"I don't think so. Could we sit for a minute?"

"Sure," Megan replied, sitting next to Rebekah on the couch.

"Are you nervous?" Rebekah asked.

"No. I'm excited. There's nothing better than spending time with you."

Rebekah leaned in and kissed Megan sweetly. "We'd better go or I won't want to leave."

"That happened to us a lot before, didn't it?" Megan said, kissing her back.

They hopped up and Rebekah drove them to the river.

"I love these places along the river," Megan said. "You remembered."

"I do. I thought we could try this new place I heard about at school and then we could take a walk along the river."

"That sounds perfect."

When they were seated Rebekah said, "Do you still love fish tacos?"

"Yes." Megan looked up.

"I hear they have the best." Rebekah looked at Megan and tilted her head. "Does it surprise you that I remember?"

"A little."

"Meg, I remember everything. You meant more to me

than you'll probably ever know, but I'm hoping to show you."

"Bekah, sometimes I can't believe you are here and this is happening."

Their server came to take their order and they decided to try several things and share.

Rebekah leaned over and took Megan's hand. "I'm not afraid to be seen with you like I was before."

"I understood, Rebekah."

"I know you did, but I thought we should talk about what we're going to do."

"Okay. I will be perfectly honest with you. I miss you and Anna if I don't see you every day."

Rebekah smiled. "I miss you, too. One reason I want my parents to meet you is because I want them to see us together with Anna."

"I want to meet your folks. Do they know that I'm gay?"

"I'm not sure that they do. I don't know exactly how to tell them about us, but I'll figure it out."

"We don't have to do everything at once. Shouldn't we see how things go with Anna first?"

"Yes, but..." Rebekah sighed.

"What is it?"

"I don't want someone to see us out together and my parents find out that way. I want to be the one to tell them."

Megan nodded. "Then we'll be careful until the time is right. I don't mind having you all to myself for a while."

Rebekah smiled. "I don't want to put you in the closet though."

"You won't be. How about we have dinner together most nights?"

"I know after staying with you tonight I'm not going to like waking up without you."

"Then let's spend weekends together too. We'll have sleepovers at both our houses when Anna is ready. We'll figure it out."

Rebekah softened. "I know we will. I'm sorry it has to be so hard."

"You are back in my life. Being without you was hard. Let's enjoy our dinner and simply be together."

"You make everything seem easier. That's another reason I love you."

Their food came and they shared just as they did years ago. Then they walked along the river and talked and caught up on each other's week.

"I have one other place I want us to go," Rebekah said as they walked to the car. She looked around and took Megan's hand. "I knew this would happen. I love holding hands with you."

"I love it, too, but..."

"It's okay, no one is watching us."

She drove them to the park that was further down the river. It was just beginning to get dark. She took a blanket out of the back of the car and reached for Megan's hand.

"I found us a spot over here," she said, leading them under a tree. "I knew there wouldn't be many people in the park this time of day."

They spread the blanket out and sat. "Do you remember when we would sit out and look at the stars?"

"Those were some of my best memories. You didn't have to worry about being seen."

Rebekah leaned back on her elbows and looked up at the heavens. "They're just beginning to come out."

Megan leaned back on one elbow, propped her head on her hand and gazed at Rebekah.

"You're missing the stars," Rebekah said.

"Oh no I'm not. I can see them sparkling in your eyes."

Rebekah lowered on to one elbow and looked at Megan and smiled. "I love you, Meg."

"Oh Bekah, I love you, too." She leaned over and kissed her gently. "Thank you for taking me out."

"I know it wasn't fancy."

"But you took me to a place I love and now this." Megan rolled onto her back and looked up. "Oh wow, look now."

Rebekah rolled onto her back and gazed at the natural light show while holding Megan's hand. "I love this time of year. It's not too cold to lie under the stars with your girl and it's not too hot during the day."

"Your girl, huh." Megan chuckled. "I like that."

Rebekah squeezed her hand.

"It won't be long until summer. You and Anna must be looking forward to that."

"What do you do during the summer? Will Anna still have therapy?"

"Yes, and we have other programs for kids during the summer."

"Maybe we could go on vacation together. You, me, and Anna!"

"That would be fun. Have you taken her to Atlanta? We could go to the aquarium, the zoo, and they have Legoland."

Rebekah rolled onto her side and Megan looked over at her. "You'd want to do that?"

Megan rolled over then and put her hand on Rebekah's cheek. "Of course I'd want to do that."

Rebekah smiled and released a contented breath. "When I look in your eyes I believe everything is going to be okay."

Megan returned her smile. "It is. We'll make it okay together."

Rebekah leaned in and kissed Megan tenderly.

"I could kiss you all night long," Megan said, her breath shaky.

"Let's go and do just that," Rebekah replied, getting up and holding out a hand to Megan.

17

When they pulled into Megan's driveway the garage door began to rise. "Go ahead, pull in. I reorganized things so your car would fit inside too. Here." Megan handed her the garage door controller.

"What?"

"Take it. I hope you and Anna will be spending a lot of time here."

Rebekah clipped it onto her visor and grinned. "Thank you."

They went into the house and Megan said, "Do you want anything to drink?"

Rebekah shook her head and set her bag on the island. She bent down and pet Wanda on the head.

Megan walked over, picked up the bag and took Rebekah's hand. She led them to the bedroom and set Rebekah's bag on a chair. "Do you need to check on Anna?"

"No," she replied, already breathless.

Megan stood in front of Rebekah and smiled.

"I'm trying not to devour you because since I saw you in the counseling center all I've wanted to do is this." Rebekah grabbed Megan's face in her hands and kissed her with fervor.

Megan lost her breath and could feel and hear her heart pounding in her ears. This kiss wasn't like the others. Rebekah claimed her and had no thoughts of letting her go. Megan was lost in the kiss when she felt Rebekah's hands at the bottom of her shirt pulling it up and over her head.

Their lips had to part to get the shirt off and as Megan inhaled deeply Rebekah took her own shirt off.

"Slow down, baby," Megan whispered. "We have all night."

"And a lot of catching up to do." Rebekah grinned. "This first time I'm going to give you all my love. Then I'm taking what's mine."

Megan remembered how passionate Rebekah could be and her mouth went dry. All she could say was, "I am yours."

Rebekah reached around Megan and unclasped her bra. "You were always the most beautiful woman I'd ever seen," she whispered.

Megan did the same to Rebekah and took just a moment to drink in this incredible woman.

"I'm different because pregnancy will do things to a body," Rebekah said, her voice suddenly nervous.

"You are even more beautiful to me, Bekah," Megan said as she reached for the button to her pants and slid them down her legs. She couldn't resist pausing for a moment on her knees and running her hands up the sides and back of Rebekah's legs. She breathed her in and rested her head against her lower stomach as her arms tightened around her.

Rebekah ran her hand over Megan's head and her fingers combed through chocolate brown hair. She held Megan to her for a moment. Then she pulled her up and removed Megan's pants. When she stood back up her lips found Megan's once again. She softened this kiss and turned Megan towards the bed, backing her up.

Megan sat down on the bed and looked up at Rebekah with a hint of a smirk. She remembered how Rebekah's confidence grew and how she liked to take over in the bedroom. Megan had no problems with that!

Rebekah raised her eyebrows as she hooked her fingers into the waist of Megan's undies. "You remember," she whispered.

"How could I forget," Megan replied as she pulled Rebekah in for a heated kiss. Any nerves were gone now as their bodies began to remember.

Rebekah pulled Megan's undies down and threw them over her shoulder while Megan glided up the bed. Then she gave Rebekah a heated look.

As Rebekah took her undies off she said, "Your eyes are saying, 'come get me.'"

Megan gave her a little smile and Rebekah began to climb up the bed.

"Oh God," Megan mumbled as she felt herself go wet. She couldn't wait to feel Rebekah on top of her, inside her, all over her.

Rebekah put one leg between Megan's and lowered down until her lips touched Megan's. Megan's arms flew around Rebekah and held her tight.

"I'm not going anywhere. I'm right here," Rebekah whispered as she inched her lips away.

Suddenly overtaken with emotion Megan said, "Promise?"

"I promise," Rebekah said firmly and then crashed her lips into Megan's.

Rebekah's hand roamed and Megan could feel the familiarity as her skin tingled under Rebekah's fingers. Megan felt her love in every touch.

Rebekah cupped Megan's breast and ran her thumb over her already hardened nipple. She pulled away and took a deep breath. "You drive me wild, Megan. I may lose control. You always did that to me."

"I love you, Bekah. All of you. And I love how you love me." Megan ran her hand over her lover's hair and wound her fingers through it as Rebekah lowered her mouth to Megan's breast. She took her nipple inside her mouth and sucked.

"Oh baby," Megan moaned as she lost her breath. Then she felt Rebekah's hand run down the outside of her thigh and then back up the inside.

Rebekah kissed over to Megan's other nipple as her hand paused between her legs.

Megan felt Rebekah everywhere. She had dreams about this and now it was her reality.

"I love you, Meg," Rebekah said softly as she raised up to look into Megan's eyes.

"I love you," she whispered.

Rebekah ran her fingers through Megan's wetness and they both moaned. Her finger roamed and circled as Megan's hips began to move and her eyes closed.

"I've got you, babe," Rebekah whispered.

Megan opened her eyes and could see the love in Rebekah's. Then she felt Rebekah push her finger inside and add another as she kissed her deeply.

"Yes!" Megan exclaimed when their lips parted.

Rebekah began a rhythm that Megan's hips matched. Their eyes were locked on each other and their breaths gasped in unison. A smile played at the corner of their mouths as they moved over and over. Megan felt herself getting close.

"Take my love, Meg, and let go," Rebekah whispered against Megan's lips.

Megan lost herself in Rebekah's eyes and the love Rebekah gave her exploded inside her body. She grabbed onto Rebekah and rode the orgasm wave after wave, her eyes never leaving Rebekah's. Then she felt tears warm on her cheeks and saw that Rebekah's were mixed with her own.

"I vow to you right here and now, Megan Neal. I will never leave you. No matter what we may face, will you help me raise Anna and spend your life with me?"

"Yes. I want that more than anything," Megan said, catching her breath.

Rebekah smiled and nuzzled Megan's neck while they held one another for a moment. "That was so much better than I remembered."

Megan chuckled. "Oh I didn't forget. I couldn't forget you." She started to push Rebekah onto her back and she resisted.

"Oh no you don't. I gave you my love, now I'm taking." She kissed Megan slow and deep.

"You can't take when I'm giving myself to you," Megan whispered.

Rebekah smiled and trailed kisses down Megan's neck, across her collarbone and then looked up into her eyes. "You take my breath away. I love you so much."

Megan ran her fingers through Rebekah's hair. "Make me yours."

There was that wicked smile that Megan often saw when they were in the bedroom. Rebekah made her feel worshiped, treasured, and oh so beautiful.

She circled Megan's nipple with her tongue and then sucked it into her mouth. Megan gasped and moaned.

"God, Bekah."

Rebekah smiled as she lavished Megan's other nipple with her kisses and licks. This time when she sucked Megan's nipple in her mouth she bit down gently.

"You're going to make me come again right now," Megan groaned, breathless.

"Hold on, gorgeous. I'm just getting started," Rebekah said as she kissed her way down to Megan's stomach. She slowly licked around her belly button and kissed a line down to her curly coarse hairs.

Megan couldn't stop her hips from moving so Rebekah put her hands underneath Megan's thighs and held on.

Rebekah took a moment to gaze at Megan's wetness and inhale her sweet scent. "You are so ready and want me."

"I do, Bekah! Take me!"

"You are mine," Rebekah said and licked the length of Megan's sex.

Megan threw one hand on the bed and searched for Rebekah's hand with the other. Her heart was beating out of her chest and all she could feel was love. She was so sensitive to Rebekah's touch, but couldn't wait for what she knew would come next.

Rebekah swirled her tongue around Megan's hard clit and then sucked her into her mouth.

Megan groaned. "Oh fuck, Rebekah!" She raised her hips as Rebekah brought out another even more intense orgasm.

"Bekah!" Megan screamed in ecstasy.

Rebekah eased Megan's hips back down and smiled. "That's right, love. It's my name on your lips." She wrapped

Megan in her arms and held her tight as her breathing calmed and her heart began to slow.

"I thought you loved me," Megan finally mumbled.

"I do!" Rebekah said, raising up and looking into Megan's eyes.

Megan smiled. "You keep doing that and there won't be any of me left."

Rebekah smiled then. "I can't help it. You do something to me."

"Well, you're about to find out what you do to me. But Bekah, I'm in this with you for everything, for all time. I won't lose you again."

18

Megan pulled Rebekah down and crushed their lips together. This time when Megan pushed her on her back, Rebekah didn't resist. She wanted to give herself completely to Megan. Twelve years ago when they were together like this was when Rebekah knew there was no way loving Megan Neal could be wrong or a sin.

Back then she'd held onto Megan so she wouldn't lose herself in the back and forth of her thoughts and beliefs. Megan had let her find her way. She simply told her what she'd been through and let her draw her own conclusions. When she would ask Megan what she should do, Megan always said she had to figure it out for herself because what might be right for Megan might not be for Rebekah.

Megan spoke, sweeping the past aside and bringing Rebekah back into the present. "You are who my heart is meant to be with. I love you, Bekah."

"My heart is yours. I'm giving you all of me." She caressed the side of Megan's face as their lips came together in a tender kiss.

The urgency of this first time together after such a long separation subsided. Megan slowed their pace and took her time kissing Rebekah with soft, loving gentleness. Her tongue explored and caressed Rebekah's mouth and then she trailed kisses down her neck.

"Oh Meg," Rebekah moaned. Megan always knew the places that made Rebekah weak. Her tongue was sliding along Rebekah's collarbone and she felt the familiar tingle throughout her body. She felt even more wetness between her legs and knew Megan would be there soon.

"I love you," Megan murmured as she kissed her way to Rebekah's breast. She caressed, kissed, licked and then sucked it into her mouth.

"Mmm," Rebekah moaned. The motion was slow and felt so, so good as pleasure pulsed through Rebekah's body. Her ears were filled with the sounds of their love, breaths full of anticipation accompanied by soft moans and satisfied sighs.

Megan didn't let her other breast wait long before turning her mouth to it. Rebekah wound her fingers through Megan's hair and moaned again.

"I feel adored," Rebekah whispered.

Megan kissed her way down Rebekah's stomach then took her finger and gently ran it along her lower abs. Rebekah could feel goosebumps erupting on her skin and she shuddered. She smiled knowing Megan once again remembered this sensitive spot on her.

She felt Megan begin to kiss down one of her inner thighs and then back up the other. She paused and looked up at Rebekah. "Oh how I've missed you."

All Rebekah could do was smile and then she closed her eyes as Megan's tongue touched her most sensitive spot. She felt Megan's tongue love her up and down and around. Then she felt Megan's finger gently push on her entrance.

"Oh yes, babe, yes," Rebekah moaned.

Megan pushed her finger inside as she took Rebekah in her mouth.

Rebekah raised up and then fell back and pushed her hips higher. Megan began a slow rhythm and then sped up just enough to build that familiar feeling inside her.

"Oh babe, oh babe," Rebekah groaned.

That's when Megan pushed inside and up to find her favorite spot as she took Rebekah into her mouth again.

Rebekah felt an explosion through her body as colored stars sparkled behind her eyelids. This was so much better than the light show the stars gave them earlier.

"I love you, I love you, I love you," she murmured over and over. "I'm yours."

Megan raised up and kissed Rebekah softly. She smiled down at her with so much love in her eyes. The most comforting and protected feeling wrapped around Rebekah. She was home. That was it; that's what she'd been missing all along.

"You." Rebekah trailed her fingers along Megan's cheek.

"I know," Megan whispered. "I feel it too."

Rebekah smiled and they simply gazed into each other's eyes for several moments. No words were needed.

Finally, Rebekah breathed in and slowly released it. "Maybe I'll see if my parents can make this a regular Friday night thing."

Megan laughed and snuggled next to her.

"By the way, Anna wanted to know if she could come over and play with Wanda."

"She can play with Wanda every day. I'm surprised she hasn't scratched on the door to get in here."

"She knew her momma needed time with me," Rebekah said.

"Oh I did and I need more." Megan nuzzled Rebekah's neck.

"I'll go pick Anna up in the morning. We can come back over and spend the day together if you want."

"That's exactly what I want. Hey, I had an idea."

"Let's hear it."

"Can we take Anna shopping? I'd like to get books and maybe a few toys to keep here for her."

Rebekah gazed at Megan and narrowed her eyes. "That's really nice. Are you thinking what I'm thinking?"

"I don't know. I want her to have things here that are hers and maybe eventually she'd want to live here. What are you thinking?"

Rebekah chuckled. "Is this what lesbians call U-hauling?"

"No way. This took twelve years!"

"We're together now, that's all that matters." Rebekah leaned over and kissed Megan.

"We are and we have a lot more catching up to do," Megan said, ending the discussion.

*　*　*

The next morning, Rebekah sat at the island and smiled when Megan handed her a cup of coffee.

"Thank you, babe. That shower is incredible!"

"I always hoped to use it like we did this morning," Megan said, wiggling her eyebrows.

"My body is so delightfully sore this morning. I may need to use your shower again this evening."

"That can be arranged."

"Do you come along with it?"

Megan leaned over and kissed her sweetly on the lips. "Absolutely." Megan's eyes widened. "We should get some bubble bath for Anna!"

Rebekah laughed. "You are something else. From sexy showers to bubble baths in two seconds."

"I want her to feel like she's home. I want her to have more than just Wanda to play with."

At the sound of her name Wanda came over and jumped up on Rebekah's legs.

"Come here, sweet girl. Did we keep you from your bed last night?" Rebekah said, picking up the puppy and letting her sit in her lap.

Megan smiled at them both and rubbed Wanda's head. "This must be what it feels like to have a family," she said softly.

Rebekah wasn't sure she heard Megan correctly. "Do you want a family?"

"Oh!" Megan met Rebekah's gaze. "Did I say that out loud?"

"You did." Rebekah nodded with a chuckle.

Megan stared at Rebekah and finally said, "Yes, I want a family. I didn't know how much until Anna came into the counseling center."

Rebekah noticed tears pooling in Megan's eyes and reached for her hand. "You have a family now, Meg. Will you share Wanda with us?"

"I think Wanda is already yours."

Wanda looked up at her and tried to lick her nose. Rebekah laughed and leaned back.

"You know, I'm only thirty-one." Rebekah took a sip of her coffee and looked at Megan over the rim.

Before Megan could respond, Rebekah's phone began to

ring. She handed Wanda to Megan and dug her phone out of her purse.

"Hi Mom," she said, smiling at Megan as she answered. Her eyes widened and she giggled. "Hi honey."

She put the phone on speaker and they heard Anna's voice. "I fooled you, didn't I?"

"Yes you did. Are you having fun?"

"Yes. We're watching TV. I just wanted to see if you were okay."

"I'm fine. You'll never guess what I'm doing."

"What?"

"I'm drinking coffee with Megan and Wanda."

"You are! Did you ask Megan if I could come play with Wanda?"

"I did and guess what?"

"I said yes," Megan said.

"Hi Megan!" Anna giggled.

"Did I fool you?" Rebekah said.

"Yes." Anna giggled again.

"I'll come get you in a little while," Rebekah said.

"Come now. I want to play with Wanda."

Rebekah chuckled. "In a little while. Grandma and Grandpa won't be ready for you to leave yet."

"Okay. Bye Megan. Bye Mommy. I love you."

"I love you, too," Rebekah said, ending the call.

"You know she's going to go right in and tell your parents what you're doing," Megan said with her eyebrows raised.

"I expect her to. She probably told them we were having dinner last night, too. Now they know we're spending time together. I'll answer their questions when I pick her up. Then we get to spend the day with you!" Rebekah put Wanda down and stood up, grabbing Megan's hand. "I'm not quite ready to share you yet."

Megan followed her back to the bedroom, unable to stop the smile growing on her face.

19

Rebekah walked through the back door of her parents' house and called out, "Anyone home?"

"Mommy!" Anna yelled from the living room.

Rebekah walked in and Anna hugged her around her legs. "Hi honey. Are you having fun?"

"Uh-huh, Grandma made waffles!"

"Oh, I know you liked that." Rebekah smiled at her mom, who was sitting on the couch.

"We watched a movie last night *and* one this morning!" she exclaimed.

"Wow, you've got the best grandparents, don't you," Rebekah said, winking at her dad.

"How was your night?" he asked.

"It was nice. Megan and I went to dinner at a new place on the river. We had the best fish tacos."

"I've heard about that place," Helen said. "What else did you do?"

"Years ago we used to love to walk the river, so we strolled along and, my, how it's changed."

"It has," her dad commented.

"You were at Megan's this morning?" Helen asked.

"Yes, she offered to make breakfast. I wasn't turning that down," she said, tickling Anna. *I'm not lying*, she thought.

"Are we going over there now?"

Rebekah nodded. "I think Megan has a surprise for you."

"You seem to be spending a lot of time with Megan," Helen commented.

"Why do we like to go to Megan's?" Rebekah asked Anna.

"Because we get to play with Wanda," she answered.

"Yes and what else?"

"Because it's fun!"

"It is fun. Megan is our friend." She could feel her parents staring at her. She looked at them both and said, "It's nice to have my friend again." Then she turned to Anna. "Are you ready to go?"

"Yes." Anna giggled.

"You can leave her clothes. I'll wash them and she'll have them here the next time she spends the night. Maybe we could do this regularly," Helen said.

"What do you think, Anna? Will you have movie night with me again?" Daniel asked her.

She nodded enthusiastically. "Yes, Grandpa."

"Okay then, give hugs and let's go," Rebekah said.

Anna hugged her grandparents.

"Thanks. We'll see you in the morning at church," Rebekah said.

"I can't wait to hear you play bells," Helen said.

"Me too," Daniel said, walking them to the door. "I'll be glad to meet Megan, too."

"I can't wait for you to meet her." Rebekah gave her dad a smile.

They drove to Megan's and Rebekah pulled into the garage.

"Mommy!"

"Megan told me to. She said she'd be in the backyard with Wanda."

Anna jumped out of the car and ran to find Megan and Wanda.

Rebekah joined them on the patio and Megan was already chasing Anna and Wanda around the yard. Laughter filled the air and it was music to Rebekah's ears.

"Hi Mommy," Megan said, running up to Rebekah and squeezing her hand.

"Hi gorgeous," she said quietly. Anna couldn't hear her over her own laughter.

They sat down and watched Anna and Wanda play for a few minutes.

"How were your parents?" Megan asked, catching her breath.

"Full of questions. They can't wait to meet you tomorrow." Rebekah raised her brows.

"I can't wait to meet them."

Anna and Wanda came running onto the patio and Wanda jumped into Rebekah's lap. They all laughed.

"Hey Anna, I was thinking we might go to the store and get Wanda a new toy."

That got Anna's attention.

Megan smiled at Anna. "What would you think if we got a few books for you to keep at my house?"

"Okay!"

"You don't really have anything to play with here, except for Wanda. Maybe we could get a few toys for you. Would that be okay?"

Anna looked at Rebekah and she nodded.

"I really like to read books and I think it would be fun to read together," Megan said.

"Mommy reads to me every night. You could, too."

"Would you read to me?" Megan asked.

"Yes." Anna giggled.

"I haven't read your books, so it would be fun for you to read them to me." Megan smiled at her.

"Let's go!"

Rebekah chuckled. "I told you she'd think this is a good idea."

Megan grinned. "I'm ready. Come on, Mom."

Rebekah drove them to Walmart and Anna headed toward the toys.

"I may not be able to keep up." Megan laughed as they followed behind her.

Rebekah looped her arm through Megan's. "Come on. I'll help you."

A half hour later Anna was shooting their purchases with the scanner gun as Megan put them in bags.

Rebekah leaned in and quietly said to Megan. "You have to let me pay for this."

"Oh no you don't. This was my idea. I want to do this, Bekah."

"Do you think you're going overboard? She'll think she's moving in."

Meg looked at her and raised her eyebrows.

"I shot all of them, Megan," Anna said.

Megan turned back around. "Let's see. Three puzzles, four books, a new doll with three outfits and a ball for Wanda. Is that everything? Are you sure we don't need another book?"

"That's plenty for now," Rebekah said firmly.

"You forgot the new pajamas," Anna said, holding them up.

Megan winked at Anna and she giggled. She paid and on the way back to the car she told Anna, "I hope you teach Wanda how to fetch."

"I will. Thank you, Megan."

"You're welcome, honey. Will you read to me tonight?"

Anna nodded as they put the bags in the car and Rebekah drove them back to Megan's house. They went outside so Anna could play fetch with Wanda.

"Anna, I need to talk to Mommy for a minute inside. We'll be right back," Megan said, eyeing Rebekah.

"Okay." Anna went back to playing with Wanda.

Once inside Megan took Rebekah's hands. "When you wonder 'what if' for twelve years, you grab a second chance if you get it. That's what I'm doing. Is this too fast for you? Tell me now." Megan studied Rebekah's face. "You seemed a little hesitant at the store."

Rebekah smiled. "I'm not. This isn't too fast. Living my life by making decisions that would please my family is not living. I can no longer be that person. This is what I wanted but didn't know how to get all those years ago. You are who I wanted all along. I loved Ben, but I honestly don't know if it would have lasted if not for Anna. I settled and got married because of what my family would think. I wasn't unhappy, but I still thought of you and always wondered. I'm grabbing this chance too!"

Megan released a relieved breath. "This will appear fast to everyone else. They don't know what we started twelve years ago. *We* know our lives are together. But there will be obstacles and doubters."

"I know that, but I have the courage to live the life I want now, Meg. The life that is best for Anna and me."

Megan tilted her head. "Not everyone will agree with that."

"Too bad. It's you and me and Anna, baby." Rebekah grinned.

"What about Wanda?"

"Of course, Wanda too!" Rebekah laughed and threw her arms around Megan's neck. She kissed her softly and rested their foreheads together. "Wanda gave me her superpower to change reality. You and me together, that is where Anna will thrive and we will too."

Megan smiled and glanced towards the back door. "Can we go play now?"

"I think I have two kids now."

"Just so you know, I have courage too, Bekah. We're doing this together."

"I know." She kissed Megan again and they went out to join Anna and Wanda.

They spent the day at Megan's playing with all of Anna's new things. As the evening wound down, Anna watched TV with Wanda fast asleep next to her while Megan and Rebekah cleaned the kitchen after dinner.

"I really don't want you and Anna to leave," Megan said softly. They were on one side of the island gazing at Anna as she stroked Wanda's head. Occasionally she'd giggle at something on the show she was watching.

"I know, but we should go home tonight. Let's talk after lunch at my parents' tomorrow and we'll figure something out."

"How about we let Anna take that bubble bath? Or should we save it for another time?"

Rebekah looked at Megan and saw such love. She knew that all Megan wanted was to make them happy.

"Let's save it. We'll do a sleepover next weekend."

Megan grinned. "I'd love that."

"Anna," Rebekah said. "I think it's time for you to put your toys away so you and Megan can read. We have to go home pretty soon."

"Aw, do we have to, Mommy? Can't we just stay here?" Anna begged.

Megan looked at Rebekah, her expression hopeful.

"How about we have a sleepover here next weekend? You have to play bells in the morning, remember?"

Anna sighed and got up. "Do you promise we get to stay next weekend?"

"You'd better ask Megan."

"I'd love for you to stay next weekend. Both nights if you want to." Megan winked at Rebekah.

Anna smiled. "You're still coming to church tomorrow, right?"

"I wouldn't miss it." Megan walked around the island into the living room. "You can leave your books on this table." Megan stacked two of Anna's books on a table by the TV. Anna picked up the others and neatly stacked them on top.

"Okay, let's get your toys and take them in here." Megan picked up the puzzles while Anna gathered her doll and clothes. She led them down the hall to the guest bedroom.

"This is supposed to be for people that come to visit me. Are you going to keep visiting me and Wanda?"

"Yes," Anna said.

"Then this can be your room. Okay?"

"Really?"

"Yep. Here, let's put your doll on the bed."

"Her name is Zoe," Anna said, placing the doll so her head was on the pillow.

"How about you put Zoe's clothes in this drawer?" Megan pulled out a mostly empty drawer in a small dresser.

"Hey, what's going on in here?" Rebekah said from the doorway.

"Megan said this can be my room!"

"She did? How nice."

"We're putting Zoe's clothes in here," Anna said, closing the drawer. "Where do you want to put the puzzles, Megan?"

She opened the next drawer to see if there was room in it. "They'll fit in here."

Anna put them inside and closed the drawer.

"That's good for this time. We'll get it the way you want it next weekend. How about that?"

"Okay," Anna said happily.

"Let's go read before you have to go home," Megan said, extending her hand to Anna.

Anna took it. "Come on, Mommy. You can read with us."

"I'd like that," Rebekah said, letting them through the door. She squeezed Megan's other hand as they went to the living room. They settled on the couch with the book Anna chose.

"Let's each read a page," Anna suggested.

"Okay. You go first," Rebekah said.

She looked at Megan over Anna's head and smiled. Her heart was full of love, but she wasn't fooling herself. Rebekah knew this wasn't always going to be easy and she could feel a sort of reckoning coming in her bones.

20

Megan was sitting at the kitchen island and smiled when she heard her garage door go up. A few moments later Rebekah walked into the kitchen.

"Hi honey, I'm home," she said with a chuckle. "That's kind of fun."

Megan laughed. "Good morning, *honey*."

Rebekah leaned down and gave her a sweet kiss. They stared into each other's eyes for a moment, just breathing.

"Would you like a cup of coffee?" Megan asked.

Rebekah looked down at her and smiled. She pushed Megan back gently and wiggled her way into her lap. She wrapped her arms around her neck and then kissed her deeply.

"Now that's a good morning," Megan said.

Rebekah got up and poured herself a cup of coffee. "I am so tempted to push you up against this island, but I'm afraid we'd be late."

"I have no self control when it comes to you."

"I remember," Rebekah said in a low voice.

"Stop!" Megan grinned, her eyes wide.

"Okay!" Rebekah said. "Are you nervous about today?"

"I'm not nervous about church. I'm looking forward to watching Anna perform. But I am a little nervous about lunch."

"Why? My parents will be nice to you."

"It's not that. I know you want to wait before you tell them about us. I'm simply afraid they are going to see the love I have for you and Anna written all over my face."

"Neither one of us can hide that. Let's hope Anna distracts them enough that they don't see."

Megan chuckled. "Maybe we shouldn't look at each other."

"I like looking at you," Rebekah said, placing her hand on Megan's cheek. "These chocolate brown eyes melt my heart and give me love."

Megan leaned in and pressed her lips to Rebekah's. She could feel her whole body go weak. Rebekah's hand slid to the back of her neck and held them together.

When the kiss ended, Rebekah rested her forehead against Megan's and whispered, "We'd better go."

Megan smiled. "Let me check on Wanda."

"Where is that little bundle of love?"

"She's outside enjoying the sunshine."

Megan got up and went to the back door and peeked out the window. "Come look." Wanda was lying on her side in the grass, soaking up the sun.

Rebekah put her arm around Megan and followed her gaze. "Aw, she's so cute."

"Let's leave her out there. She'll be fine until we get back."

Megan followed Rebekah to her car and she drove them to the church. Once she'd parked she turned to Megan. "I want you to know that I will be pretending in my head that we're a couple just like any other watching our kid play handbells in church."

Megan smiled. "Maybe someday we will be."

"My sweet, optimistic Megan," Rebekah said as she reached for her hand.

"Maybe I'll hold your hand in church someday and no one will think anything about it."

Rebekah smiled and nodded.

They went inside and Rebekah greeted several people. Megan simply smiled and followed her into the sanctuary. Helen was sitting about midway down on the left side of the center aisle.

"This is our regular spot," Rebekah said softly as she grinned at Megan.

Rebekah sat next to her mom and then Megan next to her.

"Mom, this is Megan Neal," Rebekah smiled from her mom to Megan.

"It's nice to meet you, Megan," Helen said with a friendly smile.

"It's nice to meet you," Megan said. She made eye contact with Helen and smiled.

"Have you seen Anna yet?" Rebekah asked her mom.

"No. I'm sure they will come in right before the service starts."

Megan looked around and smiled when people made eye contact. She was a new face so the regulars would be wondering about her. Rebekah's shoulder grazed against hers momentarily and she felt a moment of calm. It had been a long time since she'd been inside a church. Megan knew how important the church was to Rebekah and she'd give anything for them to be accepted for who they were in this church, but she wasn't holding her breath that that would happen anytime soon.

Rebekah leaned over and whispered, "Here she comes."

Megan followed her gaze and saw Anna walk out from a door at the front of the sanctuary. She was with several other little girls and boys about her age. When she saw them her face lit up and she gave them a slight wave.

Megan chuckled. "She is the cutest," she whispered to Rebekah.

"I know. She's very proud of that dress," Rebekah said.

"I think she had help with her hair, too."

Rebekah nodded. "She wanted to wear a bow. That doesn't happen very often."

Megan could feel her heart swell with pride and love for Anna. *Is this what it's like to have kids?* she wondered.

"You're kind of glowing," Rebekah whispered.

Megan looked sideways at her and her eyes widened. "Later," she whispered.

Rebekah nodded and Megan figured she knew exactly what was going on in her heart.

Megan smiled at Anna when she turned around in her seat to look their way. Music began to play and she turned her attention to the front of the sanctuary when Rebekah's father took his place in the pulpit.

He looked down at Helen and Rebekah and smiled. Then he made eye contact with Megan and gave her a slight nod. She smiled at him and for a moment it felt like he could see straight into her heart. An uneasy feeling passed through her and she tried to temper it with a deep breath.

"Good morning," Daniel said to the congregation and began the service.

About halfway through the service it was time for Anna

and her group to play. Rebekah bumped her shoulder and she leaned in and whispered, "I'm nervous for her."

"I'm so glad you said that because I am too," Megan whispered back.

The group took their place behind the tables that held their bells. Once they all had their bells and were ready, the instructor led them through the song.

Megan couldn't keep her eyes off Anna, who was focused on her instructor and when to play her bells. As the song continued Megan noticed that Anna began to relax. It was obvious that she enjoyed what she was doing. By the end of the song Anna had a small smile on her face as the congregation applauded.

The kids were allowed to sit with their parents after the performance and Anna hurried toward them.

"You were awesome," Megan said quietly to Anna when she reached them.

Anna gave her a quick hug and then hugged Rebekah tightly.

"I'm so proud of you," Rebekah whispered as she kissed Anna's cheek.

"Can I sit here?" Anna whispered, wiggling between Megan and Rebekah.

When Megan looked up Rebekah gave her a smile full of love. She squeezed Megan's shoulder then put her arm around Anna.

Anna grabbed Megan's arm and grinned. As they quieted down Megan looked back up to the pulpit and Daniel Mathews' eyes were locked on them.

The uneasiness was back and Megan could feel her cheeks pinken. *Holy shit!* she thought. Lunch was going to be interesting.

Megan settled in and sang along with the congregation.

She recognized the hymns from her church in California. Rebekah's church was very similar to the one Megan had grown up in. The denomination was the same, but California was more liberal. Megan appreciated the similarities though so she didn't feel quite so out of place.

Having Anna holding onto her arm helped and a glance at Rebekah always made her heart smile inside.

Rebekah's dad was preaching about time. "Do you take time with God every day? He does with you. He's waiting for you to stop and have a conversation with Him. If you don't know what to say to Him, how about thank you? Don't you have something to be thankful for everyday? I know I do."

He continued. "Do you take time to help others? That is what our church is all about. Our mission is to help others and while we're doing it we can tell them about Jesus."

"I love the word time," he said. "Do you have the time? We run out of time? Is it time for a change?"

When he said the last sentence he looked straight at Megan.

He gazed back over the congregation and smiled. "I know some of you are thinking it's time for him to wrap it up. I'll leave you with this: make time with God every day this week and see what changes. I'm simply suggesting a minute or two of your time."

Then he announced the next hymn. After they sang he gave the benediction and the service was over.

Rebekah leaned over and smiled. "You made it."

Megan released a big breath and nodded.

Rebekah told her mom they would see her at the house and they walked out of the church. Several people told Anna what a good job she had done and said hello to Rebekah.

On the way to the car Anna grabbed Rebekah's hand

and then reached for Megan's. *How could holding a little kid's hand make your heart feel this full*, Megan wondered.

She looked down at Anna. "That is a pretty dress you're wearing."

"Thank you." Anna grinned up at her. "It's my favorite."

"I can see why."

Rebekah grinned over at her.

"Mommy fixed my hair and put the bow in for me," Anna said.

"It looks very pretty." Megan said, swinging their arms.

Anna giggled. Megan thought that might be the best sound in the world.

21

Once in the car Rebekah turned to Anna. "You did such a good job."

"Thanks."

"You looked like you were having fun. Do you like playing handbells?" Megan asked. Anna nodded.

Rebekah pulled into her parents' driveway and her mom's car was already there.

"Wow, Grandma got home fast," Rebekah commented.

Anna got out and went ahead while Rebekah waited for Megan to walk around the car. She reached for Megan's hand and squeezed it. "If you feel uncomfortable, just look at me and I'll give you a smile."

Megan chuckled. "Thanks. Why would I feel uncomfortable? Are they going to ask about my intentions with their daughter?"

Rebekah's eyes widened and she playfully slapped Megan on the arm. "No!" Then she whispered, "They don't have a clue about us."

Megan nodded. The way Daniel had looked at her in church made Megan think otherwise, but she was probably being paranoid. Why would Daniel think that anyway? Megan shook those thoughts out of her head.

Rebekah and Megan walked into the kitchen where Anna and Helen were talking about Anna's performance.

Megan listened to their exchange and then felt something hit her leg. She looked down to see a beautiful calico cat rubbing against her leg. The cat looked up at her and meowed.

"Oh my gosh," Megan said. "Neal! You grew!"

"He remembers you!" Anna yelled.

Megan bent down and rubbed the cat behind the ears and he immediately began to purr. She went to one knee and picked the cat up. Megan cradled it in her arms and he purred even louder.

"You are such a beautiful boy," Megan said as the cat nuzzled the side of her face.

"Oh no, Meg. Your allergies!" Rebekah exclaimed.

"It's okay. I took an allergy pill this morning before you picked me up."

"Oh good. I'd hate to watch your eyes swell up."

"And the sneezing! Remember!" Megan chuckled.

"Oh I remember." Rebekah laughed, her eyes sparkling.

"I can't believe he remembers me. Surely he's just a friendly cat. It was a long time ago."

"He is friendly," Helen said, smiling at the scene. "But he seems to know you."

"Thank you for giving him such a good home. He's obviously living his best life," Megan said. She put Neal down and he went to rub on Rebekah's legs next.

"What were we to do? Rebekah begged us to take him."

"He's a great cat. I knew it when we rescued him," Rebekah said as she smiled down at the cat and then at Megan. "Plus we got to be friends."

"We did," Megan said softly.

"Hello family," Daniel said as he walked in the back door.

"Grandpa, Neal remembered Megan!" Anna told him excitedly.

"He did! How about that." He held his arms open and Anna ran into them, giving him a hug.

"Dad, I'd like you to meet Megan Neal," Rebekah said as she put her hand on Megan's shoulder. "Megan, this is my dad, Daniel."

"It's nice to meet you, Megan. We have heard so much about you."

"It's nice to meet you," Megan said with a friendly smile.

"We should thank you for the work you've done as Anna's counselor," Daniel said.

"Dad," Rebekah admonished him.

"It wasn't just me. Crystal is my partner and we're a team, but Anna did all the work."

"What did I do?" Anna asked.

Megan kneeled down to face Anna, wishing she could smooth away the confusion on her face. "You created beautiful paintings for your Mommy. Do you remember why you chose those colors?"

"Yes." Anna nodded. "They were the colors of my feelings. Sometimes they were blue because that's Mommy's favorite color and that's how I felt."

"Right," Megan praised her. "Do you remember what color you painted when you played with Wanda?"

"Yes, I painted light blue because I was happy."

"And what color did you use when we rode bikes?"

"I painted bright blue because it made me happy to think about Daddy."

"You were happy about your daddy?" Helen asked.

"Yes. I remembered riding bikes with Daddy and he would sometimes tickle me when we stopped to rest. Now when Mommy puts her hands on me like she's going to tickle me, I remember Daddy and I'm not sad, I'm happy."

"I'm not sure I understand," Daniel said.

Rebekah sat in one of the kitchen chairs. "Come here, Anna, we'll show them." Anna walked over and turned around so her back was facing Rebekah. "When I put my hands on her waist like this she can close her eyes and remember Ben tickling her."

"Right." Anna nodded. "It makes me happy, not sad."

"That's right. You still miss your daddy, but he's near you," Megan said.

"Right here." Anna pointed to her heart.

Rebekah tickled Anna and said, "I don't know about everyone else, but I'm ready for lunch. How about you?"

"Yes ma'am." Anna chuckled.

Megan noticed Rebekah gave her dad a look. Why did it feel like he was trying to upset Anna by calling Megan her counselor? He must know Rebekah tried not to use that word around Anna. Besides, she was here as their friend, not Anna's counselor.

"What can I do to help?" Megan asked Helen.

"Not a thing. We're going to eat in the dining room. All I have to do is put the food in bowls. Rebekah, will you get the drinks, please?"

"Sure, Mom. Come on, you can help me," Rebekah said to Megan.

Rebekah poured the drinks and Megan helped her carry them into the dining room. When everything was on the table they all sat down. Daniel was at one end and Helen at the other. Rebekah and Anna sat on one side of the table with Megan across from them.

"This smells so good," Megan said. "I don't know when I last had roast. Probably the last time I went home."

"I think it's the only thing we ever have on Sundays," Rebekah teased.

"We talked about that last week," Helen said defensively.

"I know! We talked about it while we were eating roast!" Rebekah laughed.

Megan looked down at her plate and chuckled.

"Anna, would you like to pray for us?" Daniel asked.

"Not really," she replied, hiding her face behind Rebekah's shoulder.

"I'll do it," Rebekah offered. "Dear Lord, we thank you for this food that was prepared with loving hands. And we thank you for this opportunity to share love and fellowship with family and friends. Amen." She looked up at Megan and smiled.

Megan smiled back and then her eyes widened when she saw Rebekah wink.

"What is fellowship?" Anna asked as they began to pass the food around and fill their plates.

"It means spending time together, like we're doing now. We're spending time with Grandma, Grandpa, and Megan."

"Oh. Were we having fellowship yesterday at Megan's?"

"We were," Rebekah replied. "This piece is just your size." Rebekah placed a piece of meat on Anna's plate and gave Megan a quick glance.

"Tell me, Megan, do you spend time with other kids outside the counseling center?" Daniel asked as he passed her the rolls.

So this is how it's going to be, Megan thought. It was becoming clear that Daniel Mathews did not approve of her friendship with Rebekah or Anna.

Megan took a roll and then passed the basket across the

table to Rebekah. She could see Rebekah's cheeks pinken and anger spark in her eyes.

"Generally no," Megan said. "Occasionally I'll run into clients when I'm doing other things. Crystal and I have attended different events where the kids might be performing or playing ball of some sorts. If you're asking because I came to hear Anna play today…" Megan paused, looked at Anna and smiled. "I came to hear Anna because she invited me, and Rebekah and Anna are my friends."

Rebekah looked at her and smiled. Megan knew that look. Rebekah was saying *I love you* with her eyes.

"I see. Rebekah said you hadn't kept in touch all these years and then reconnected when Anna came to the counseling center."

"That's right. It was quite a surprise to both of us. A very happy surprise I might add."

"Dad," Rebekah said. "You know all this. I told you about Megan after that first day. You seem surprised by our friendship. We spent a lot of time together that summer."

"We did," Megan added.

"It's natural that we'd pick back up," Rebekah said.

"I understand you have a dog with superpowers," Daniel said, changing the subject.

"Did Anna tell you that?" Megan chuckled and looked at her.

"She does have superpowers. She makes people feel better," Anna said.

"I think most puppies make people feel better, honey," Daniel said.

Fuck, Megan thought. *This guy isn't showing the love he preaches about.* It's just like she thought: everything is different when it comes to your own family.

"I guess we need to bring Wanda over to meet your

grandpa, Anna. Then he can see her superpowers for himself."

"Can we go get her now?"

Rebekah chuckled. "No, honey. You'll get to see her when we take Megan home."

"Oh goodie!" she squealed. "Can we ride bikes, too?"

"We'll see," Rebekah answered.

"Why don't you come by the counseling center sometime? I'd be happy to give you a tour and then you can see what we do," Megan said to Daniel.

"Thank you," he said.

Megan noticed his surprise at her offer. He covered it quickly, but not before she saw it.

"This roast is delicious," Megan said to Helen.

"Thank you."

"Rebekah said that you originally came here from California," Daniel said.

"Yes I did. Crystal, my business partner, and I went to college together and she convinced me to come to Georgia."

"You must like it here then," Helen said.

"There are some things I really like." Megan smiled. Out of the corner of her eye she could see and feel Rebekah staring at her. "And then there are some things I love."

"Oh?" Helen raised her eyebrows.

"I really enjoy walking the river and the parks along the way," Megan said.

"Uh-huh," Rebekah murmured softly.

Megan wondered if anyone else heard her and stifled a chuckle. "Crystal came here when she finished her Masters degree and loved it. Of course she also met her partner and didn't want to leave. We had always dreamed of opening a place like the counseling center, so that's when she stepped up her efforts to get me here." Megan decided to be honest about Crystal's relationship with Kim. She said partner, so they could draw their own conclusions.

"I've heard good things about the counseling center. I think Athens is fortunate to have you both," Helen said.

That made Megan relax slightly. "Thank you."

22

Megan felt like Daniel was giving her some kind of reprieve and let Helen continue the conversation.

"I think it's great that you work with the school district. You reach more kids that way," Rebekah said.

Megan turned to Daniel. "Your after school outreach program is doing great work, too. Bible Zone, isn't it? We adjusted our schedule at the center because we have several younger clients that attend. On Wednesdays, we now have group and one-on-one sessions with the older kids."

Megan wasn't necessarily trying to find common ground with Daniel, but wanted him to know that she recognized the contributions the church was making to the community and especially children.

"It continues to grow," Helen said.

"My grandfather always said if you get the kids to come to church then the parents will follow," Megan said.

"Was your grandfather a leader in the church?" Daniel asked, his curiosity evident.

"My church is the same denomination as yours. He

served on all the different committees in the leadership of the church over the years and was very active all his life."

"So you grew up in the church?"

"I did."

Daniel studied Megan for a moment and she was afraid of his next question. She did not break eye contact and was ready for him to ask why she didn't attend church now.

"Is everyone ready for dessert?" Helen asked.

Megan wondered if she could feel the tension that suddenly hung in the air.

"I am!" Anna shouted.

"Me too," Rebekah agreed.

"Come on, Anna, you can help me," Helen said.

"Where do you ride bikes?" Daniel asked, once again changing the subject.

"I live in the Pine Hills area. They have several bike trails that connect two parks on each end of the subdivision. It's a great place to ride bikes, especially with kids."

"Anna told us all about it. Is that part of counseling?" Daniel said.

"No." Megan gave him a wry smile. "Anna has therapy at the center, but sometimes situations come up and the day we rode bikes is a good example. Rebekah handled it."

"With your help," Rebekah cut in. "Sometimes I don't know what to do for her. I'm glad you were there."

"I didn't notice anything when she spent the night. She is more talkative and happier. I can tell whatever you're doing has helped," Daniel said.

"Thank you," Megan replied earnestly.

Anna came back carefully carrying two bowls. She set one down for Megan and then one for Rebekah.

Helen set a bowl down for Anna and one for Daniel as well as for herself.

"Thank you. Is this banana pudding?" Megan asked excitedly.

"It is," Helen replied with a smile.

"I feel like I'm back home in California." Megan took a bite and moaned. "This is delicious!"

"I'm glad you like it. Rebekah may have told me it was one of your favorites."

Megan looked up at Rebekah and smiled.

"Yes, I remember. We went to that little cafe that served homestyle cooking. You went crazy for their homemade banana pudding," Rebekah said as she returned her smile.

"Thank you," Megan said to Helen. "That's so nice of you."

"We happen to love banana pudding, too," Helen said with a pleased smile.

The rest of the meal was more relaxed. Anna gave them instructions on how to play handbells and even demonstrated her technique. When Rebekah tried to mimic her actions Anna very seriously corrected her.

Megan couldn't stifle the smile that grew on her face. Anna could be so serious about some things and happily carefree about others, like when she suddenly began telling everyone about the book she and Rebekah were reading at bedtime.

Helen wouldn't let them help with the dishes and she invited Anna to stay for the afternoon.

"I have dozens of cookies to bake for Bible Zone this week and could use Anna's help," Helen explained.

"I've helped Grandma with it before," Anna assured Megan.

"Those are lucky kids that get to eat your cookies," Megan said.

Anna giggled.

"Okay then. I'll check with you later, Mom."

"Thank you again for having me," Megan told Helen and Daniel.

"I hope you can come again," Daniel said.

"We won't have roast," Helen teased.

Megan chuckled and gave Neal one last pat between his ears.

Once they were in Rebekah's car Megan released a relieved breath.

"I don't know what is going on with my dad," Rebekah said as she backed out of her parents' driveway. "He's not usually like that."

"He doesn't like our friendship or me being involved in Anna's life. I felt it the first time he looked at me from the pulpit."

"What?" Rebekah said, glancing over at Megan.

"Yep. I thought I was being paranoid, but now I know I wasn't. Right before he started the service he gave me a look and nodded. I'd hoped he was welcoming me, but I don't think so now."

"I'm so sorry, babe." Rebekah pulled into her own driveway. "Do you mind if we stop here so I can change?"

"Of course not. And there's no need for you to apologize," Megan said as she got out of the car.

She followed Rebekah into the house.

"Come in here with me," Rebekah said as she walked down the hall to her bedroom.

Megan lay back on the bed and watched Rebekah kick her shoes off. "This could be fun if it were under different circumstances."

Rebekah looked at her with a smirk. "I don't know why Dad would treat you that way."

"I do. He knows, Bekah."

Rebekah swung around and looked at Megan. "What? How could he know?"

"Maybe it's the way we look at each other. Maybe it's because you and Anna talk about me. Maybe..." she paused. "Did he know about us twelve years ago?"

"No," Rebekah said. "I never told anyone about you, about us, until Ben."

"It felt like he was trying to turn Anna against me or at least upset her by continuing to talk about counseling."

"He knows I try not to use that word around her; however, Anna and I have talked. She knows you're a counselor, but she also knows that outside of the center we're friends. She loves you because of the things we do together outside of counseling."

Megan smiled as Rebekah sat down on the bed next to her. "Your dad was acting like that because it was his way to protect you and Anna. I think he will say something to you about me being older. And also me being an influence on Anna outside of counseling. And he'll encourage you to make new friends or look up other old friends that still live here."

Rebekah had a sad look on her face when she took Megan's arm and put it around her. She laid her head on Megan's shoulder and rested her arm across Megan's stomach. "When I was a little girl I always wanted to help people. I don't specifically remember my parents telling me to be good, but it was understood that I was the preacher's daughter and I was supposed to behave a certain way. We were always helping others in some way and I loved it."

"That's why you're such a good teacher. You want to help your kids."

"I was part of a group of girls that grew up together from elementary school through high school. A couple of them could be mean and it was always me that pointed out when they should stop. Sometimes they would tease me about having to be good because of who my dad was. I remember when we were in high school there were a couple of times when they talked about the boys they were dating and what they did with them. I thought my dad would die if I did some of the things they said." Rebekah chuckled.

"But that didn't mean you didn't want to do those things," Megan said.

"Exactly. When I went to college that's when things started to change. For one, I could breathe. I wasn't always worried about doing something that would reflect on my parents."

"I get that."

"I was always curious about gay people, but didn't know anyone that was gay. One of the first friends I made on campus was a guy that happened to be gay. We had so much fun and he introduced me to people that I would have never met otherwise. That's when the things I'd been taught about sin started to crumble."

"It's scary and exhilarating all at the same time when you get to think for yourself."

"Yeah it is. I had so many friends that were like no one here in Athens. I learned about other denominations. I had a friend that was Jewish. And I knew people who had never been to church. It was so much fun."

Megan smiled. "I remember those days. I bet they all fell in love with the preacher's daughter."

Rebekah chuckled. "No, but it didn't matter to them that my dad was a preacher."

"Did you tell your parents about your new friends?"

"Not at first, but then I started to ask questions," Rebekah said.

"What did your dad think of that?"

"He would listen. I didn't challenge him, but I do remember telling him it was hard for me to imagine that God didn't love them even though they were different from me. Wait a minute—" Rebekah sat up.

"What?"

"When I told Dad that I had reconnected with you he said he remembered that summer."

"He did?"

"Yeah, he said I was questioning and he and Mom were afraid they'd lose me and that I would leave the church."

"There you have it. He thinks I'm the one that put all those crazy notions in your head," Megan said with a southern parental accent.

Rebekah chuckled. "He has no idea that all you did was listen. I'd already made up my mind that if kissing you was a sin then I was going to hell. I'd also decided that hell couldn't be bad if we were there together loving each other."

"Oh baby." Megan pulled Rebekah closer. "I will find a way to make him like me. I won't make you choose between your family and me."

"*You* are my family, too, Megan," Rebekah said earnestly. She turned her head and looked into Megan's eyes. "I love you and I'm not living my life without you."

"I think you're going to have to tell your parents sooner than you wanted."

"You're right." Rebekah blew out a breath. "Wow, I didn't have a clue."

"He may not, baby, but he definitely feels threatened somehow."

"I'll have to set him straight then. He doesn't realize what he's missing because you are someone that he would love."

Megan's eyebrows shot up her forehead. "You'll set him straight?"

Rebekah laughed. "Seriously, you both have big hearts that want to help people. He'll love you when he gives you a chance."

Megan smiled at Rebekah and gently cupped her cheek. "I think we've talked enough for now." She brought her lips to Rebekah's and kissed her tenderly.

"I'm not finished just yet," Rebekah said. She sat up and pushed Megan down on the bed. She straddled her hips and pinned her hands to the bed on either side of her head. "I love you, Megan. Now I'm finished talking."

Rebekah kissed the smile from Megan's face.

23

"Hi Mom," Rebekah said as she answered her phone.

"It's me, Mommy. I'm ready for you to come get me."

"Oh, hi honey. Are you finished baking cookies?"

"Yes ma'am. Can we go play with Wanda?"

"Yes we can. I'll be there in just a minute."

Rebekah ended the call and turned to Megan. "This was a fun way to spend a couple of hours."

"I'll say." Megan nuzzled her neck. "I could kiss you all day long."

"Anna wants to go play with Wanda."

"Wanda will love that." Megan sat up. "Hey, we'll figure it out. You don't have to say anything to your parents until you're ready."

Rebekah sighed. "Will you talk through this with me? If I tell them we have to be prepared to talk to Anna, too."

"Let's go get her and she can play with Wanda. Anna may be a kid, but she knows we all love each other. That matters."

Rebekah kissed Megan softly and got up. "Okay love, let's go."

They picked Anna up at Rebekah's parents and went to Megan's.

"I brought clothes for you to change into, sweetie. You don't want to get your favorite dress dirty," Rebekah said as they walked into Megan's house.

"Okay. I'll go change in my room." Anna took the clothes from Rebekah and walked down the hall to the guest room.

Megan chuckled. "I think Anna feels at home here."

"She has claimed that room." Rebekah laughed and shook her head.

Anna walked back into the living room. "Is this the night we get to have a sleepover?"

"Uh—um," Rebekah stuttered. "Well, you have to go to school tomorrow."

"So? Can't I go to school from here? You have to go to school and Megan has to go to work."

"You still have to go to sleep at your regular time," Megan said.

"Okay. We can all read together," Anna stated.

Megan and Rebekah looked at each other and shrugged.

"Let me think about it," Rebekah said.

"Come on, Mommy. That means no. Please," Anna begged.

"Okay. I'll run home and get us clothes for tomorrow."

"Yay!" Anna shouted. "Thank you, Mommy!" Anna ran outside to play with Wanda.

"Is it okay?" Rebekah asked Megan.

"You know I'm going to say yes. I want you and Anna to stay over every night."

"Okay. I'll be right back."

"Do you want us to go with you?"

"No. It's fine," she said. "What a day and it isn't over yet."

"Wait." Megan reached out and placed her hand on Rebekah's arm. "Let's go get your stuff and then we can go to the park down by the river. It's a beautiful day. Let's show Anna a place we love. Together."

"Are you sure?"

"Yes. We can go by that ice cream shop and really spoil Anna." Megan walked over and took Rebekah's hands in hers. "Let's spend the rest of the afternoon together and have some fun. We'll talk tonight after Anna goes to sleep about your parents and us."

Rebekah looked into Megan's eyes. When she had struggled at nineteen Megan could ease her anxiety with a look or a touch; surprisingly, she still could. For a moment she was angry with herself because she didn't have the courage to be with Megan then. She believed that they had been given this second chance because this time it could work, if they were both strong and believed.

"I'm not going to lose you," Rebekah stated.

"What?" Megan asked, confused.

"Sorry, I was thinking about how you always calmed me back then, and Meg," she said, squeezing her hands, "I'm standing up for us with my parents, the church, and anyone else. I'm not losing you again."

"Oh Bekah, you are not going to lose me." Megan put her arms around Rebekah and held her tight. "I'm sorry you're having to go through this."

"I'm strong enough now to fight for us. But babe, you're going through it with me."

Megan sighed. "I wish it didn't have to be this way." She pulled away far enough to look into Rebekah's eyes. "We will find the place where you are at peace with the church and our love."

"I am at peace with us."

"Then we will find the church that wants us exactly the way we are. I know that's important to you and part of who you are."

"My sweet Megan." Rebekah cupped her face. "You're right, we'll find a way, but right now, let's take our girl to the river."

The smile that grew on Megan's face left no room for anxiety in Rebekah's heart at this moment. She peeked around Megan to look out the window and saw Anna at the back of the yard with Wanda. Then she kissed Megan softly. There was nothing wrong with their love and she didn't want to hide it, especially from Anna.

"Let's spend the rest of this day as a family because that's what we are," Rebekah said. She went to the back door and called Anna and Wanda.

They came running up to the back door and both were panting as they bounded into the living room.

"Do you remember when we were talking about the river at Grandma and Grandpa's?" Rebekah said to Anna.

"Yes. There are parks and you ate tacos."

"That's right." Rebekah chuckled. "Megan and I would like to take you to the river and show you why we love it."

Anna's eyes brightened. "Now?"

"Yes, right now," Megan said.

"Oh wow!"

Rebekah laughed. "We'll go by our house first and get clothes for tomorrow and then it's off to the river."

"Guess what?" Megan said to Anna

"What?"

"Wanda gets to go, too!"

"Yippee!"

Megan handed Anna Wanda's leash. "Here you go."

They all got in Megan's car and began their first family adventure.

At Rebekah's house she quickly packed a bag for her and Anna then Megan drove them to the river.

They started at one park and crawled through tubes and over brightly colored obstacles that were just Anna's size. Wanda even got in on the fun when they created a game just for her. Anna crouched in the opening of one end of a tube and called to Wanda at the other end. When Megan let her go she ran through the tube to Anna. Then she followed Anna over obstacles and they did it all again.

Laughter was the music of the afternoon as they played and played and played some more.

"Let's sit for a minute," Rebekah said, indicating an empty bench near the sidewalk that meandered parallel to the river.

"Are you having fun, Anna?" Megan asked as she plopped down next to Rebekah.

Anna giggled. "Yes," she said, a little breathless. "Wanda is too."

Rebekah leaned down to rub Wanda's head. "Look at her! She's smiling!"

Megan laughed. "I know! She's the happiest little dog, especially when her favorite playmate is near."

"I love Wanda," Anna said, leaning back on the bench and swinging her legs.

They sat together for a moment, catching their breath and taking in the scene. Rebekah rested her arm across the back of the bench and squeezed Megan's shoulder. She released a contented breath and smiled at her little family.

"Are you ready to see the next thing we love at the river?" Megan asked Anna.

"I'm ready," Anna said, hopping up and holding Wanda's leash.

They walked the short distance along the path to the area that had shops and restaurants.

"This is where we ate the other night," Rebekah explained to Anna.

"And here's where we want to shop today." Megan stopped in front of the ice cream shop.

Anna looked up at Rebekah with a big smile on her face.

"Let's go in," Rebekah said, opening the door.

"Can Wanda come in, too?"

"Yes. They have ice cream for dogs, too," Megan said.

They made their selections and went outside to sit at one of the outdoor tables.

"Can I feed Wanda?" Anna asked.

"Sure." Megan handed the small paper cup to her.

They sat in the sun, ate their ice cream, and watched the people stroll down the river walk.

"What do you think of the river so far?" Rebekah asked Anna. "Do you see why Megan and I love it?"

"It's fun. I like it."

"We're not through yet. There's another park just around that corner," Megan said, nodding towards the river.

"Another park? Let's go!" Anna exclaimed.

Rebekah and Megan laughed as they made their way down the sidewalk. Anna skipped ahead of them with Wanda. Joy filled Rebekah's heart and she couldn't resist the urge to reach for Megan's hand. When she curled her fingers between Megan's, she looked up at Rebekah, surprised. Rebekah smiled and nodded, holding Megan's hand firmly.

They continued on the sidewalk and Rebekah noticed no one looked twice at them. When people they met did make eye contact they simply smiled and continued on their way.

"I see it," Anna said, turning to wait on them.

"What do you want to do first?"

"Let's go down the slides. All of them!" she exclaimed.

"Let me have Wanda so you and Mommy can go slide," Megan said, reaching for the leash.

They played on the slides and the swings, then the monkey bars and the see-saw. Anna climbed up in the tower and slid down a chute to land in the cedar shavings below.

Megan and Rebekah took turns with Anna and playing with Wanda.

"We're going to sit under this tree," Rebekah told Megan and Anna. "Wanda's getting tired."

A few minutes later Megan walked over and sat down next to Rebekah.

"She's having so much fun," Megan said, her eyes on Anna.

"I think you are, too." Rebekah smiled at Megan.

"I am. How about you?"

"This has been the best afternoon. I'm so glad you thought of this!"

Anna skipped over and fell down on the grass in front of them.

"I love the river," Anna said, contentment in her voice.

"Hey honey, do you see that family over there?" Rebekah pointed to two kids who were eating ice cream with who she assumed were their parents.

"Yes," Anna answered.

"Do they look like us?"

"What do you mean?" Anna's brow furrowed.

"Do you think you, me, Megan and Wanda look like a family?"

Anna studied the family and then looked from Megan to Rebekah and finally to Wanda.

"I think we are a family. Megan, do you and Wanda want to be a family with us?"

Megan smiled. "Anna, do you and your mommy want to be a family with Wanda and me?"

Anna looked at Rebekah and nodded. "Yes, we do."

"Nothing would make Wanda and me happier than to be your family. Except..." Megan paused. "Could I have a hug to be sure?"

Anna got up and curled her little arms around Megan's neck.

Rebekah could see the joy and the tears pool in Megan's eyes. "Don't forget Wanda," she said as Anna let Megan go.

"You have to hug Megan, too," Anna said to Rebekah.

"I'd love to." Rebekah leaned over and wrapped her arms around Megan. For a moment she rested her head on Megan's shoulder and took a deep breath.

"Okay, our first family adventure is over. Let's go home," Rebekah said.

"It's not quite over," Megan said to Rebekah. "There may be a surprise for Anna later this evening."

Rebekah realized Megan meant a bubble bath in her big tub and smiled. "Oh that's right."

"What is it? What is it?" Anna exclaimed.

"Do you promise not to complain when it's time to go to bed?"

"I promise, I promise," she replied, jumping up and down.

"Then Meg, I guess you'd better take us home."

Megan held out one hand to Anna and the other to Rebekah.

24

When they got back to Megan's house, Wanda went to her bed in the living room, curled up, and immediately closed her eyes.

"Wow, Anna, I think we wore Wanda out," Megan said. "That doesn't happen very often."

"She's not the only one," Rebekah said. "I'm sitting on this couch and watching the *Kids Baking Challenge*. Would anyone like to join me?"

"I do," Megan said, dropping on the other end of the couch and putting her feet up.

"What about me?" Anna asked from where she stood in front of them with her hands on her hips.

"How about this?" Megan sat up and pulled the ottoman in front of them so they could all prop their feet up. She scooted closer to Rebekah but left enough room for Anna to sit between them.

Anna stepped on top of the ottoman and dove into the space between them. She giggled when Megan and Rebekah both tickled her.

"Does anyone need anything?" Megan asked as she

leaned up and looked at Rebekah and Anna. "A pillow? A blanket?"

"Ooohh, a blanket might be nice," Rebekah purred.

"Kick your shoes off and I'll be right back." Megan disappeared down the hall and came back with a blanket. She spread it out over Rebekah and Anna and then bowed. "Can I get you ladies anything else?"

Rebekah looked at Anna, her eyebrows raised, and Anna shook her head.

"Thank you, ma'am. Would you join us?" Rebekah asked in a queenly accent.

Anna threw one end of the blanket back so Megan could snuggle under with them.

Once they were all settled Megan leaned over and said to Anna, "Don't you dare fall asleep."

"That's right," Rebekah said, sitting up. "We still have to eat supper and have bathtime."

Anna giggled. "I won't." She looked at the TV and asked, "Okay, who do you think will be leaving tonight?"

They watched the show and commented on the different bakers' offerings. Anna rested her head on Rebekah's shoulder for a while and then Megan's. When she got quiet Rebekah looked down to make sure she wasn't asleep.

When the episode was over, Anna asked, "Can we watch another one?"

"Let's have supper and you still have to take a bath. You played hard today."

"I had fun at the river. Can we do it again?"

"It's one of our favorite places. Of course we can do it again," Rebekah said.

"Is that where you and Megan used to go when you were friends before?"

"We did." Rebekah looked at Megan and smiled.

"You know, Bekah, I think it was more fun having Anna with us. What do you think?" Megan looked down at Anna and grinned.

Rebekah pretended to be thinking and furrowed her brow and then she looked up and down before finally laughing. "Yes, it was definitely more fun with Anna."

"You're both funny sometimes." Anna giggled.

"Funny? What do you mean funny?" Megan asked, feigning seriousness.

Anna giggled.

"Do you mean funny like this?" Rebekah tickled her and Anna's laughter echoed around the room. Wanda jumped on the couch and joined in, licking Anna's face.

"Stop! Stop!" Anna cried breathlessly.

Rebekah stopped and Megan grabbed Wanda while they all laughed with Anna.

Megan went to the kitchen and set out sandwich makings for supper. They each created their own sandwiches and ate at the island sharing chips.

Rebekah helped Megan put everything away and tidied the kitchen.

"Is this what it would be like?" Megan mumbled aloud.

"What it would be like?"

"To be a family? Would we get to do this every night?"

Rebekah smiled and leaned against the counter. She looked into the living room where Anna and Wanda sat on the couch. Then she met Megan's gaze. "I'd love to do this every night."

"Let's make it happen."

Rebekah smiled and nodded. "Anna, are you ready to take a bath?"

Megan grinned. "How about a bubble bath?"

That got Anna's attention. "In your big tub?"

"In my big tub." Megan nodded. "I'll go start the water."

Anna and Rebekah went into the bedroom to get her pajamas and then went to Megan's bathroom.

"Your bubble bath is ready, Princess Anna," Megan said with a flourish of her arm towards the tub.

Anna giggled and started to take her clothes off. Megan threw a couple of bath toys into the tub and Rebekah picked her up and lowered her into the bubbly water.

"Is it too hot?" Megan asked.

"No, it's fine."

Anna sunk down into the bubbles and laughed.

"Okay, I'll let you play for a few minutes," Rebekah said. "Keep the water in the tub."

"Okay." She giggled.

Megan and Rebekah left the bathroom and sat down on the bed.

Rebekah fell back and sighed. "So you want this family, huh?"

"Very much," Megan answered.

"Since moving here it has become apparent to me that this is God's plan. I intend to tell my father just that, this week."

"Moving here is the plan? Or moving here and being with me is the plan?" Megan asked, narrowing her eyes.

Rebekah raised up on her elbow and rested her head in her hand. "Loving you, raising Anna with you, creating a life together. That is the plan."

Megan gazed into Rebekah's eyes.

"Oh wait. That *is* what you want, too. Isn't it?" Rebekah asked, a moment of uncertainty creeping into her thoughts.

"Yes! That's what I've wanted all along."

"So this could be God's plan for you, too."

"I will tell you what I think of God's plan and me after Anna goes to sleep," Megan said.

"And that's why I love you. We don't have to see things the same way to be together."

"We all have to come to terms with what we've been taught and then what we've learned on our own."

Rebekah leaned over and kissed Megan softly. "I love you," she whispered.

"Mom! Will you come wash my hair?" Anna yelled from the bathroom.

Megan chuckled and blew out a contented breath. "You heard Princess Anna."

Rebekah helped Anna finish her bath and they went back into the living room.

"It's bedtime," Rebekah said. "Get two books and we'll come and read with you in bed."

Anna picked out two books and followed Rebekah to the bedroom. Then she turned around to find Megan. "Are you coming?"

"I'll let Wanda in and be right there," Megan said with a grin.

With Rebekah on one side, Megan on the other and Wanda at the foot of the bed, they took turns reading. When they finished the first book Anna yawned.

"Can Wanda sleep in here with me?"

"Yes she can," Megan answered. "Hey, if you wake up in the night, you remember where my bedroom is, right?"

Anna nodded. "Are you going to sleep with Megan, Mommy?" Anna asked.

"Yes. You can come in there if you get scared."

"I won't get scared. Wanda will be with me." Anna looked down at the blanket. "I saw you holding hands at the river."

"We were."

"Does that mean Megan is your girlfriend?"

"It does." Rebekah smiled at Megan. She knew Anna had seen them holding hands and wondered when she would say something.

"I love your Mommy and I love you, Anna," Megan said.

Anna looked up at Megan. "I love you, Megan, and Mommy loves you too. I can tell."

Megan smiled at Anna and waited.

"It's okay, because I don't want Mommy to be sad without Daddy. Now she has you and she can be happy again like me. You helped me be happy about Daddy."

"Oh Anna, you make me very happy," Megan said, her voice hoarse.

"And Wanda!"

"And Wanda." Megan chuckled.

"Now that we all love each other, it's time for you to go to sleep my sweet girl," Rebekah said around the lump in her throat.

"But you said two books, Mommy."

"She did," Megan said as she leaned back. "I'll read first."

They finished the second book and kissed Anna goodnight.

"I'll leave the door open in case you need to go to the bathroom or come to Megan's room," Rebekah said.

"Okay," Anna said around a big yawn. She rolled over and closed her eyes.

Rebekah and Megan left, leaving the door open a crack. They held hands as they went back to the living room.

Megan poured them both a glass of wine and they settled on the couch.

Rebekah took a sip and looked at Megan. "A lot has happened today."

"Yeah it has. Were you surprised by what Anna said?"

"I knew she saw us holding hands and would say something eventually. What did surprise me was what she said about my happiness."

"She is very attuned to you, babe; especially now with Ben gone. Your happiness shows her it's okay to be happy."

"Everything has felt right today. We started by watching Anna perform in church and you were right by my side. And then lunch with my folks felt right even though my dad was acting weird. To go to the river and share the things we love with Anna seemed like something we'd do all the time. Reading books at bedtime together could be our normal routine. But Anna knowing we love each other and knowing we're a family is the icing on the cake."

Megan smiled. "I didn't think she would have a problem with us, but she seemed happy about it. I want Crystal to talk to her Tuesday just to be sure."

"What are you worried about?"

"I'm not worried at all. She's had to navigate moving to a new town and a new school. She's also learning how to live with the memories of her dad. And now her mom has a new partner. I want Crystal to check in with her, that's all."

"Does it seem too good to be true? Are you afraid something is going to happen?"

"I'm thankful every day that you are back in my life, but, Bekah, something is going to happen. It's not going to be this easy when you tell your parents about us. It was obvious to me today that your dad is feeling protective."

"Can Anna come home with you Tuesday after counseling? That would be a good time to talk to my parents."

"Of course. Do you want me to go with you?" Megan asked warily.

Rebekah chuckled. "I can tell that is something you *would* do, but don't *want* to do. So no, babe, you don't have to come with me. I need to do this alone."

"I think your parents would appreciate it if I wasn't there, but if you need me for support I'm yours."

"I know you are." Rebekah finished her wine and looked at Megan. "Right now, I need you for something else."

"Oh?"

"I know the perfect ending to this day," Rebekah said, raising her eyebrows.

25

They checked on Anna on their way to Megan's bedroom. Wanda raised her head and then snuggled back down next to Anna.

"That is the smartest dog," Rebekah said softly.

"She knows Anna needs her more than we do tonight."

Once inside the bedroom, Megan took Rebekah in her arms and nuzzled her neck. "I'm glad you're here. My bed was so empty last night."

Rebekah ran her fingers through Megan's hair. "I missed you too." She looked into Megan's eyes and then began to undress her.

"Are you sure? I mean..." Megan quietly stammered. "Anna's just down the hall."

Rebekah smiled. "I'm sure that I need to show you how much I love you right now. Let me end this day loving you."

That's all Megan needed to hear. She firmly pressed her lips to Rebekah's and kissed her with the love that had smoldered all these years. She could now let it burn hot and fast because Rebekah was here to receive it and give it back to her.

Between kisses they finished undressing and fell into bed, limbs wrapped around each other. Heated kisses, coupled with moans and gasping breaths echoed around the bedroom.

Rebekah crawled on top of Megan and smiled down at her. "Slow down, my love," she panted. "I'm going to savor each kiss, each touch, and each heavenly moan."

Megan watched Rebekah's eyes sparkle in the darkness as she told her what she was going to do. Rebekah commanded their lovemaking in a way that made Megan feel worshiped, treasured and loved.

"Love me," Megan whispered.

Rebekah smiled and nibbled Megan's earlobe. "I trust you, Meg. I know you'll cherish and protect my heart. Feel my love."

Rebekah ran her tongue around the inside of Megan's ear and made her shudder. Then she slowly kissed a path down Megan's neck and paused at her pulse point. "I can feel my love flowing through you with every heartbeat," Rebekah whispered as she sucked gently on Megan's neck.

"Good God, Bekah," Megan moaned.

"That's right, my love. Tell me you feel it." Rebekah kissed then licked along Megan's collarbone. She kissed down Megan's chest and cupped one breast in her hand as her tongue swirled around her other nipple.

"You are making my body tingle all over," Megan whispered as her chest heaved up and down. She felt Rebekah smile against her nipple and then bite down on it. "Ohhhhh. Yes!"

When Rebekah sucked, licked, and bit her nipple Megan thought she might come undone, but her lover knew her body better than Megan did herself. After all this time

Rebekah knew exactly what to do and when to do it to give Megan the utmost pleasure. *She just knew.*

Rebekah began to kiss down to Megan's stomach. This gave Megan the opportunity to take a much needed deep breath. She ran her fingers through Rebekah's hair and could see the rust colored strands shine from the moonlight coming in the window. It reminded Megan of a halo. If she ever believed in angels then Rebekah was certainly hers and she was thankful she'd returned.

Rebekah kissed her way across Megan's stomach to her hip bone where she found a smattering of light flecks on her skin.

"I love these little freckles," Rebekah said as she kissed Megan's skin gently.

"They seem to be very sensitive when your lips touch them." Megan took a sharp breath in.

Rebekah grinned. "They are a little roadmap for me to follow to make you purr."

"Oh I'm purring all right," Megan said breathlessly.

"We'll see about that."

"Fuck, Bekah," Megan moaned as Rebekah's tongue followed the path her lips just kissed from Megan's hip back across her stomach and lower.

Megan bent her knees and dug her heels into the bed when Rebekah's tongue touched the tip of her hardened clit. Then she licked Megan from one end to the other, spreading her wetness. She couldn't stop writhing under Rebekah's touch.

"You are magical," she moaned. Megan felt Rebekah chuckle against her.

"No honey, I'm in love," Rebekah said softly. Then she sucked Megan's sensitive clit into her mouth and grabbed her thighs.

Megan's whole body flexed and one of her hands flew across her mouth to stifle a loud groan while the other slapped against the bed. Her hips rose into the air and Rebekah held her there until a soul absorbing orgasm coursed through her body. Megan was sure her whole body must be glowing from the inside out because she felt such heat and love rushing through it.

She didn't dare take a breath because she didn't want this feeling to end. Rebekah's love was everywhere. It was wrapped around her, inside her, it became her. When she couldn't hold on any longer her hips fell to the bed and she reached for Rebekah's head. Her breath came in gasps and although she was spent, she needed Rebekah's lips on hers.

Once again Rebekah knew what she needed and claimed Megan's lips with a firm, assertive, and possessive kiss. Megan groaned and ran her hands up and down Rebekah's back.

When Rebekah eased her lips away, Megan took a deep breath. "Oh, I love you so."

"I know, babe. I could feel your love. I could taste it. I could see it."

"Don't ever leave me again, Bekah. Promise?" Suddenly Megan felt very vulnerable. She knew they would be facing challenges that they could only imagine. They had no idea how hard it could be.

"I promise."

"I don't care what we have to go through. We can make it this time."

"We already have, Meg. We already have."

Megan tightened her arms around Rebekah and held her to her chest.

"Don't ever let go," Rebekah whispered.

"I won't."

* * *

The next morning Megan walked into the counseling center. The smile that played at the corners of her mouth had been there since she'd woken up that morning with her arms around Rebekah. A little early morning cuddling and kissing was a wonderful way to start the day.

Anna had woken up and played with Wanda as if she did it every morning. She sat at the island while Megan made breakfast and told her all about a project she was working on at school. When Rebekah walked in the kitchen and kissed Anna on the head and Megan on the cheek it seemed like the most natural thing in the world.

Megan let out a contented sigh as she set her bag on her desk. She hoped this would be how her mornings started every day going forward. There would be challenging times ahead with Rebekah's parents, but surely they wanted her to be happy.

She sat down in her chair and couldn't keep from smiling. Megan would do anything to make Rebekah happy and she knew Rebekah would do the same for her.

"What's put that smile on your face?" Crystal asked from the doorway.

Megan hadn't heard her come in as the happy thoughts floated through her head. "Good morning."

Crystal narrowed her eyes and perused Megan for a moment. Then a smile grew on her face. "You're downright glowing, partner. What do you need to tell me?" She sat down in the chair opposite Megan's desk and waited.

Megan chuckled. "*Need* to tell you?"

"Oh yeah, come on. I'm guessing Rebekah has put that smile there. Now, tell me why."

Crystal was right. Megan couldn't wait to tell her about

the weekend. She recounted all that had happened from her date with Rebekah that started the weekend to this morning making breakfast for them.

"Wow! That's great, Megan. No wonder you're so happy."

"Would you visit with Anna? She's had so many changes in a short time and I want to be sure she's okay, you know?"

"That little girl is much better. I'll chat with her Tuesday. Before I forget, Kim and I would like you and Rebekah to come over for dinner Friday night."

"That would be fun. Let me ask Rebekah. I don't know if Anna will be at her grandparents' house or not. They mentioned her spending Friday nights with them."

Crystal nodded. "So you think her dad knows about you and Rebekah?"

Megan nodded. "Or he just doesn't like me. He was very protective and asked a lot of questions."

"I can't imagine him not liking you. I mean, if he'd spent time with you and didn't like you that would be one thing, but inviting you to his home and asking a bunch of questions seems suspicious."

"Exactly. Rebekah plans to talk to them tomorrow while Anna is with us."

"Wow! That's a big step for her."

"I know. I told her she didn't have to tell them yet. She could do it when she was ready."

"Sounds like she's ready."

Megan sighed. "Yesterday was almost perfect. It will all change when she tells them."

"Yes it will. For a while it may be a challenge, but it's always better to be honest. You know that."

Megan nodded.

"Tell me something. I know you don't really like going to church, so why do you go with Rebekah?"

"It's important to her. It's like it's a part of her. I go to be supportive and because I love her. I'm not sure she'll still want to go when she tells her parents, but I'm going to look into other churches. I know there are churches that are welcoming to the gay population and some are right here."

"That's not the church she grew up in though," Crystal cautioned. "Maybe you'll be the couple to open their eyes and show the congregation we're just like them."

Megan raised her eyebrows, but before she said anything they heard the front door open.

Crystal got up. "That's probably my nine o'clock appointment."

We'd love to be the first gay couple accepted into that church, Megan thought. "One step at a time," she said aloud to herself.

"Hey," Crystal said from the doorway. "There's someone here to see you."

Megan couldn't mistake the strange look on Crystal's face as she got up and walked out of her office. She went to the waiting area and then understood why Crystal looked that way.

"Hi Megan," Helen Mathews said.

26

"Mrs. Math—"

"Call me Helen," she said, holding up her hand.

Megan smiled. "Helen. How nice to see you," Megan said as she tried to regain her composure. The last person she expected to see here was Rebekah's mother.

"Did you come for a tour?" Megan asked. Her heartbeat had certainly picked up in her chest.

"Uh, actually, I hoped to visit with you. Do you have time?"

"Of course. Right this way." Megan led them to her office and instead of sitting behind her desk, she guided them to the couch and chair on the other side.

"Please, have a seat."

She waited for Helen to sit on the couch and Megan sat across from her on the chair.

"Can I get you something? Coffee or water? We might have tea?" Megan offered.

"No, thank you," Helen said. She held her purse tightly in her lap. Then she looked up at Megan. "Rebekah thinks you and Daniel would have a lot in common, but I suspect you and I might have more than she thinks."

Megan looked at Helen and could see where Rebekah got her blue eyes from now. But she also saw kindness. The look Helen gave Megan made her pounding heart start to slow. Megan smiled and nodded.

"I know about the counseling you do here to help children and adults, but I also know about the work you do to help queer youth," Helen said.

"Oh!" Megan said, surprised.

Helen smiled. "Most folks think that preacher's wives are meek and unassuming. While there is some truth in that, it doesn't necessarily mean we have always led quiet lives."

Megan raised her eyebrows and waited.

"I was raised in a small town in southern Georgia. We went to church like most of the people in town did. My brother and I thought that everyone went to church because there wasn't anything else to do."

Megan chuckled.

"One summer," Helen continued, "I was around twelve or so and my brother was fourteen, I guess. I thought he could do no wrong and hung the moon."

Megan watched as Helen appeared to be swept back in time. She suddenly couldn't wait for her to continue the story and leaned forward a little.

Helen looked at Megan. "One evening we were all down at the river swimming and I had to go to the bathroom. I didn't want to *go* right next to my friends, so I waded around a small bend. I was hidden behind a branch that hung over the water and was about to do my business when I heard voices. I looked a little farther down the shore and could make out my brother talking quietly to someone else. Then

I saw them kiss. When he pulled back I could see that he was kissing another boy."

Megan's eyes went wide, but she didn't say anything.

"Let me tell you, I no longer needed to use the bathroom. I tried to quietly slip away, but my brother saw me." Helen smiled and looked away. "The look he gave me!" Helen looked back at Megan. "Let me put it this way, I knew not to say a word."

"What happened?"

"When we got home that night, he waited until our parents had gone to bed and he explained to me what he felt inside. He didn't try to tell me I was seeing things; he told me the truth." Helen smiled at Megan. "You can probably imagine the fear of being a gay teenager forty years ago, deep in the rural south of Georgia."

Megan nodded.

"He was careful and got out of our little town as soon as he graduated from high school. I can still remember the whispers I occasionally heard after he left."

"What happened to your brother?"

Helen chuckled. "He moved to California and has lived happily as a gay man all these years. He never came back to our small town and my parents rarely talked about him. It was like they didn't know what to do. I learned quickly not to ask questions about him."

Megan anxiously waited for her to continue.

"When I left to go to college I contacted him. He invited me to come visit, but I wasn't brave enough to ever go. We checked in with one another occasionally. He told me all about his struggles and that he was safer in San Francisco than he'd ever be in Georgia."

"He was in San Francisco?"

"Yes, that's where he ended up. He did come to my

wedding. That's when I found out that he called our parents several times over the years, but he didn't want to put them in an awkward position by coming home. So he chose not to. And at home... Well, we simply didn't talk about him."

Megan tried to digest all that Helen had told her. She couldn't imagine rarely speaking to her sister or not coming home so as not to put her parents in a delicate situation.

"Rebekah doesn't know about any of this," Helen added.

"She doesn't know she has an uncle?" Megan asked, surprised.

"She knows I have a brother, but has never met him. She doesn't know he's gay."

Megan's mouth fell open, but she didn't say anything.

"I'm sure you're wondering why I'm telling you this," Helen said.

Megan nodded.

Helen leaned forward slightly. "I know you're in love with my daughter and she's in love with you."

Megan nearly fell out of her chair. Her cheeks felt hot and she was sure they were flaming red.

"I'm not asking you to betray Rebekah's trust. I intend to talk to her, but what I want to tell you is this: don't be afraid."

"Don't be afraid?" Megan repeated, finally finding her voice.

"My brother was afraid to come home and give me and my parents a chance. He doesn't know how we or our town would have reacted because he stayed away. Don't be afraid to give us a chance. Don't be afraid to give the church a chance. Times have changed and views are changing."

Megan shook her head. "I don't know what to say."

"Daniel challenged you at lunch yesterday, but you didn't falter. It is obvious that Anna loves you and I can see that you love her like your own. I suspect that Daniel may have seen what I saw when you and Rebekah look at one another. Or he may have noticed the joy in Rebekah's voice when she talks about you. We have not discussed it, but we will."

"Won't it put him in a tough situation at your church?"

"Preachers are always in tough situations." Helen chuckled.

"But this is his family. It's easy to believe in something when it doesn't affect your family. But when it does, beliefs change."

"That's true in some situations, but Daniel has a superpower similar to your dog—Wanda, is it?"

"Yes, her name is Wanda." Megan chuckled. Then she narrowed her eyes and stared at Helen. "I think his superpower is the meek and unassuming preacher's wife."

Helen smirked. "Maybe."

"Rebekah plans to talk to you and Daniel tomorrow," Megan said.

"Were you going to keep Anna for her?"

"Yes ma'am."

"I think we'll do it today."

Megan found herself speechless again. How many times had that happened since Helen Mathews walked in the front door?

"The reason I said we have more in common than Rebekah thinks is because I know you were there for Rebekah when she struggled years ago, just as I was there for my brother. I'm sure you listened, told her your beliefs and supported her as she discovered her own. I can't imagine how hard that must have been for you when she left." Helen looked at the ceiling then back at Megan. "I'm thankful you've found one another again. Surely it's part of a plan."

Megan scoffed. "Oh my God, you sound like Rebekah."

When Helen burst out laughing, Megan realized what she had said and joined her.

"I pick Anna up from school on Mondays for Rebekah. I'll drop her off here, if that's okay, and then make sure Daniel is home when Rebekah gets there."

Megan smiled. "I'm happy to keep Anna anytime."

Helen studied Megan and then remarked, "I imagine Anna feels at home at your house since they weren't home this morning when I went by there before school."

"Uhh," Megan stammered.

"It's okay. I had a pretty good idea where they were."

Megan smiled and then suddenly felt very protective of Rebekah. "I can't keep this from her, Helen. I don't want her walking into your house and being blindsided."

Helen tilted her head and gazed at Megan. "I can understand your concerns. But believe me, all I'm going to do is love her."

"What about Daniel?"

Helen shrugged. "I can't speak for him. He loves Rebekah and I imagine there will be several debates, but that's nothing new."

Helen got up and Megan hurried to her feet.

"Everything will be all right." Helen put her hands on Megan's shoulders and gave her the kindest smile. Then she walked out of the office and out of the counseling center's front door.

Megan wanted to believe her, but she couldn't let Rebekah walk into her parents' house not knowing what was about to happen. Before she could decide what to do next, her first client of the day came in.

When she was finally able to take a short break between clients, Megan remembered that she and Crystal were leading a group activity at the middle school after lunch. That would provide the perfect opportunity to go by Rebekah's room for a quick visit.

She couldn't believe Helen's story and the courage it took for her to come here. But now that she thought about it, Helen had a twinkle in her eye when she confronted Megan about her and Rebekah's love. It felt like she was rooting for them and would do all she could to champion them.

Megan chuckled. "A meek and unassuming preacher's wife, indeed."

"Hey, are you ready to go?" Crystal asked, popping her head in Megan's office.

"Yeah. When we get back, do I have a story for you!"

27

Rebekah strolled around the room as her students worked individually on an assignment. She stopped when someone had a question and helped when needed. Something caught her eye and when she looked up at her closed door she saw Megan's face grinning at her through the window.

She knew Megan and Crystal were doing a group session for one of the classes this afternoon and hoped Megan could stop by. Returning her smile, Rebekah went to the door and quietly opened it. She slipped through it and stepped into the hall.

"Hi honey," she said softly.

"Hi." Megan beamed a smile. "How's your day going?"

"It's better now," Rebekah replied.

"Your mom is bringing Anna to me at the counseling center after school."

"Why?" Rebekah asked, her brow furrowed.

"I can't explain here, but go to your parents and speak your truth, baby," Megan said cryptically.

"What?"

"Your mom came by to see me this morning," Megan answered, nervously looking around the hall. "Everything will be all right."

"Psst," Crystal said from the end of the hall. "Come on," she whispered loudly.

"I've got to go." Megan squeezed Rebekah's hand and kissed her on the cheek.

"Megan?"

"You've got this. I love you."

"I love you, too," Rebekah mumbled to Megan's back as she hurried away. *That was weird,* she thought.

Rebekah went back into her classroom and before she could think about what Megan said, two students had questions.

An hour later the release bell rang and her students hurried into the hall.

Rebekah grabbed her phone and called Megan. When it went to voicemail she realized that she must be with a client. She huffed out a deep breath and replayed their earlier conversation in her head.

Mom went by the counseling center this morning. Why? She bit her lip nervously. *Go to your parents and speak your truth.* "Speak your truth," Rebekah said aloud. Her voice echoed around the room and her heart began to pound in her chest. Realization dawned. It was time to tell her parents about Megan and her. She'd planned to talk to them tomorrow, but something must have happened.

Oh well, she was excited to tell them about Megan. They may not be happy about it, but Rebekah didn't want to hide her feelings for Megan and in reality, she couldn't anyway.

Everything will be all right. That was the last thing Megan had said. Rebekah smiled. She took a deep breath and felt a wave of courage pass through her. "Everything *is* all right, now that we're together again, Meg," she said.

Rebekah gathered her things and drove to her parents' house. She pulled in the driveway and thought back to several nights in high school when she'd gotten home just before her curfew. How many times had she heard her father say what she did reflected on their family? She was the preacher's daughter and had to be an example for others.

She sighed. Looking back, she knew she had been a good kid. There wasn't one time that she remembered thinking "I can't do this because of who my parents are." Even when she was first with Megan, it wasn't her parents that made her question her actions. It was God and what the church taught about homosexuality.

"Well, let's see what they think of the preacher's daughter now," she said, getting out of the car.

She looked up and quietly said, "Please help them to understand. I love her so and I know that's okay with you."

Rebekah walked in the back door to find her parents sitting at the kitchen table.

"Hey," she said with a nervous smile.

"Where's Anna?" Daniel asked.

"I took her to Megan at the center," Helen said. "Come sit, sweetheart."

"Rebekah, is everything all right?" Daniel asked with concern in his voice.

Rebekah released a deep breath and smiled at each of her parents. "Everything is finally right again, Dad."

"You girls are confusing me," Daniel said, sitting back in his chair. "What are you talking about?"

"Mom, Dad. Megan and I are in love and we are creating

a life together, with Anna," Rebekah said, looking each of them in the eye.

Helen reached over and took Rebekah's hand and smiled at her.

Daniel stared at her then shook his head. "Rebekah."

Rebekah returned her mom's smile and turned to her dad. "Yes Dad?"

"How? Have you thought about Anna? What..." he sputtered.

"Of course we've thought about Anna. She is my number one priority. You know that," Rebekah answered, her voice rising.

Helen squeezed her hand. "I think what your father means is how did this all happen?"

Rebekah nodded and took a moment before responding. "When I was in high school I started having these feelings. I won't go into all of it, but when I realized what was happening it scared me to death. I just knew I was going to hell and that God had to be angry with me. That's what I'd learned in church and it was quite a struggle. I pushed all those feelings down and actually believed what I'd heard: that it was a choice. But when I got to college I did what you taught me, Dad, and I talked to God. I also read the Bible and you know what I learned?" Rebekah paused.

"Go on," Daniel urged her.

Rebekah smiled. "I learned that you can find anything in the Bible to support your views if you look hard enough and twist the words to fit your agenda."

Helen smiled and nodded.

"I came back home that summer and knew in my heart that even though I was attracted to women, God still loves me. Where I still struggled was with the church. I had a hard time sitting in church knowing that if the congregation knew who I was they'd refuse to let me in."

"Now Rebekah—" Daniel started.

"That's how it felt, Dad. I know that wouldn't have happened, but nineteen-year-old me didn't. Anyway, then I met Megan. That's when I knew for sure that the church had it wrong because there was no way the love we had could be a sin. It's hard to explain, but I felt like I was home." Rebekah had to pause because a lump had suddenly formed in her throat. The love she had for Megan sometimes slammed into her heart and she had to steady herself.

"We understand, honey. Your dad and I have that love, too," Helen said. She squeezed Rebekah's hand then looked over at Daniel and smiled.

"Megan had been through a lot of the same struggles. But at first all she did was listen and then finally she told me some of the things she'd gone through. Ultimately, she told me it didn't matter what she thought or what happened to her. I had to figure it out for myself. I had to find my truth, who I was, and what I wanted."

"What happened?"

"Although I was in love with Megan there were other things I wanted. I wanted to finish school. I wanted a family. I couldn't figure out how I could have those things with her. So I went back to school and then I realized that we could figure anything out together."

"That's when you came back for the weekend," Helen said.

Rebekah nodded. "I came back to tell Megan that I believed in our love and that we could make it work. But I couldn't find her. The apartment she'd been living in was Crystal's. She moved and I thought she'd decided to leave town."

"I was worried about you going back to school. I knew something had happened, but you wouldn't talk to me," Helen said.

"I was devastated. I was afraid you'd be disappointed, so I went back to school and put it in God's hands. I decided if it was meant to be that we would find our way back to each other. I focused on my studies and anytime I came home to visit I hoped somehow I'd run into Megan even though I didn't think she lived here anymore."

"What about Ben?" Daniel asked.

Rebekah smiled. "Ben and I met when we both needed a friend. He knew all about Megan. I loved, and still love, Ben. Please don't doubt that. But Megan has always had my heart."

Daniel sighed.

"When I saw Megan in the counseling center that day it was the first time I felt like maybe Anna and I could get through this. I thanked God that night for giving me this second chance and I'm not going to lose Megan again."

Rebekah looked at both her parents and sighed. "Dad, I know this is a lot, but please try to understand. I don't mean to hurt you or put you in an awkward position at the church."

"Rebekah, you are my daughter. I love you. Don't worry about the church right now. What about Anna?"

"Can you not see how much Anna loves Megan? And how Megan loves her? Anna knows about Megan and me." Rebekah chuckled. "She's only eight and in her words, she knows Megan is my girlfriend."

Helen chuckled.

"I know about Megan's work and the good things she and her partner have done with kids. But I don't know her," Daniel commented.

"That's why I wanted her to come for lunch yesterday. You asked a lot of questions, Dad, and you weren't very nice to her."

Daniel sighed. "I'm protective of you and Anna."

"But you don't have to protect us from Megan. She loves us, she wants a life with us!"

"We know that now," Helen said calmly. She looked at Daniel then back to Rebekah. "Why don't you give us some time to sit with this?"

Rebekah nodded. "You always told me that you wanted me to be happy. Megan is my happiness."

Helen smiled. "Why don't you, Megan and Anna come to Sunday lunch? We won't be having roast."

Rebekah laughed. "Okay, Mom. I'll let you know."

Rebekah got up to leave and Helen grabbed a container off the counter.

"These are extra cookies Anna and I made yesterday. I brought them by this morning before school, but..."

Rebekah closed her eyes and dropped her head. She could feel her cheeks pinken. "We were—"

"I know," Helen said with a sweet smile.

"Thanks, Mom. Bye, Dad."

Helen hugged Rebekah then put her hands on her cheeks. "Everything will be all right."

Rebekah tilted her head. "That's what Megan said."

28

Rebekah walked into Megan's kitchen from the garage and saw Anna and Megan sitting on the couch watching TV. "There are my girls."

She walked over and kissed the top of Anna's head and sat down next to Megan. Rebekah put her arm around Megan and kissed her on the lips.

Anna glanced at them and giggled.

"Mommy, Megan has never watched *Barbie* before!" Anna exclaimed. "I'm showing it to her."

Rebekah ran her hand through Megan's hair and gazed at her face and into her eyes. "Everything is all right," she said quietly, then kissed her cheek.

"I have some things to tell you," Megan started.

"It's okay," Rebekah whispered. She gently pushed Megan's head onto her shoulder. Then she rested her head on Megan's and closed her eyes. The floral scent of Megan's shampoo tickled Rebekah's nose and brought with it a comforting feeling of being exactly where she should be.

"Mommy, do I have to tell Grandma and Grandpa when

I get a girlfriend or a boyfriend?" Anna asked, her eyes never leaving the TV.

"Uhh." Rebekah arched an eyebrow at Megan.

Megan shrugged. "I explained that you wanted to tell Grandma and Grandpa that we're girlfriends."

"Anna," Rebekah said. "Can you please pause the show?"

Anna reached for the remote and punched the button. Then she looked at Rebekah.

"It doesn't matter to me or Megan if you have a girlfriend or a boyfriend someday."

"Or neither," Megan added.

"I wanted to tell Grandma and Grandpa about Megan and me because I'm happy. Are you happy?" Rebekah asked.

"Yes. Grandma and Grandpa are happy too, aren't they?" she asked.

Before Rebekah could answer Anna added, "Megan and I made you something!"

"You did?" Rebekah looked at Megan.

"You can get it." Megan smiled at Anna. "It's on the kitchen table."

Anna hopped up and grabbed a small canvas off the table. She brought it over and held it in front of Rebekah.

"These are mine and Megan's happy colors today. We wanted to put them together for you, so we did blue as the sky and then painted yellow across the bottom like a sunset," Anna explained. "Then we added some darker blues and yellows to make the lighter colors stand out."

"Honey, it's beautiful!" Rebekah said with awe in her voice. Amazed, she looked at Megan.

"We did it together." Megan smiled. "Anna has become quite the artist. What she just explained to you were her words. She understands colors and shades. We would like to invite you to come watch us paint some evening."

"I'd love that." Rebekah put her arms around Anna and pulled her into her lap. "How did you do this? It's incredible."

"Anna, can you tell your mommy what you told me about the colors and painting?"

"Well, Megan thought it would be nice to make you something. I wanted to paint, so we decided to do it together. I always do blue paintings for you and wanted to add another color. Since you love Megan I thought her happy color and your happy color in the same painting would make you happy." She giggled.

"That's a lot of happiness, kiddo." Megan chuckled.

"Dark colors don't always mean you're sad and bright colors don't always mean you're happy. Just like me. I'm not always sad or happy; sometimes I'm lots of colors inside. But your painting is full of happiness, Mommy, because you're happy again since Megan is your girlfriend."

"You're happy again, too," Rebekah said, hugging her close.

"I get sad because I miss Daddy, but I can be happy again and painting helps me be happy."

"I miss Daddy, too, but this painting makes me happy. I want to hang it somewhere that I'll see it every day."

"You could hang it here," Megan suggested, her voice laced with hope.

Rebekah cut her eyes to Megan and raised her eyebrows.

Anna turned to look at Rebekah. "I think Megan wants us to move here. Can we?"

"Uhh," Rebekah stammered.

"We have fun here, Mommy. Besides, Megan and Wanda are here."

"What did you tell your parents earlier?" Megan asked.

Rebekah smiled. "I told them that we're in love and want to create a life together with Anna."

"Then don't we need to live in the same house?" Anna asked as she raised one hand and shrugged.

"We don't have to live here. We can find a house together," Megan said.

"Have you two been conspiring?" Rebekah asked suspiciously. Then she chuckled. "I love it here!"

"Me too!" Anna said excitedly.

Megan tilted her head. "Welcome home?" she asked with a grin.

Rebekah and Anna looked at one another and they both grinned and nodded. With Anna still in her lap, Rebekah put an arm around Megan and hugged them both.

"Why don't you finish watching *Barbie* while Megan and I fix dinner," Rebekah said to Anna.

"I'll show you more *Barbie* later, Megan," Anna told her as she reached for the remote.

Anna sat on the couch with Wanda snuggled next to her and watched TV. "We're going to be living here. We'll get to play all the time," she said to the little dog.

In the kitchen, Megan poured them both a glass of wine. "Let's order pizza."

Rebekah raised her eyebrows. "To celebrate?"

"Oh yeah." Megan leaned over and kissed Rebekah. "What happened at your parents'?"

Before answering, Rebekah took a sip of her wine and studied Megan over the rim. "When I told them it was as if my mom knew. She grabbed my hand and squeezed it. Why did she come see you today?"

Megan smiled. "She figured it out from the way we look at each other and the way you talk about me."

"Imagine that." Rebekah smiled.

"Your mom is incredible. During our conversation it was clear to me that *she* is your dad's superpower."

Rebekah chuckled. "She always has been."

"How did your dad react?"

"He was surprised, but he loves me and I made it clear that you are my happiness." Rebekah leaned in and kissed Megan softly.

"What about the church?"

"He didn't want to talk about the church. Mom asked to let them process it all." Rebekah took another sip of her wine. "Oh, and she invited us to lunch on Sunday. Don't worry, Dad will be more welcoming this time."

Megan chuckled. "I couldn't believe it when your mom showed up at the center today."

"Thanks for warning me, although it was a bit cryptic."

"Sorry. I couldn't let you walk into your parents' house not knowing what was happening."

Rebekah set her glass down and put her arms around Megan's neck. Then she brought their lips together in a firm kiss that settled her soul. *These are the lips I'll be kissing for all time,* she thought.

"What's for dinner?" Anna asked as she walked into the kitchen.

Megan pulled away and looked down at her. "Pizza is on the way."

"*Barbie* and pizza. I love it here." Anna looked at them both and giggled. "Come on Wanda, let's go outside and play so they can keep kissing."

Anna opened the back door with Wanda on her heels.

"That kid." Rebekah shook her head.

Megan put her arms back around Rebekah and pulled her close. "She's a great kid and I'm going to do what she said and keep kissing you."

Megan brought their lips together and Rebekah sank into the kiss. She counted her blessings and said a silent thank you.

* * *

Later that night, Rebekah and Megan tucked Anna into bed. As they walked back to the living room Rebekah asked Megan, "You never did tell me what you think God's plan is for you."

"If you'll remember, we were a little busy." Megan took Rebekah's hand and pulled her over to the couch.

"Oh, I remember. But I still want to know; it's important to me. Just because we've had similar struggles doesn't mean we necessarily believe the same thing."

Megan smiled. "The church matters more to you than it does to me. You know that. But I know who I believe." She gazed into Rebekah's eyes. "For me it isn't necessarily God's plan. When things get hard or something happens that I don't understand, what I do is take a breath. I pray and tell God that I know He's there and I know He can see the big picture. Someday, maybe not until I get to heaven, I'll see the parts that I couldn't see then."

"What do you think the big picture is now?"

Megan grinned. "I have no doubt that we've been given a second chance, and since seeing you again in the counseling center that day..."

"Don't you dare say this is fast. It took twelve years! I wanted you and a family. I've got that now. What did you want, Meg?"

"I wanted you," she answered softly. Megan scooted closer to Rebekah and put her arms around her. "I wanted this sweet little southern girl that stole my heart."

Rebekah brought her face closer to Megan's. "But now I come with a kid."

"She's part of you. She's a gift." Megan stared at Rebekah's lips. Her heart pounded in her chest and her breath quickened.

"What if we had another?" Rebekah asked with a twinkle in her eye.

"The gifts just keep coming." Megan couldn't resist her any longer. She claimed Rebekah's lips and slid her tongue inside. It was met with a more than eager match and their tongues danced to the rhythm of their thumping hearts.

Rebekah's hands framed Megan's face as they pulled apart to take a breath. "Are you going to take me right here on this couch?"

A wicked grin grew on Megan's face. She stood and snatched Rebekah up into her arms. "You aren't always in charge." She gave her another soulful kiss and hurried them to the bedroom.

She quietly closed the door and turned to find Rebekah already taking her clothes off. "Hurry up."

"There you go again. Always in control," Megan said as she took her clothes off.

"When I left my parents' house today, I finally felt like I could be myself; the person I am inside. No more hiding."

"You never had to hide with me," Megan said, jumping onto the bed.

"I couldn't. You saw the real me the first time we met." Rebekah began to crawl up the bed.

"I love what I see. Just like I did then. Come here." Megan leaned against the pillows and held her arms out for Rebekah. She placed her hands on either side of Rebekah's face and pulled her into a fiery kiss. This kiss was full of passion, desire, and lust.

"Straddle me," Megan panted.

Rebekah did as Megan asked and leaned down to kiss her.

Megan's heart was racing and she knew Rebekah's was too. This was a kind of new beginning for them. Rebekah was always honest and her whole self in their bedroom but she could be that in public now.

Megan palmed both of Rebekah's breasts. "You always love to be on top," Megan murmured between kisses.

"I love *you*," Rebekah panted as she looked down at Megan. "I really need you right now."

"You have me." Megan ran one hand down over Rebekah's stomach and cupped her sex. She slid her finger through Rebekah's wetness and then inside her.

Rebekah groaned. "Oh fuck, baby. Yes!" Rebekah reached for the wall over the bed and flattened her palms against it.

Megan looked up into the most beatific face. *God, she loved this woman.* Megan could see what her touch did to Rebekah and all she wanted to do was bring her the ultimate pleasure. She added another finger and with her other hand she pinched Rebekah's nipple.

Rebekah looked down at her and they locked eyes.

"Don't scream, love," Megan said softly.

Rebekah nodded her understanding.

"Let's go."

Rebekah began to move her hips and threw her head back. Megan kept her hand steady and cupped Rebekah's butt with the other. This erotic tango was more than sex. It was trust mixed with love.

"I've got you, baby."

"Oh God, Meg," she said breathlessly.

"Show me your love," Megan whispered loudly.

"Ohhhhh," Rebekah groaned as she stilled and pushed down on Megan's hand.

Megan could see the orgasm ripple through her and felt it in her fingers.

They stayed like this, fixed in this moment, and then Rebekah collapsed on top of Megan. They were both breathing hard and Megan held Rebekah to her chest. "I love you so much," she whispered.

"Mmm, I love you, too," Rebekah groaned. Her chest was still heaving for air.

After a moment she raised up enough to see into Megan's eyes. "You can be in charge anytime you want."

Megan chuckled and kissed her softly. "Oh darling, you're always in charge and that's just the way I like it."

29

Rebekah and Anna stayed at Megan's every night that week. They fell into an easy routine and Rebekah brought more of their things over every day.

"I've packed you a bag to take to Grandma's tonight," Rebekah told Anna when she picked her up from school.

"Okay. I wanted to take one of my books with me. It's at Megan's," Anna replied.

"You know what? Let's go to our house tomorrow and pack up the things you want to move to Megan's. Then we'll have your stuff in one place."

"Okay. What are you and Megan going to do tonight without me? You could come watch the movie with me and Grandpa. Wanda's going to be sad."

Rebekah held back a chuckle. "I'll make sure Wanda isn't too sad. Megan and I are going to Crystal's house for dinner."

"I like living at Megan's. She does funny voices when we read at bedtime."

Rebekah smiled. "I like living at Megan's, too." *I especially like waking up in her arms,* she thought.

"You know, Megan wants it to be our house too."

"We are a family."

Rebekah smiled. "We are."

"Then, I like living at our new house with our new family."

Rebekah looked in the rearview mirror and met Anna's eyes. "I love our new family."

Anna grinned. "Me too."

Rebekah pulled into her parents' driveway and went inside with Anna.

"Hi Mom" she said, bending down to pet Neal.

"Hi honey. Anna, I have a snack waiting for you on the table," Helen said.

"Thanks Grandma."

"Wait, give me a hug. I'll pick you up tomorrow, sweetie." Rebekah opened her arms.

Anna walked into them and Rebekah held her for a moment. "I love you," she said softly.

"Love you," Anna said and walked over to the kitchen table.

"I'll walk out with you," Helen said as she followed Rebekah out the back door.

"How's Dad doing?" Rebekah asked.

"He has a lot on his mind, as you can imagine," Helen replied.

"I'm sure he does. I've been thinking about the church, Mom. I don't want to put him in a difficult position."

"I know you don't. We can talk about it Sunday. You're still coming to lunch, right?"

"Yes ma'am. We'll be here."

Helen reached for Rebekah and hugged her. "I'm sorry you didn't feel like you could come to me back then."

"Oh, Mom. I couldn't talk about it to anyone but Megan. I simply didn't have the courage. Thank God, I do now."

Helen nodded and smiled. "See you tomorrow."

* * *

Megan pulled into Crystal and Kim's driveway and smiled over at Rebekah.

"Are you sure we didn't need to bring anything else?"

"This is one of their favorite bottles of wine. Are you nervous?"

"Why do you ask? Do I look nervous?"

Megan smiled. "No, I can tell though. But you don't need to be nervous. You already know Crystal and you'll love Kim."

"It's not that, babe. This is kind of a big deal for me. I had a few gay friends in college, but not like this. We're two couples, that happen to be gay, having dinner together."

"And they are our friends. They know you've had my heart all these years. Crystal tried to help me get over you, and now she understands why I couldn't." Megan chuckled. "Kim can't wait to meet you. They want to be your friends."

Rebekah softened and let out a breath. Megan leaned over and kissed her softly.

"Thanks," Rebekah said as they pulled away. Megan could calm her or light her on fire with a simple kiss.

"Don't ever thank me for kissing you. It is entirely my pleasure." Megan grinned.

"Come on. Let's go meet my new friends."

Once inside and after introductions were made Rebekah

began to relax. They went outside on the back patio and shared the bottle of wine.

"I have great respect for your mother, coming to see Megan the way she did," Crystal said as she lit the grill.

"My mom is a polite, easy-going preacher's wife, but she has quite a bold streak," Rebekah said.

"Does that mean you were the nice little preacher's daughter? Or were you a wild one?" Kim asked in a playful voice.

"Oh, you can see I was the quiet one with the big secret." Rebekah reached over and took Megan's hand.

"I can't imagine how hard that was for you." Crystal shook her head. "My parents were supportive, but I was still afraid to come out to them."

"Add in the weight of the church on your shoulders and it had to be such a burden," Kim added.

"It was heavy, but then I met Megan."

Megan smiled at Rebekah.

"My partner to the rescue," Crystal cheered as she gave Megan a high five.

"It wasn't like that," Megan said.

"God sent you when I needed you the most." Rebekah squeezed Megan's hand.

"I don't know about that either. We're together again and that's all that matters."

"Are you going to continue to go to your dad's church?" Kim asked.

Rebekah glanced at Megan. "I'm not sure. Honestly, I love my church, but it's hard for me to sit there knowing I'm not treated the same as other parishioners. Megan is so good to go with me, but I know she feels it, too."

Megan sighed. "I know God loves me, but I don't get how

the church *says* they love me, but then put conditions on my membership."

"Have you thought about going to another church?" Kim asked.

Rebekah and Megan looked at each other and shrugged.

"I've been working on a project at a non-denominational church that's been here for around ten years," Kim said.

"Oh, that's right. You have your own construction company," Rebekah said.

Kim laughed. "I know. I'm such a lesbian conundrum. I have this butch construction company and I'm as femme as they come."

"I find that extremely hot," Crystal said, leaning over and kissing her.

"How long have you been married?" Rebekah asked as she smiled at them.

"Almost ten years," Kim said. "Anyway, you and Megan might like this church."

"How so?" Megan asked.

"They welcome everyone, have an active youth group, and the pastor is a woman. I think she may have come from the Methodist church."

"Hmm. I know several pastors left a few years ago after the big vote on gay marriage in the Methodist church," Rebekah commented.

"What kind of project are you doing there?" Megan asked.

"They wanted to renovate their youth room, but were short on funds. I agreed to help with the costs if the youth would help with the labor. We're teaching them basic construction skills and how to work with others. It's been fun."

"The kids keep asking Kim to come to Sunday service.

We thought about going this Sunday. Would you both like to come with us?"

Megan raised her eyebrows at Rebekah. "I'll do whatever you want."

Rebekah tilted her head. "See what I mean? She's so supportive."

"Think about it. We can go together. Maybe lightning won't strike if Rebekah is with us," Crystal teased.

"I want to hear all about Anna and this newly discovered artistic talent," Kim said, smiling at Rebekah.

The rest of the evening was spent in lively conversation and Megan was right. Rebekah loved Kim and felt like she'd made a new friend.

On the way home Rebekah turned to Megan. "I had such a good time." She grabbed Megan's hand. "We have friends!"

Megan laughed. "You say that like it's a surprise."

"Think about it. We didn't have friends before."

"That's because we didn't go anywhere."

"I know, I was afraid."

"It wasn't that. We couldn't get enough of each other." Megan glanced at Rebekah with a salacious grin.

Rebekah chuckled. "Are you saying it isn't that way now?"

"I'm saying when I'm not with you, I'm thinking of you. When I am with you…" Megan sighed. "This week was just about perfect. Starting the day with you and Anna and ending it the same way, well—"

"I get it, babe. I feel the same. By the way, I told Anna we would go get her stuff from the house tomorrow. Is that all right?"

"Yes! What about your stuff? What do you want to do? I was serious when I said we could get another house."

"I know you were. Let's get Anna's stuff tomorrow and I'll get more of my clothes."

"How about we look at your things and blend our two houses? I want this to be *our* home. It can't be my stuff and your clothes. We'll store the things we don't need right now."

"It'll be like redoing the house, only we already have the stuff."

"Exactly. We could paint, too."

"Hmm, now that's an idea. It feels more like home already."

"We'll paint Anna's room whatever color she wants," Megan said excitedly.

"Careful. You never know what our budding artist will choose."

Megan chuckled. "That's true."

"Hey, what do you think about going to church with Crystal and Kim on Sunday? And don't say you'll do whatever I want."

"I think we should try it. I know how important church is to you and if I'm being honest, I'd like for us to find a church we can go to as a family."

"Really?"

"Yeah, it surprised me when I realized it. All this time I said I didn't go because I didn't like to attend alone, but last Sunday when I was sitting in church with you and Anna was between us, it did something to my heart." Megan glanced over at Rebekah. "This is going to sound weird, but it felt like God was saying 'I'm glad you're here, Megan.' Is that crazy?"

"Not at all," Rebekah said, squeezing her hand. "I feel God nearby sometimes. Or at least that's what I think it is. You know, it doesn't matter because that's what I feel."

Megan nodded. "I'm so glad you get me."

Rebekah laughed. "Of course I get you, You're the one God made for me, Megan!"

Megan laughed along with her. "Let's go to church with them Sunday."

"Let's do it."

30

Kim and Crystal were waiting for Megan, Rebekah, and Anna outside the church.

"What a sweet family," Crystal said, tickling Anna when they walked up. "Anna, this is my wife, Kim."

"Hi Anna. I've heard wonderful things about you," Kim said.

"You have?" Anna looked at her skeptically.

"I heard that you take really good care of Wanda and that you create beautiful paintings. I'd love to see them sometime."

"They're at Megan's—" Anna stopped and corrected herself. "They're at *our* house. You can come over and see them."

"I'd love that."

"We get to redo our house," Anna added excitedly.

"Oh?" Crystal said, looking from Anna to Megan and Rebekah.

"Yep. We're going to put all our favorite things in the same house so it will be our home."

"I can't wait to see it!" Crystal said. "I am invited, aren't I?"

Anna giggled. "Yes, you and Kim are both invited."

"Thanks." Kim grinned at her. "We'd better go in."

They went inside and were welcomed at the entrance to the sanctuary by several friendly faces. After they found a seat, several kids came by and said hello to Kim.

The service started with lively music and they all joined in. After several songs they took their seats and Anna said quietly, "This is like our church in Miami."

"It is," Rebekah whispered. She leaned over to Megan. "We went to a more progressive church and these songs are familiar."

"I love these songs," Megan whispered back. "I have two of them on a playlist on my phone."

Rebekah's eyes widened. "That's what I love about us. We know each other, but there are always new things to learn."

"Shh!" Anna sent an irritated look at both of them.

Megan winked at Rebekah as they both tried not to laugh.

During the service, the children were called down to the front for the children's chat. Anna got up slowly.

"Do you want me to go with you?" Megan asked.

Anna smiled at her and nodded slightly. Megan offered her hand and Anna took it. They walked down to the front and the kids sat cross-legged at the feet of the leader while Megan sat in the front row a few feet away.

When they were finished they walked back to their pew hand in hand. Megan couldn't believe how full her heart felt. If she thought God had welcomed her last week in church, this week He'd stepped it up and had her heart overflowing.

Megan felt Rebekah's hand on her shoulder and glanced over at her. The smile on Rebekah's face said it all: She felt it too.

The pastor preached on patience and it felt like she was talking to Megan and Rebekah. A lot had happened since they'd been reunited and now they were hoping for more. They were moving in together, they wanted Rebekah's parents to accept their relationship and they wanted to find a church home.

After the service, the pastor was shaking hands at the back of the church.

"Kim, I saw several faces light up when you and your friends walked in."

Kim chuckled. "Hi Dawn. This is my wife, Crystal." Kim waited for them to shake hands then said, "And these are our good friends Megan, Rebekah, and Anna."

"I'm Dawn Peterson. It's nice to meet you. Welcome." She held out her hands.

"My grandpa is a preacher like you," Anna said.

"He is?"

"My dad is Daniel Mathews," Rebekah explained.

"Oh, I know Daniel. We've worked together on the community ministerial alliance. He was quite a help to me when we founded the church."

"You have such a welcoming vibe here," Rebekah said.

"I love the music," Megan added.

Dawn smiled. "It's different from your dad's church. But the average age of the congregation is younger here. How is Daniel? There are changes coming for him."

"What do you mean? Are you referring to the vote on gay marriage? I thought that was over."

"They are having another vote later in the year. It hasn't garnered much attention yet, but I expect it will."

"Hmm, he hasn't mentioned that," Rebekah said as she glanced over at Megan.

"You are all welcome here and I hope you'll come back." Dawn smiled warmly at the group.

On their way out Kim said, "Thanks for coming with us."

"Thanks for inviting us," Megan replied. "I really enjoyed the service."

"I did too," Rebekah added.

"Don't forget I want to see those paintings, Anna," Kim said.

Anna giggled. "Okay."

"See you tomorrow," Crystal said to Megan as the two groups parted ways in the parking lot.

They went to their cars and Megan drove them to Rebekah's parents' house for lunch.

"Did you like that church, honey?" Rebekah asked, turning around to look at Anna in the back seat.

"Uh-huh. I knew some of those songs from our church in Miami."

"I knew some of those songs, too," Megan said, looking at her in the rearview mirror. "Listen." Megan punched a few buttons on her dashboard and a song began to play through the car speakers.

"That's 'Bless My Soul'!" Anna yelled. Then she started singing.

"It is!" Megan smiled at Rebekah and they all sang along.

"That was fun!" Anna exclaimed as they pulled into Rebekah's parents' driveway a few minutes later.

Megan and Rebekah exchanged a look.

"Maybe we should go to church there again." Rebekah said.

Anna jumped out of the car and ran ahead.

Rebekah came around the front of the car and grabbed

Megan's hand and bumped their shoulders together. "I liked that church."

"I did, too." Megan glanced at Rebekah.

She stopped before they walked in the back door. "This lunch will be much better than last week."

"Last week wasn't so bad. Look where we are now." Megan grinned.

"I love you," Rebekah whispered.

"I know." Megan winked and opened the back door.

* * *

"I hope you like lasagne," Helen said as she placed the pan on the table.

"I love it, but Helen, I loved your roast last Sunday," Megan said.

Rebekah brought the bread in from the kitchen and sat next to Megan.

"Someone keeps complaining about roast so I thought we'd have something else this Sunday," Helen said as she sat on one end of the table.

"Mom, I wasn't complaining. I was just pointing out what seems to be a Sunday tradition."

"Maybe we should let Rebekah cook Sunday lunch next week." Daniel chuckled as he sat on the other end of the table.

Rebekah sat up and looked at Megan. "I think that's a great idea. You can come to our house."

"I was just teasing," Daniel said.

"I know, but I'd like that. We are combining houses," Rebekah said, her voice tentative. "We're going to live at Megan's but blend our things so it will be our home."

"That sounds exciting," Helen said.

"Let's say thanks and then you can tell us all about it," Daniel said, bowing his head.

Rebekah wasn't sure she'd heard her parents correctly. She'd meant to ease into the conversation of them moving in together, but it had just come out.

Daniel said a quick prayer and then they began to fill their plates.

"Megan, I'm glad you came back for lunch today," Daniel began. "I apologize if I made you feel unwelcome last week."

"Not at all, Daniel. I know you're protective of your girls. I am, too." Megan looked at him and smiled.

He nodded and returned her smile. "Now what's this about you moving again?"

"I get to paint my room!" Anna exclaimed.

"It's silly to keep two houses when we're starting a life together," Rebekah explained.

"So we're moving all our favorite things into our house," Megan added.

"We'll store what won't fit and figure it out as we go." Rebekah smiled lovingly at Megan.

"I'll be glad to help. Let me know when you're ready to move," Daniel offered.

"Thanks, Dad. I may take you up on that."

"Oh, before I forget. Anna's handbell leader asked me to pass along that she has practice this week after Bible Zone," Helen said.

"Thank you. I wondered," said Rebekah.

"Tell us about the church you went to today," Daniel said.

"We met Dawn Peterson. She had good things to say about you, Dad," Rebekah said.

Daniel smiled. "I've known Dawn for a long time. She

was very active in our church."

"She said you were very helpful to her."

"Dawn is a good pastor. Did you like the service?"

"We did," Rebekah said quietly.

"I imagine you felt very welcome and comfortable," Helen said.

"They sang songs I knew," Anna said.

"They did! I imagine that was fun," Daniel said as he smiled at his granddaughter.

"Dad, Dawn mentioned that there is going to be another vote later this year on gay marriage and gay clergy," Rebekah said.

Daniel nodded. "It's more like a vote on separation. It's inevitable that the church is going to split. The church has already allowed some congregations to leave with their property and assets."

"Does each church vote?" Megan asked.

Daniel nodded again. "They will have guidelines on how to exit. The conservatives have already formed another denomination called the Global Methodist Church."

"Will the churches that don't leave still be the United Methodist Church?" Rebekah asked.

"I think so. It's a sad day, but it's been brewing for many years," Daniel explained.

"Which way will our church vote?" Rebekah asked.

"I don't know. Two years ago our church was leaning toward the conservative side, but you never know."

"What does that mean for you, Dad?"

Daniel sighed. "I'm not sure about the pastors or about the church. Either way, our church will not be the same in a few months."

A heaviness fell over the room.

"Megan, I would still like that tour of the counseling center," Daniel said, changing the subject.

"Come down any time. I'd love to show you around," Megan said with a kind smile.

"You haven't met Wanda yet either, Grandpa," Anna said.

"I have a lot to look forward to then, don't I?" He grinned at Anna.

Rebekah could tell the looming church vote was weighing on her dad. Her relationship with Megan was probably adding to his stress level. Maybe she needed to sit down and find out how he was doing. As much as she wanted him to accept her relationship with Megan she hadn't really thought about all the other things he had to deal with as the pastor of the church. She made a mental note to visit with him while Anna had handbell practice Wednesday.

31

"Is that okay with you?" Megan asked. When Rebekah didn't respond she looked over at her. They had been watching Anna and Wanda play in the backyard.

Megan was excited to get this move underway. She planned to start packing up the things from her house to move to storage to make room for Rebekah and Anna's things this week. Then next weekend they could have a moving party. She thought Crystal and Kim would help along with Rebekah's parents.

As she stared at Rebekah she knew something had been on her mind all afternoon. They'd had a great time at lunch with her parents. Daniel was a different person. She really enjoyed their conversations and felt like he and Helen were welcoming her into the family. But Rebekah was definitely contemplating something.

"Baby," Megan said softly as she intertwined their fingers.

"What?" Rebekah looked at her, surprised. Then she sighed. "I'm sorry, babe."

"Do you want to tell me what's going on or do you want me to guess?"

Rebekah smiled, then she narrowed her eyes. "Knowing you, you'd probably guess."

Megan kissed the back of Rebekah's hand. "I can't decide if you're scheming or just wondering about something. I know it has nothing to do with the move because I've been rattling on about it for the last fifteen minutes and you haven't heard a word I've said."

"I'm sorry." Rebekah sighed. "I know you're excited about the move and so am I."

"Are you sure?" Megan asked seriously.

"Yes! I want us to make this our home more than anything, babe." Rebekah got up and sat in Megan's lap. With one hand caressing Megan's cheek she said, "This is a dream coming true for me. I've wanted us to spend our lives together as a family. I can't tell you how much this means to me."

Megan smiled. "Okay. Then will you please tell me what's bothering you?"

Rebekah kissed Megan softly then got up and sat back down in her chair. "I've been thinking about the church and my dad."

"Oh. I really had a good time with your folks today, but I am surprised about this vote coming up."

"I am too. I can't imagine how that must weigh on him. I wonder if our situation just adds to it."

"Our situation? Do you mean our *relationship*? Because we are not a situation. We are a happy bundle of love that is new and fresh as well as old and familiar."

Rebekah's face lit up with delight. "You are amazing, Megan Neal! My apologies, we are not a situation."

"At first we may have added stress to your dad, but he

seemed really happy we were all together today. I think you, my love, are worried about the church."

"You're right, I am. However, I'm also happy because I loved Dawn's church. I could see us happy there, can you?"

Megan nodded. "Anna sure liked it."

"You felt comfortable, too. I could tell. Your face was bright enough to light the entire sanctuary when you came back from the Children's Chat with Anna." Rebekah grinned.

"Oh Bekah, I thought my heart was going to explode."

"Kids are wonderful, but it's a whole different ball game when they're yours, isn't it?" Rebekah chuckled.

Megan looked at Rebekah wide-eyed. "You could've warned me!"

"Oh darling, I couldn't have warned you that she was going to steal your heart. She already had it!"

"Who stole your heart?" Anna said, running up with Wanda on her heels.

"You did!" Megan pulled Anna into her lap and giggles filled the air.

* * *

The next day Megan walked back into the counseling center after lunch to find Daniel talking to Crystal.

"Is this the famous Wanda?" he asked when Megan walked towards them.

"Here she is," Megan said.

Wanda wiggled her tail and licked Daniel's fingers as he bent down to pet her. "Show me your superpowers, you little darling," Daniel said as he stroked Wanda's head.

"Have you come for a tour?" Megan asked.

"I have," he said as he stood up with Wanda in his arms.

She licked his chin and he laughed. "Anna was right. This is one special little puppy."

"She loves Anna, but just between you and me, Rebekah is her favorite. She sleeps with Anna every night, but anytime Rebekah sits on the couch Wanda is snuggled next to her if she isn't in her lap."

"I'm not surprised. Neal always goes to her when she comes into the house. Cats usually can't be bothered," he said.

"Let me show you around. I even have a couple of Anna's paintings in my office."

Daniel followed Megan around the space and she explained some of the things they did in each area. They ended up in Megan's office where she showed Daniel two of Anna's paintings.

"You know, I don't know anything about art and she is my granddaughter, but they are beautiful and seem advanced for an eight-year-old."

"Oh they are. It has been amazing to watch her blossom to the point of not just existing, but thriving. Over a few weeks it's like she's figured it out. Whatever she was feeling, whether it was sadness or despair or simply longing, she has learned how to cope on her own terms."

"That seems like so much for an eight-year-old."

"Losing your dad is hard at any age. I'm most proud because Anna is no longer afraid to talk about it or ask questions. She'll tell Rebekah or me when she misses Ben and then we can talk about it. Or sometimes we do things that they did which turns a sad memory into a happy one."

"I'm not sure she could have done all that without you, Megan," Daniel said earnestly.

Megan smiled. "Thank you, but Anna did all the hard work. I'm so proud of her and I love her so much."

Daniel put his hand on Megan's shoulder and nodded. "I know you do. We could see that and we could see that she loves you, too."

Megan nodded and they both sat down on the couch. "Rebekah and I were surprised to hear about the split the church is facing. Has it intentionally been kept quiet?"

"Well, it's not good news that you want to report about your church, that's for sure," Daniel said. "But it was imminent with how the vote went in 2019. Were you aware of what was happening then?"

"Oh yeah. I mean, it was important to me. Of course, I was hoping they would approve gay marriage. I don't know what the problem with gay clergy is. There are already so many gay pastors in the church that the whole issue seemed backwards to me."

"Is that why you've never been married?" Daniel asked.

Megan smiled. "I haven't been married because..." She paused, taking a deep breath. "I've always been in love with Rebekah and hoped somehow, someway we'd find our way back to one another."

"Does it matter that you can't get married in the Methodist church since that's the church you grew up in?"

"Uh, to be honest, it does. Rebekah and I haven't even talked about getting married and one reason is because I know she'd love nothing more than to get married in your church."

"It hurts me because I know it hurts her. But"—he slapped his hands on his knees and stood up—"maybe someday that will change." He bent down to pet Wanda then turned to Megan. "I've taken up enough of your time. Thank you for the tour. I really enjoyed our visit."

"I'm so glad you came by," Megan said sincerely.

"Let me know when you're moving. I was serious about helping," Daniel said as they walked to the front door.

"I will," Megan assured him.

She watched him leave and felt like she'd made a friend. When she was at lunch on Sunday they'd made her feel like part of the family, but she knew it was for Rebekah as well as for her. This felt different. Daniel wasn't just Rebekah's dad today, he felt more like a new friend that was getting to know her. She smiled as she walked back to her office. Whatever it was, it sure felt good.

* * *

When Megan got home from work Rebekah and Anna were already there. As soon as she walked in from the garage Anna grabbed Wanda and headed for the back door.

"Hey, don't I even get a hello?" Megan asked Anna.

Anna giggled. She ran back to Megan and gave her a quick hug. "Hello and goodbye." Then she was gone.

Megan laughed. "Hi babe."

"Hello yourself." Rebekah put her arms around Megan and pressed their lips together. "Mmm, I think that's what I've needed all afternoon." She tilted her head. "Let me do that again." This time Megan felt her knees weaken when Rebekah deepened the kiss.

"Now that's a hello," Megan said, holding on to Rebekah.

"How was your day?"

"Your dad came to see me," Megan said as Rebekah walked over to the table. She had papers spread out, along with her computer.

"He did?"

"Yeah. I gave him a tour. He met Wanda and we had a really nice visit."

"My dad's a great guy. I'm glad you're getting to see that now."

"He was fine before. I don't know. Today felt different. We talked about the schism."

"Excuse me?" Rebekah said, looking up from her papers.

"That's the official name they're calling the split. It makes the separation sound like an exorcism or something. At least it does to me. How often do you hear that word used? I mean really."

Rebekah chuckled. "I've never really thought about it."

"I'd wager not many people have. Anyway, we had a nice visit."

"I've been thinking about the schism as well," Rebekah said.

"Can we call it something else?"

"I've been thinking about the split."

"That's better."

"I wonder what will happen to all the pastors and the other people."

"What do you mean?" Megan said.

"Well, take Dad's church for example. If it splits, does the majority get the building and stay there? What happens to the other people? Do they form a new church or go to another one?"

"Hmm, those are all good questions. Surely they have instructed the pastors or will."

"You'd think. But right now I have more pressing issues, like these papers to grade."

"Then I will go change and play with the girls," Megan said, leaving Rebekah to her work.

Later that evening, after Anna had gone to bed, Megan sat on the couch with Rebekah's head in her lap. She stroked her silky auburn locks while Rebekah watched TV.

"Your dad asked me why I wasn't married."

Rebekah looked up into her eyes. "What?"

Megan chuckled. "We were talking about the ban on gay marriage in the church and he asked me if that's why I wasn't married."

"What was your answer?" Rebekah asked.

"I told him the truth. I am not married because you are the one I've loved and I hoped we'd be together again someday."

Rebekah smiled.

"He asked if it bothered me that I couldn't get married in my church."

"I know it does," Rebekah said.

"I don't know why it has to be so hard." Megan sighed. "I think that's why I quit going. I mean, what does it matter who I love? I'm just a person who wants to sing a few songs, hear a message, and give God a little praise." Tears sprang to Megan's eyes.

Rebekah sat up and threw her arms around Megan and held her. "You're a good person, baby, you're *my* person."

"Thank you," Megan whispered. "Who needs church when I have you?"

"It matters, baby. We matter." Rebekah gently kissed below Megan's ear and pulled her closer.

"Let's go to bed. I think I've had all the church talk I can stand today," Megan said.

Rebekah got up and held out her hand to Megan. "I'm going to marry you someday, Megan Neal."

"What? Did you just propose to me?"

"No." Rebekah chuckled as she led them down the hall. They peeked into Anna's room and saw her sleeping contentedly with Wanda. "But I am going to marry you someday in our church, wherever that may be."

Megan hadn't allowed herself to think about marriage because she knew how Rebekah felt about it, but hearing her proclaim it into the world did something to her heart. She smiled. *Rebekah could be her wife someday. She was going to be Rebekah's wife!*

"I can feel those wheels turning in your head. Get used to it, babe," Rebekah said as she walked into the bathroom.

Megan fell onto the bed and looked past the ceiling to the heavens. "Thank God!"

32

"I feel like all we do is pack boxes," Megan said as she carefully put Rebekah's plates into a box.

"That's because all we've done this week *is* pack boxes," Rebekah replied. "Has the excitement of us moving in worn off?"

"No way! I love coming home to my girls every day."

"Your girls look forward to you coming home every day. Hmm," Rebekah said as she looked into another kitchen cabinet.

"What's wrong?"

"I'm not sure I want to put my grandmother's dishes in a box. I wish you could've met her. She was a wildfire."

"Oh yeah?"

"Yes, she always told me to follow my heart. I didn't always do that, but I am now and look what I've got." Rebekah walked over and kissed Megan softly.

"I like your grandmother," Megan mumbled.

Rebekah chuckled. "You like my kisses."

"No, I love your kisses," Megan said, grabbing Rebekah and kissing her again.

Rebekah giggled and walked back over to the dishes and set them on the counter.

"Why don't you pack those in one of the plastic bins? They'll be safe," Megan suggested.

"I used the last plastic bin last night."

"Then let's go buy another. We could use a break."

"I'll feel better when we can move some of this stuff," Rebekah said.

"Let's run to the store and get a few more bins. Then we can take a load to storage. This will be done by Sunday evening. Keep looking forward, babe," Megan encouraged her.

"I'm glad Mom offered to keep Anna all weekend. She's going to be so surprised when she sees her room at *our* house."

"When are we going to paint it?"

"That is my and Anna's first project this summer."

"It won't be long until school is out. What are you planning for the summer?"

"I have a few ideas I'm kicking around," Rebekah said stealthily.

Megan chuckled. "Well, don't forget to save a week in July to go see my family. They can't wait to meet you and Anna in person."

"Video chats are fine, but I can't wait to hear all the embarrassing stories about you growing up," Rebekah said.

"There are no embarrassing stories about me," Megan deadpanned.

"I'm sure your sister and mom will have a few for me."

"Anna is quite good at entertaining them with video calls."

Rebekah chuckled. "She's had a lot of practice. She's been video chatting with Ben's folks since she was tiny."

"When is she going to visit them?"

"In June. For an eight-year-old her summer is beginning to fill up."

Megan put the lid on the box she'd been packing and said, "Okay, let's go."

"I'm ready."

Megan drove them to the store and they found the bins.

"Let's go down the clearance aisle," Megan said. "There might be something that Anna needs."

"Anna doesn't *need* anything. You've got to stop buying her everything you see."

Rebekah put her arm through Megan's as she turned the basket into the clearance aisle. They were both laughing when they almost ran into Dawn Peterson.

"Well hello," Dawn said in a friendly voice. She looked at the bins in their basket. "Let me guess. Reorganizing or storing?"

"Hi Dawn," Rebekah said. "Moving. Anna and I are moving in with Megan and we have too much stuff."

"Oh, combining households. That should be fun."

Rebekah and Megan looked at one another. "Maybe ask us in a week or two." Megan chuckled.

"Got it." Dawn laughed.

"You probably won't see us Sunday. We're hoping to have all this done by Sunday night."

"We'll save a seat for you whenever you can come back."

"Thank you," Rebekah said.

"I'll let you get to it. Good luck," she said as she squeezed Rebekah's forearm and moved past them.

"I really like her," Rebekah said.

"I do, too."

* * *

"We got a lot done, honey," Rebekah said as they walked into the house.

"I know. If we keep this up we might finish tomorrow. That would give us all day Sunday to clean your house and maybe unpack a few boxes."

"Right now, I'm starving." Rebekah set the sack of food on the island. "Here's a burrito for you and a taco for me."

"Thanks, babe. Here's your rice." Megan slid the container over to Rebekah.

"Do you have the chips and salsa? They didn't forget the queso, did they?"

"No, here it is. Are you going to share those chips?" Megan asked.

Rebekah grinned. She dangled a chip in front of Megan. "Open up."

"Thank you," Megan mumbled as she crunched.

"Okay, we move the furniture from this house to storage first and then we can get Anna's room in one load," Rebekah said between bites.

"Yep. We'll get the rest of your furniture moved here and then what's left goes to storage."

"Sounds like a plan." Rebekah nodded.

They finished up their meal and threw the trash away.

"It seems weird without Wanda here," Rebekah commented.

"I couldn't believe your folks wanted to keep her too," Megan said.

"She is adorable and will give Anna someone to play with."

"Yeah, but are you sure your mom said she wasn't a bother when you called her earlier?"

"Babe, my parents are capable of taking care of their

granddaughter and her dog. After all, they've taken care of Neal for twelve years."

Megan laughed. "You're right. I'll have to do something special for them."

"No you don't. That's what family does and you're family."

"Family," Megan said softly. "Sometimes this is so surreal."

Rebekah walked over and put her arms around Megan. "I know what you mean. All day long I've said little prayers of thanks. I'm so happy and so thankful and right now I'm so…" Rebekah leaned in and nibbled on Megan's bottom lip. Then she pressed her lips to Megan's and slid her tongue inside Megan's mouth. She heard Megan moan and their tongues danced the dance of lovers.

"Mmm, I'm about to worship at the altar of Megan," Rebekah mumbled as she kissed up and down Megan's neck.

"That sounds lustful and sinful," Megan said softly as she leaned her head back to give Rebekah better access.

"Oh, it's full of lust, but there's nothing sinful about me loving you or how I show you my love." Rebekah took Megan's hand and led them down the hall. "You know, I've been waiting for the right time to try out that huge shower of yours again." She paused. "With you in it."

They quickly got out of their clothes and stepped into the shower. Megan had all the showerheads streaming warm water.

"Get your hair wet," Rebekah told Megan as she stepped into the shower. She grabbed the shampoo and began to wash Megan's hair. Her fingers gently massaged her scalp as the suds cascaded down her body.

"That feels so good," Megan hummed.

Rebekah guided her head back under the water to rinse the shampoo out.

"Your turn," Megan said as she switched places. She lathered the shampoo through Rebekah's hair. "I know there's something going on in this beautiful head." Megan gently wiped suds away before they could get into Rebekah's eyes. "I know you'll tell me eventually."

Rebekah leaned her head back into the water. "You have always let me work through things and never pushed."

"That's because I know you'll share when you need to."

"But you always tell me things up front," Rebekah said. She began to spread soapy suds over Megan's body.

"Because that's how I deal with things. We're two different people, babe."

"That's why we're so good together. You give me the space to be who I am and you're always honest with me."

Megan washed Rebekah's body with her hands and stopped to look into her eyes. "I trust you with all my heart. Together we're pretty damn amazing, babe."

"Turn around," Rebekah said with a firmness to her voice and a glint in her eye. Sometimes she felt like she might explode if she didn't touch Megan.

Megan did as she said and turned her back to Rebekah as she placed her hands on the wall.

"Are you sure you trust me?" Rebekah asked, her voice low in Megan's ears.

Megan turned her head. "Always," she said emphatically. Then she captured Rebekah's lips in a heated kiss.

Rebekah pushed up against Megan and could feel her hardened nipples press into her back. She took a deep breath and eased away just enough to run her hand from Megan's neck down the middle of her back and around to her stomach.

Her lips parted and she gently bit down between Megan's neck and shoulder as she ran her hand up and cupped Megan's breast.

Megan leaned her head back and groaned as Rebekah pinched her nipple and bit down harder.

"This is kind of erotic, isn't it, babe," Rebekah whispered over the sound of the water as it sluiced down their bodies.

Megan suddenly turned around, surprising Rebekah. "Let's do this together."

"Can your legs hold you?" Rebekah asked as she started to put her arm around Megan's waist.

"You'll hold me up," Megan said with a look that made Rebekah weak.

"Good God," Rebekah breathed. Her hand shot between Megan's legs and she cupped her sex. She could feel the heat and wetness radiating from Megan's core.

Megan put one hand on Rebekah's shoulder and the other traced down the front of her body until she mirrored Rebekah's hand.

"Can you feel how much I want you?" Rebekah said, her chest heaving.

Megan nodded.

Rebekah crashed her lips into Megan's and at the same time eased two fingers inside her. She could feel and taste Megan's moan in her mouth. Following Rebekah's lead Megan pushed two fingers inside Rebekah.

For a moment they held each other like that, letting their tongues explore, wrestle, and caress.

They found a slow intense rhythm as steam rose around them, water streamed over them and the air was filled with love.

Megan pulled her lips from Rebekah's and hissed. "I'm close, babe."

"Hang on, baby, hang on," Rebekah said, her eyes now locked on Megan's. "Watch what our love can do."

With one more push and curl of their fingers they both exploded into bliss. Rebekah swore she could see the colors bursting behind Megan's eyes at the same time they ignited in hers. Such an intense feeling built and then rushed through her body. She tingled from her head to her toes and out her fingers that were inside Megan. She was sure Megan could feel it too as it shot into her.

"I've got you," Rebekah said to Megan with a grin.

"I love you." Megan pushed the words out in a big breath.

"I know what we're doing every Friday while Anna's at my parents." Rebekah giggled.

Megan turned the water off as Rebekah got out of the shower and reached for a towel. She held it open for Megan and she walked into it.

"I love you so much," Rebekah said as she dried Megan's body. Then she put the towel over her head and began to dry Megan's hair. She wrapped the towel around her shoulders and then reached for a towel for herself.

"Let me," Megan said, securing the towel across her chest.

Rebekah handed Megan the towel and she gently wiped the water away. She looked into Rebekah's eyes and then kissed a couple of water droplets off her shoulder. She dried Rebekah's hair before wrapping the towel around her shoulders.

"I got a little carried away," Rebekah said as she reached out and gently touched the red spot she'd left on Megan's shoulder.

Megan smiled. "You've marked me as your own." She raised her eyebrows. "I'm yours, now and always."

Rebekah looked into her eyes and held Megan's chin in her hand. "That's right." Then she pressed her lips softly against Megan's. She pulled back and studied Megan's face. How she loved the little freckles here and there. The fine lines that crinkled around her eyes when she smiled. That sexy little dimple. Those lips that said the most wonderful things and gave her such pleasure.

"No one will ever doubt that I'm yours, Megan. I am a child of God, but my heart was made to abide with yours, always." A grin spread across Rebekah's face. "And so it shall be."

Megan nodded. "Amen."

33

"We did it." Megan plopped down on the couch and put her feet on the ottoman.

"I can't believe we got everything moved," Rebekah said as she sat down next to Megan.

"Don't look at the boxes stacked over there, but look around the rest of the room. I like your TV table better than mine and your chair looks great over there."

"My grandmother's table is perfect there," Rebekah said as she gazed around the room. "Wait, it's not yours, it's ours."

"*Our* TV table is much better than the one we had there. And I can imagine Anna reading books with me in that big chair."

"Much better. Our living room looks good, babe."

"That was so nice of your mom to feed us lunch," Megan said as she blew out a breath.

"It was her way of helping," Rebekah commented. "That was really sweet of you to suggest that Anna go with us on one load."

"I wanted her to feel like she was a part of this big move and I knew she thought she was missing out."

Rebekah chuckled. "It only took her one trip to figure out it was work and not fun."

"But she helped," Megan said. "You may not have noticed, but Anna likes to run things, much like someone else I know."

"I don't know what you're talking about," Rebekah said innocently then laid her head on Megan's shoulder.

Megan chuckled. "Uh huh."

"Thanks to Dad helping us move the big stuff, we now have all day tomorrow to unpack and get Anna's room just right," Rebekah said. "But I'm hungry."

"You know, since we got so much done today, we could go to church in the morning."

"I figured you'd want to sleep in."

"I know what will happen. We'll wake up and think about all the boxes waiting to be unpacked."

"Then we'll get up and start in Anna's room."

"Exactly. So, I can make us a sandwich, but I'd really like to shower first," Megan said.

"You know what I want? A beer," Rebekah said as she got up and walked to the kitchen. She opened the refrigerator and stared inside. "You've got to be kidding me!"

"What?" Megan got up and walked to the kitchen.

"There isn't one bottle or can of beer in here!" Rebekah turned to Megan, her eyes wide.

"Oh no! I remember Kim telling me she took the last one. I meant to stop on our way home."

"That's okay, babe. You go shower and I'll run down to the corner store and grab a six-pack."

"Are you sure? I can go," Megan said.

"I'm sure." Rebekah pecked Megan on the lips. "I'll be right back. Go shower." She walked out to the garage, hopped into her car, and backed out of the driveway.

A smile played on her face as she thought back to all they'd accomplished today. She was glad all the moving was done. Now they needed to unpack and rearrange a few things. Anna was going to love her room and it touched her heart how much Megan wanted to make it special for her. There was no doubt in her mind that Anna would one day feel like Megan's daughter as well as hers.

She ran into the store and looked at the beer choices.

"Decisions, decisions," a voice said from behind her.

Rebekah turned around and found Dawn Peterson smiling at her.

"Hey Dawn. How are you?"

"I'm probably better than you. How's the move going?"

"It's actually done. Well, the moving part is done. Now we get to unpack."

"Oh that's the fun part."

"Yeah, we're tired, smelly, and out of beer." Rebekah chuckled. "Do you live around here?"

"I do. I'm around the corner on the next street over."

"We probably ride bikes by your house," Rebekah said with a smile.

"You do. I've seen you from my backyard."

"We got more done today than we thought, so Megan and I will probably be at church in the morning."

"We're happy to have you." Dawn smiled.

"Do you think it would be possible to visit for a few minutes after church? I don't want to keep you, but I would like to talk to you about something."

"I'd be happy to visit with you and Megan."

"Okay. Thanks." Rebekah opened the door to the cooler and took out a six-pack of beer.

"Let me get that for you. Call it a housewarming gift."

"I can't let you do that," Rebekah objected.

"You're not. Welcome to the neighborhood."

Dawn took the beer from Rebekah and they walked to the front. After Dawn paid for it and her items, Rebekah opened the door for them both.

"Thank you again. We'll drink a toast to you," Rebekah said.

"See you tomorrow."

On the drive back home Rebekah thought about what Megan had said in the shower last night. Megan knew her like no other person. Sometimes she thought that Megan knew her better than she knew herself. It was time to share with Megan what had been weighing on her mind.

"I have a cold beer for my gorgeous lover," Rebekah said when she walked into the kitchen.

"Are you talking to me?" Megan said. She winked at Rebekah as she combed her fingers through her hair, still wet from the shower.

"Ha ha," Rebekah said. She put the beer on the island and draped her arms around Megan's neck. "You are gorgeous *and* you are my lover." She exaggerated the last word.

Megan cocked one eyebrow. "Then kiss me like you mean it."

Rebekah's face lit up in surprise. She slowly brought her lips to Megan's as she stared into her eyes. Their lips touched softly and Rebekah slid her tongue over Megan's bottom lip. When Megan leaned towards Rebekah she backed away slightly and raised her eyebrows. Then she pushed Megan against the island and pressed her lips to Megan's firmly. Her lips were soft and pillowy and hers for the taking. She devoured Megan's lips then slid her tongue inside her mouth and continued to caress and explore until Megan moaned.

Rebekah pulled back and asked, "Can you tell I mean it?"

Megan gave her a devilish grin. "Maybe."

Rebekah threw her head back and laughed. She opened a beer for each of them and put the others in the refrigerator. "We'll see about that later."

Megan chuckled.

Rebekah held up her beer for a toast and waited on Megan.

"What are we toasting?"

"This is for Dawn Peterson. I ran into her at the store and she bought us this six-pack."

They clinked bottles and each took a long drink.

"Ohhh, that's good," Megan said.

"She lives one street over."

"Really? I didn't know that."

"She said she's seen us riding bikes."

Megan began to get the makings for sandwiches out of the refrigerator and then got the bread out of the pantry.

"Let's eat outside. It's so nice tonight," Rebekah said.

"Okay."

They took their food and beer out to the back porch. When they'd settled down, Rebekah took a long drink from her beer.

"I asked Dawn if we could visit with her after church." Rebekah took a bite from her sandwich.

"Oh?" Megan asked as she looked up at Rebekah.

"I can't stop thinking about this vote coming up in the church. I've done some research and I want to do something that's proactive." Rebekah gazed at Megan and saw the most compassionate look.

"Tell me."

Rebekah sighed. "You may not like it and you don't have

to do it if it makes you uncomfortable." Rebekah scooted her chair closer to Megan and grabbed her hands. "The last thing I ever want to do is upset you."

"Baby." Megan smiled. "What is it you want to do?"

"I've been thinking about what you said about getting married in your church. You said that you would invite a lot of those people to your wedding and they'd come even though you couldn't have it in your church."

"Right."

"The same thing holds true for me. Even though I haven't lived here in a long time, most of the church knows who I am."

"But they don't know you just happen to be in love with a woman."

Rebekah nodded. "I think the people that would vote against gay marriage are the ones who don't know any gay couples or gay people."

Megan smiled. "So we're going to be the gay couple they meet and grow to love."

Rebekah shrugged. "It could happen."

Megan nodded. "Hmm."

"I know you didn't feel welcomed at my church the way we were last week at Dawn's."

"That's not true. The way your dad looked at me that day kind of put a damper on things. It wasn't the church."

"Would you be willing to try and change their minds?"

"Oh Bekah, I don't know about that. I'd be willing to let them see that I'm a woman who is in love with another woman and we have this adorable little girl. We worship God just like they do and God loves us just like He loves them. If that changes minds, it's all well and good."

"It's hard to vote against something when you can put

faces and names to it. Especially when they are nice people, like you and me."

"What if they vote against it?"

"Then we go to Dawn's church or find another church that wants us for who we are."

Megan sighed. "I don't want you to get hurt."

"I don't want any of us to get hurt. I feel like God gave us this opportunity because He knows we're good people and maybe, just maybe, we can open their minds. We can show them that we may be different, but that doesn't mean our love and our desire to be married are any different than theirs."

"Oh baby."

"This is my way of saying thank you to God for helping us find each other again."

Megan smiled. "Have you told your dad?"

"No." Rebekah shook her head. "I had to discuss this with you first. We are in this together. I don't expect you to serve on the church committees or teach Sunday School or anything like that."

"Oh, well, good thing!" Megan chuckled.

"I just want us to go to church as a family and show up for God. Let's see what happens if we do."

"Have you ever thought about being a preacher? You have a good message and you are definitely passionate about it."

"Don't tease me." Rebekah squeezed Megan's hands.

"I'm serious! People would listen to you."

Rebekah smiled. "What do you think?"

Megan paused and sat back in her chair. She reached for her beer and took a drink. Rebekah never took her eyes off her.

"I'm a believer!" Megan exclaimed. "Did you really think I wouldn't go to church with you?"

"I didn't want you to go for me if it made you uncomfortable."

"I won't be uncomfortable if I'm with you. However, everything you said makes sense. Most of the time fear is the culprit."

"What do you mean?"

"People are oftentimes afraid of people that are different from them. I'm not sure what scares them about letting gay people marry if they've accepted them into the church. It's probably some kind of fear that God's wrath will rain down on them, but that's not our God."

"Well, we'll show them they have nothing to fear."

Megan nodded. "Wait a minute, I thought you said we were going to Dawn's church tomorrow."

"We are. I want to run all this by her and see what she thinks. She was once a part of Dad's congregation."

"What about your dad?"

"I hope we can go by and talk to him one night this week."

"You really have thought this through, haven't you?"

Rebekah nodded. "It's important to me. I'm trying to save my church."

"It scares me a little, Bekah. If they don't vote the way you hope…"

"I'll be all right. I promise. I have to try."

"Then I will be right beside you, my love. What was it Ruth said, 'where you go, I will go.'"

"'Where you live, I will live; your people will be my people,'" Rebekah said, continuing the verse from the Bible.

34

"That is a bold undertaking," Dawn said to Rebekah.

"Do you think it will work?" Rebekah asked. "You were a member of Dad's church and still know a lot of the congregation."

"It's been over ten years since I was a member there, but I do know many of the members."

"And?"

"How are you going to reach the members with your message?"

"Well, when school is out, parents often scramble to find activities for their kids," Rebekah began. "I hope to do some kind of program that teaches the basic tenet of love one another."

"Go on," Dawn urged her.

"We can study different cultures, ethnic groups, and include gender and sexual orientation. We can't be afraid to talk about it."

"My youth minister has worked with your church before

in several different programs. He might be interested in this. What did your dad have to say?"

"We're talking to him this week."

"How do you plan to reach the adults that don't have kids?"

"I am simply going to work with the church members through volunteering, but I also thought I might speak to the women's group."

"What do you think?" Megan asked. "Do we have a chance to open their minds?"

Dawn studied them both before smiling. "I think you will be an asset to the church. I expect you will get some push back from conservative members."

"I realize that, but when they see we aren't going away, maybe our actions will speak louder than words."

"Let me know if there's any way I can help. I'll be praying for you."

Rebekah smiled and reached for Megan's hand. "Thank you. We're going to need it."

They walked to the car hand in hand. Megan looked over at Rebekah. "How do you think that went?"

"I know it's going to be hard, but at least we know she'll support us. That's something."

"I think it's encouraging that their youth minister might be interested in the summer program. You know I'll help with that, right?" Megan asked.

"You don't have to take that on."

"Bekah, you are my partner. We are in this together. No, I don't want to serve on a church committee, but you know I'm committed to helping kids. I think your summer idea is enlightening and just what this community needs."

"Thank you, babe. That means so much to me."

"Why don't we tell your parents when we pick up Anna. I mean, why wait?"

"Hmm, I guess we could," Rebekah said.

"Do you know how much TV Anna has watched this weekend? One more show while we talk to your folks won't hurt her."

Rebekah chuckled. "She's been living her best life."

"Yeah she has. I'm sure your mom did other things with her, but you know how much she and Daniel love to watch movies."

"Let's go home and finish her room and maybe we'll have time to unpack the boxes in the kitchen."

"Yes ma'am," Megan replied.

Rebekah reached for Megan's hand. "Thank you, babe."

"For what?"

"For supporting me. For helping me open minds. For always listening."

"Oh baby. This is what love looks like."

Rebekah kissed the back of her hand and sighed contentedly.

* * *

"Mommy!" Anna exclaimed when Rebekah and Megan walked into Daniel and Helen's living room.

"Hi honey," Rebekah said, holding her arms open. Anna ran to her and hugged her tightly.

Wanda looked over the arm of the couch, her eyes on Anna. It took her a moment to notice Megan standing next to her. The little dog hopped up and ran to Megan. She jumped up on Megan's legs while her tail wagged ninety miles an hour.

"Hi, honey bear," Megan said as she leaned over and

rubbed the dog's head. She picked her up and rubbed her stomach to Wanda's little grunts of love.

"She missed you," Anna said.

"What about you?" Megan asked her.

Anna giggled. "I missed you, too."

"I could use a hug," Megan said as she put Wanda down.

Anna hugged her around the waist while Wanda jumped on Rebekah's legs.

"I'd say you were both missed," Helen said.

"Are you watching a movie?" Rebekah asked.

"Yes, but it's almost over," Daniel replied.

"Would it be okay for Anna to finish it while you two visit with Megan and me in the kitchen?"

"It's fine with me," Daniel said, getting up from his recliner.

"Come on, Wanda," Anna said, sitting back on the couch.

Megan, Rebekah, and her parents sat around the kitchen table.

"What's up? Is everything all right?"

"Yeah, Dad. We're okay. We wanted to talk to you about church."

"Oh, I see. I suppose you're here to tell me that you've decided to attend the community church with Dawn." Daniel sighed.

"Nope," Rebekah said. "We're coming to your church."

"You are!" Helen exclaimed. "That's wonderful."

"But Dad, I'm not hiding who I am. Megan, Anna and I are a family and that's how we'll attend."

"I don't want you to hide who you are, Rebekah," Daniel said.

"Megan and I are hoping to open the minds of your more conservative members. When the vote comes around at the end of the summer, hopefully they will vote to allow gay marriage."

Daniel looked from Rebekah to Megan. "How do you plan to do this?"

"By being an active part of the church."

"Will it put you in an awkward position, Daniel?" Megan asked.

"I don't know. We have not talked about the vote yet."

"How would you vote, Dad?"

"I am in favor of allowing gay clergy and gay marriage."

"We were for it even before you moved back home, Rebekah," Helen said.

Rebekah smiled at both her parents.

"I also want to start a summer program for the kids when school is out, but for now we want to come to church."

"You are always welcome at the church. Both of you," Daniel said with a smile.

"Thank you," Megan said, returning his smile.

"It won't be easy," Daniel said.

"I know it won't, but it's something I have to do. I want the church I grew up in to last."

"I can tell you now, that won't be possible. But a church similar to that one is certainly within reach, if, as you said, we can open their minds."

"You are invited to Sunday lunch at our house next week," Rebekah said with pride.

"How lovely, will we be having roast?" Helen asked with a twinkle in her eye.

* * *

"What do you think?" Rebekah asked as Anna walked around her room.

She ran her little hand along the dresser and over the toy box under the window. Her stuffed animals were lined up on a small couch on the other wall. Two of her dolls rested on the pink pillows at the head of her bed.

"I love it!" she exclaimed.

"Are you sure?" Megan asked. "We can change it."

"No, it's perfect. Look Wanda, you even have a little bed. You can nap while I play."

Rebekah looked at Megan and winked. She had suggested they put a bed for Wanda in here.

"Does this feel like your house now?" Megan asked.

Anna turned around and looked at Megan and Rebekah. "Nope."

Megan and Rebekah looked at her, confusion on their faces.

"It feels like our house!" She giggled.

"Oh, you little kidder," Megan said as she took two steps toward Anna and tickled her.

Wanda jumped up on them both and joined the action.

Anna's laughter echoed around the room. "Okay, okay," she yelled as she tried to catch her breath.

Megan patted her on the back and let her breathe. When Anna's laughter died down she threw her arms around Megan. "That was fun. Thank you for my room."

"It wasn't just me," Megan said. "Mommy helped, too."

Anna stepped back and looked at Megan and Rebekah. "Thank you, Mommy. I love our new family."

Rebekah walked over and put one arm around Anna and one around Megan. "I love our family, too."

Megan grinned down at Anna then gazed into Rebekah's eyes. With all the big ideas and plans Rebekah had, Megan realized there was one thing missing. She intended to take care of that this week.

35

"How's the new house, Anna?" Crystal asked as Anna came into the therapy center.

"It's great. You should see my room," Anna replied happily.

"I will this weekend because I'm coming over for dinner."

"Hey Anna banana," Megan said as she walked up to them.

Anna giggled. "Hi Mama Meg."

"What?" Megan chuckled.

"I need a name for you, too."

"Mama Meg sounds great, Anna," Crystal said as she smiled at Megan.

Megan grinned at Anna. "Come on, let's go paint."

Megan couldn't believe Anna had called her 'mama.' She'd never dreamed Anna would ever call her that. A smile played at the corner of her mouth as she enjoyed the moment. It wouldn't be long until school was out and Rebekah started her summer program. She was afraid there might be struggles with getting it started. But she had plans to give her new family a little happiness before that happened.

When the art therapy session ended Anna ran to Megan's office while Megan and Crystal put the supplies away.

"Hey, where's Wanda?" Anna asked.

"We have something to do as soon as we finish here and Wanda can't go with us," Megan replied.

"What are we doing?"

"It's kind of a surprise. You could help us, so we could leave sooner," Megan suggested.

Anna quickly helped them put the rest of the art supplies away and they were in Megan's car in no time.

Megan parked the car and when they got out Anna said, "I remember this, it's the river, isn't it?"

"It is." Megan held out her hand and Anna took it. Joy ran through Megan's heart as they walked along the river toward the shops.

Anna skipped as she held Megan's hand and they both giggled.

"Where are we going?" Anna asked.

"Right here," Megan said as she stopped them in front of the ice cream shop. Anna's eyes widened. "Come on. I'm getting a cone, how about you?"

They went inside and each of them got a cone. Megan led them back outside to a table in the front of the store.

"I need to talk to you about something important," Megan began.

Anna looked at her and tilted her head. "Okay... Is it bad?"

Megan smiled. "No, it's not bad. It's very happy, at least it is for me."

Anna began to eat her cone while Megan took a lick of hers.

"You know how we're a family now," Megan said.

"Yeah."

"Do you know what proposing is?"

Anna paused. "I'm not sure."

"It means asking a question."

"Oh, okay."

"It usually means asking someone to marry you."

"Oh! I've heard of that. You get down on one knee."

"Yeah, well, I want to ask your mommy to marry me."

Anna smiled. "She'll say yes."

"You think so?"

Anna nodded. "She loves you. I hear her tell you all the time."

"But what I need to know is if it's okay with you."

Anna chuckled. "Duh, yes, it's okay with me."

Megan smiled. "Thanks, I appreciate that."

"I'll help you," Anna said as she kept eating her ice cream.

"You'll help me?"

"Yeah, we should ride our bikes to the park by our house. That's where you helped me not be so sad about Daddy. Remember?"

"Yes, I remember."

"We can ask her together. She'll be so surprised!" Anna squealed.

Megan couldn't help but laugh at her exuberance.

"Oh I know! Grandpa and Grandma can pick me up at the park and then you can take Mommy somewhere special with candles and stuff," Anna said as she finished her ice cream.

"Candles and stuff? That sounds like a great idea."

"We can do it Friday. That's when I stay at Grandma's anyway." Anna grinned at Megan. "And don't worry, I'll keep it all a secret."

"Okay." Megan finished her ice cream. She wasn't sure about what had just happened, but she couldn't keep from smiling. She made a mental note to let Rebekah's parents in on Anna's master plan as soon as possible.

* * *

Rebekah sighed happily as she turned into the driveway. Friday had finally arrived, and she was looking forward to having Megan all to herself tonight.

"Mommy," Anna said as they pulled into the garage. "Let's ride bikes when Megan gets home."

"You're spending the night with Grandma and Grandpa. It's Friday, remember?"

"We can ride bikes before I go." Anna opened the door to the kitchen and Rebekah followed her inside.

"Megan's had a busy week, honey. I'm not sure she'll want to ride bikes."

"I think she will," Anna said as she walked down the hall to her room. "I'm going to change. You should too."

Rebekah furrowed her brow but went to change anyway. A bike ride would be a nice way to calm down from the week. Her students were getting more unruly as the end of school neared.

"Come on, Mommy!" Anna yelled from the living room.

"What's the hurry? Megan isn't even home from work yet," Rebekah said as she walked into the room.

They heard a car door slam and Anna grinned. "She is now."

Megan walked into the house and set her things on the island. "Hello family."

"Hi babe," Rebekah said. She walked over and gave Megan a kiss. "This one"—she nodded towards Anna—"wants to go on a bike ride."

"Oh good. Let me change clothes."

"I thought you'd be tired. It's been a long week."

"A bike ride sounds perfect." She grinned, kissed Rebekah and hurried down the hall.

A moment later Anna followed behind her. Rebekah looked on suspiciously, but then Wanda scratched at the back door so she went to let her in.

* * *

"Don't forget the ring," Anna whispered when she walked into Megan's bedroom.

"I've got it."

"Okay, I'll get Mommy and meet you in the garage."

Megan couldn't keep from laughing. "I'm not sure who is more excited, me or Anna," she mumbled.

After she changed clothes, Megan walked back into the empty kitchen and went to the garage.

"I don't know what's going on with her, but she's determined to ride bikes today," Rebekah said.

"It's a beautiful day. Right, Anna banana?"

"Right, Mama Meg. Let's go!" Anna took off down the driveway.

"Mama Meg?" Rebekah looked at Megan, her eyes wide.

Megan shrugged. "She's just started calling me that."

"Wow!"

"I melted the first time she said it."

"Come on!" Anna yelled from the street.

They jumped on their bikes and took off to catch Anna.

"What is with her?" Rebekah asked.

"Let me catch up and see," Megan pumped her pedals and caught up to Anna. "Hey, slow down. We have to give everyone a chance to get to their places."

"Oh, I didn't think of that." She immediately slowed down and turned around to ride next to Rebekah.

"Let's turn here," Megan suggested. When Rebekah and Anna caught up they cruised down the street.

"I think this is where Dawn lives," Megan pointed to a house.

"She is close to us," Rebekah said.

"Is that the preacher of the other church we visited?" Anna asked.

"That's her."

"I liked that church. Should we turn here, Mama Meg?"

Megan chuckled. "Yes. Do you want to go to the park?"

Anna turned around and gave her a confused look, then realization dawned on her face. "Oh! Yeah, let's go to the park."

"We always go to the park. She's up to something," Rebekah said to Megan.

"Why do you say that?"

"She was adamant about this bike ride before you got home. Hey, I just realized, you're home early."

"I'm happy it's Friday. Aren't you?"

"Yes!"

"This is a great way to start the weekend," Megan said as they rode into the park.

They followed Anna down the path and when she stopped Megan and Rebekah pulled up next to her.

"Let's take a little rest," Anna said. "This is our family spot."

"Oh, okay." Rebekah leaned her bike against a tree and looked over at Megan and chuckled.

Megan leaned hers on the other side of the tree. She took a deep breath.

* * *

"What a nice day," Anna said as she spread her arms out wide and looked out over the park.

"It is," Rebekah said. When she started to sit down Anna grabbed her arm. "No, Mommy, you can't sit down."

"I can't?" Rebekah couldn't figure out why her daughter was acting so strangely.

"Megan wants to ask you something." Anna looked at Megan and nodded. "Now."

Megan knelt down in front of Rebekah and looked up at her with a smile. Rebekah covered her mouth with one of her hands and Megan grabbed the other one.

"This is the most awkward proposal of all time. I think this one is about to explode." Megan reached for Anna and pulled her next to her.

"I have loved you all my life. I know that because God made me for you. I feel it in my heart. I love you with all I am, Bekah, and I love Anna with all my heart. Will you marry me?" Megan smiled up at Rebekah with tears in her eyes.

Rebekah couldn't believe the sight before her. The woman she loved more than life itself on one knee with her daughter standing next to her, unable to contain her excitement as she jumped from one foot to the next.

"Say yes, Mommy, say yes!" Anna squealed. "I told Megan you would!"

Rebekah had tears in her eyes now. "Yes! Yes, babe, I'll

marry you." She reached for Megan's face and pulled her up into a kiss. When their lips met Rebekah felt all her worries fade away. This was her safe space, this was her happy place, this was her home.

She pulled away when she felt Anna hugging them both and jumping up and down.

"Give her the ring, Mama Meg, the ring!"

"Oh, I do have a ring, but I can't take my eyes off you," Megan said softly.

Rebekah smiled, put her arms around Megan's neck and pulled her in for another kiss. "God, I love you so much," she said, holding her close.

Megan pulled away and reached for Rebekah's hand. She slipped the ring on her finger and it fit perfectly.

Rebekah's eyes widened as she looked at the ring. "Oh Meg, it's beautiful!"

"It was my grandmother's. If it's not your style that's okay, we'll get you whatever you want."

"It's perfect. I love it. Look, honey." Rebekah bent down to show Anna.

"I've seen it. I knew you would like it. Why did you take so long to answer? I told Megan you'd say yes and you took forever!" Anna said dramatically.

"It's because I want to always remember this. I have the most glorious memory of you and Megan looking up at me with your faces full of love."

"I told Megan this was the perfect spot, under our tree," Anna said.

"You were right." Rebekah couldn't stop looking at her engagement ring. "This is stunning."

Megan reached for Rebekah's hand and looked down at Anna. "Thanks for your help."

"I told you she'd say yes." Anna giggled then waved to

someone in the distance. "There's Grandma and Grandpa. Time to go."

"What?" Rebekah said.

"It's all part of the plan, baby. Come on."

They walked their bikes to where Daniel had parked his pickup.

"Your parents are going to take our bikes home and Anna is going with them. The proposal isn't quite finished."

"I can't wait for what's next." Rebekah beamed a smile at Megan then hurried to show her mom her engagement ring.

36

After accepting congratulations from Rebekah's parents, they got in Megan's car and left the park.

"How did your car get here?" Rebekah shook her head. "And you said the proposal wasn't finished. What's next?"

"You'll see." Megan glanced over at Rebekah and grabbed her hand. "I had a few things I wanted to say to you, but I knew Anna couldn't wait any longer."

Rebekah chuckled. "What you said was all true." Rebekah kissed the back of her hand. "I was made for you, too. Tell me how this all came about."

"I wanted to ask you as soon as I saw you again, but thought better of it. All I knew was that I couldn't let you get away again. I figured the right time would come along. But when you started talking about wanting to go back to your dad's church and open minds, it hit me. We're fighting for the right to get married in the church and we aren't even engaged! It's time, don't you think?"

"I would've said yes the first time we saw each other again."

"You would?" Megan said dreamily, then gazed at Rebekah.

Rebekah smiled and nodded. "How did Anna get involved?"

"Well, I had to make sure she was okay with it. So I told her I wanted to propose. She said you would say yes because you tell me you love me all the time."

Rebekah chuckled. "I do say that a lot and I'm going to keep saying it to you."

"Oh I hope so. Anyway, she said she would help me and she immediately came up with this plan. I couldn't have stopped her even if I'd wanted to. This next part is called 'candles and stuff.'"

"What?" Rebekah asked, laughing.

"You'll just have to trust me, baby."

"I've always trusted you."

Megan pulled to the curb near the park on the river.

"We have a short walk," Megan said. She reached for Rebekah's hand when they got out of the car and started towards the park. "Since Anna thought our tree in the park near the house was the best place to propose, I thought the place you took me on our first date would be the best place to tell you what you mean to me."

"Oh babe, you're going to make me cry," Rebekah said, putting her arm through Megan's and pulling her close.

They turned off the path and walked through the trees to the clearing where they'd reconnected under the stars.

"What's this!" Rebekah exclaimed. There were fairy lights draped between two trees and under them was a blanket with pillows waiting for them. Next to the blanket was a picnic basket and Crystal and Kim were ready to greet them.

"Congrats! You did say yes, right?" Crystal teased. "We

have this special part of the park reserved just for you tonight."

"We're so happy for you both," Kim said, then hugged each of them.

"Of course I said yes. I can't believe all this. Wait! You have to see my ring," Rebekah said, dangling her hand in front of Kim.

"Beautiful. Nicely done, Megan." Kim winked at her.

"Wow, that's gorgeous," Crystal said.

"Thanks. We'll see you tomorrow night. We're still having dinner at our place," Rebekah said, looking at her ring. "We have to celebrate!"

"Can't wait, but for now, we should be going," Crystal hugged them both and she and Kim walked away.

"Shall we?" Megan eased down on the blanket and Rebekah sat down next to her.

She gazed into Megan's eyes and smiled. "You really surprised me."

"You know, we don't have to get married. I just want to spend the rest of my life with you," Megan said, taking Rebekah's hand in hers.

"I know we don't have to, but I want to marry you. I want to commit our lives to one another in front of God, our families and friends. I want Anna to hear our promises to one another that include her."

"Even if it isn't in the church you grew up in?"

"I'd marry you anywhere." Rebekah leaned in and touched their lips together in a sweet kiss.

"Some people go to church and some people don't." Megan looked up at the fairy lights. "I didn't think it mattered to me when I stopped going. I still prayed most days and occasionally read the Bible. As I told you, I'd go with my parents when I went for a visit, but when I went to church with you it felt different."

"What do you mean?"

"Something about sitting there with you and Anna made it more meaningful. I know you think I'm just going along with this idea of yours to change minds, but I want this as badly as you do, Bekah. I think about the people that came before us and fought for gay rights, including the right to marry. We're just one little church in the grand scheme of things, but that's what it takes. Opening minds, one at a time, leads to change."

"I didn't think I could possibly love you more," Rebekah said fiercely. She launched towards Megan and when their lips met she pushed Megan back onto the blanket. Her lips were full of passion and love that she let flow into Megan. When Megan's arms tightened around her she knew this must be what forever felt like. In each other's arms, wrapped in love: this was their forever.

"I'm going to get us arrested." Rebekah giggled.

"Do you think they'd put us in the same cell?" Megan teased.

Rebekah laughed and sat up. She propped the pillows up behind them so they could lie back and look at the sky as the sun began to set.

"No more church talk," Rebekah said while she held Megan's hand.

"It's kind of a big part of our lives."

"I know, but it's not everything."

"Okay. Let's talk about the wedding."

"Oh, will your family want to have a big wedding for you?" Rebekah asked.

"This is not my family's wedding, it is my wedding, so no."

"I like the idea of destination weddings, but..."

"If we can't get married in your dad's church then maybe Dawn's?" Megan suggested.

"Let's talk 'what-ifs.' If the marriage vote passes, we'll get married in Dad's church. If it doesn't, we'll adjust."

"Agreed. What if we went to a beach for our honeymoon?"

"You know I love the beach. Agreed." Rebekah propped up on her elbow. "My parents thought I got pregnant on my honeymoon."

Megan reached up and twirled a strand of Rebekah's hair. "What if Anna had a little brother or sister?"

Rebekah tilted her head and looked into Megan's eyes. "I think Anna would love that."

Megan raised her eyebrows in question.

"I would, too." Rebekah ran her finger down Megan's cheek.

"Those stars had better hurry." Megan breathed out a contented sigh.

"Maybe we'll start the honeymoon when we get home." Rebekah wiggled her eyebrows.

Megan pulled her down for a kiss and Rebekah felt like the rest of her life would be a honeymoon because she was living it with her love.

* * *

"Thank you for your help with the big proposal yesterday. It was certainly a team effort," Rebekah said to Kim. Megan and Crystal were playing with Anna in the backyard while Rebekah and Kim looked on.

"You're welcome. I'm glad we could make it special for you. Did you like the wine?"

"Very much. I figured that was your choice."

"Are you sure I can't help with dinner?" Kim asked.

"No, we're just waiting for the grill to heat up. I'll cook the burgers and everything else is ready inside."

"The house looks fabulous. I'm telling you, it's like Megan knew you were coming back."

Rebekah tilted her head toward Kim. "What do you mean?"

"Out of the blue she decided it was time to buy a house. Then she moved in and didn't do much to decorate. Crystal and I couldn't figure out what she was waiting on. I know you two have a powerful faith, so it must have been a God thing or something. When we got here earlier, it was like walking into a home, not a house."

"We didn't change that much," Rebekah said.

"It must be how your things go together, just like your lives. Because this feels like a happy home now."

"It didn't before?'

"Not like this. Even Wanda is happier, look at her!"

"Wanda is always happy," Rebekah said, smiling at the little dog as she ran across the lawn.

"That's what I mean. Happy little Wanda is even more joyful."

"Thanks, Kim. I feel like this must be a little slice of heaven."

"Tell me all about this summer program you're planning," Kim said.

"I want to give kids a place to go when school's out. But I want it to be based on Jesus' commandment: love one another. I want to showcase differences in people and teach tolerance, inclusion, and respect."

"That sounds amazing, but how are you going to pull it off?"

Rebekah chuckled. "With a lot of help. I've talked to a few teachers at my school and you'd be surprised how many want to help. I'm hoping I can get members of my dad's church on board, too. I envision a rotating group of volunteers with a core group that are there every day."

"Let me know how I can help. Maybe there is some kind of building project we can do."

"That would be great! I want to do all kinds of crafts, field trips, and projects around town helping others. There are so many places we can take the older kids to volunteer."

"Mommy, save me, save me!" Anna screamed. She ran onto the porch and hid behind Rebekah. "Mama and Crystal are after me."

Rebekah held out her arms and looked over her shoulder at Anna. "Why would they be after you?"

Megan ran onto the porch and stopped in front of Rebekah, panting.

"What happened to you?" Rebekah asked, not able to hold back a laugh.

"Anna banana is what happened to me!" Megan reached around Rebekah on one side and then the other as Anna squealed. "She turned the hose on Crystal and me."

Crystal walked up, soaked from the top of her head down her shirt and shorts.

"Whoa." Rebekah chuckled. "Let me get you a towel."

"I'll get it," Anna said. She quickly dashed into the house before either Megan or Crystal could grab her.

Megan threw her head back and laughed. "She really thought I was going to get her."

"I still may!" Crystal said. She sat down and laughed. "She snuck up on us."

"I may have to rethink this idea of more kids. I thought you would be more capable." Rebekah grinned at Megan.

"More kids!" Crystal exclaimed.

"Who's having more kids?" Anna handed Crystal and Megan each a towel. "Are we having a baby? Please, please, please say we are."

Rebekah looked at Megan. "Well, I think we know what Anna thinks of the idea."

"You want to be a big sister?" Megan asked. She pulled Anna onto her lap. "Are you going to sneak up on her or him and drown them with a hose?"

"No! No! I'll get her to help me spray you!" The grin on her face made Megan laugh.

Megan wrapped Anna in a hug and held her tight. "Thank goodness Mommy will save me."

Rebekah chuckled. "That's right. I'm always saving my girls." She jokingly puffed out an exaggerated breath.

Megan held her hand out for Rebekah to grab. When she took it, Megan pulled her into her lap as well. Anna and Rebekah both squealed.

"I'm the luckiest Mama in the world!" Megan exclaimed, her arms around both of her girls.

37

As the end of school neared, Rebekah lined up leaders and volunteers for her Love One Another Project. She talked to several churches and teachers from other schools. Today, she was talking to the United Methodist Women's group at her church. She knew most of the women in the group and she was nervous. Her mom would be there along with several of the younger women she'd grown up with in the church, so there would be friendly faces as well as familiar faces.

She made her presentation to the group and answered several questions. Most of the women seemed excited about having the children at their church. She stressed that this was a community-wide effort and it would be a chance for their church to shine.

"I want the kids to learn to be considerate and compassionate. We plan to put them in situations where they can practice it and not just talk about it. To love one another doesn't necessarily mean you have to like one another. But to learn respect and empathy at a young age will serve them all their lives. Hopefully, the kids can pass this along at home to their parents and other family members."

Rebekah answered a few more questions and explained how to contact her if they were interested in helping.

"I've noticed you and your friend have been regulars in church on Sunday mornings," a woman commented from the back.

Rebekah peered through the group and smiled. "Well hi, Mrs. Wiley. It's nice to see you." Virginia Wiley had taught Sunday School when Rebekah was about Anna's age. She had to be in her seventies now.

"Megan is my friend, but she's also my fiancée." Rebekah replied. "She would be with me today, but she and Anna are at the counseling center. You may not know this, but Megan and her partner created the counseling center and they do great work with kids and adults as well."

Rebekah looked around the room. "I can share some information with you but I'm sure you'll be hearing more about this from my dad over the summer. At the General Conference, which takes place at the end of August, there will be a vote to split the church into those congregations that accept gay clergy and allow gay marriage and those that don't. Megan and I are hopeful our church will vote for this and we can get married right here in the church I grew up in." Rebekah smiled brightly at the faces and tried to make eye contact with most of the women.

"I thought they ruled on that in 2019," a woman who appeared to be around Rebekah's age said.

"It's being brought before the General Council again. My dad will bring everyone up to date on it. But I hope you know that Megan and I love one another just as you do your spouses and want to be married in the same way."

"I'd better get an invitation to the wedding," Mrs. Wiley said.

"You certainly will." Rebekah grinned. "Do you have any other questions about the summer project?"

A bit later, the meeting ended and several women gave Rebekah their contact information and signed up to help.

"That went well," Helen said to Rebekah as they left the church.

"I thought so, too. Mom, did you notice any looks when I told them about Megan and me hoping to get married here? I gazed around the room and only saw a few stern faces."

Helen sighed. "I can probably tell you the ones who will vote against it."

"How about Mrs. Wiley! She's something! I've got to remember to invite her to the wedding no matter where we end up having it."

"I think she was trying to help you."

"I do too. You're okay with me marrying Megan, right?" Rebekah asked quietly.

"Of course I am." Helen squeezed Rebekah's arm reassuringly.

"I just hate putting you and Dad in an awkward position with some of the members."

"Your dad and I have been in favor of gay clergy and gay marriage the entire time. The members should know that. I'm glad that you are living your life in the open and with happiness. I miss Ben, but I know he's looking down on you and Anna and helping Megan any way he can."

"Oh, what a nice thing to say, Mom. Thank you." Rebekah stopped and hugged her mom as they reached their cars.

"We don't hug enough," Helen said, hugging her tight again.

* * *

"Yippee! School's out!" Anna screamed when she ran into the counseling center.

Megan laughed. "Mommy doesn't look as happy as you are about it."

"Mommy will be happy tomorrow when she is finished." Rebekah smiled.

Megan gave her a kiss and said, "One more day, you can do it!"

"Then the real work starts with this summer program," Rebekah said.

"You have a week before the kids start coming and lots of help. It's going to be great. I just know it."

"I love your enthusiasm and hope you're right."

"You'll see, but before that happens, guess where we're going, Anna?" Megan asked.

"Um," Anna murmured as she furrowed her brow. "To the river to get ice cream?"

"Hmm, that's not a bad idea, but do you remember the first time you met me?"

"Yeah, it was here."

"That day you told me something two boys were talking about at school and it made you sad. Can you remember what?"

"Yep, they were talking about camping."

"That's right. Tomorrow when Mommy gets through with school, we are picking you up from Grandma's and..." Megan paused.

Anna's eyes got big. "Are we going camping?" she exclaimed.

"Sort of," Megan began. "I've never put up a tent in my life."

"I offered to show her how," Crystal chimed in.

"We're going to a cabin on the lake. We'll still do the same things, but we're sleeping inside in a bed," Rebekah stated firmly.

Megan chuckled. "I don't think Mommy wants to sleep in a tent in a sleeping bag."

"That's okay. I can't wait!" Anna said, jumping up and down.

Rebekah chuckled. "Me too."

The next day, Rebekah and Megan picked Anna up from Helen's and they were off on their first family trip.

"I'm so glad Wanda gets to go too," Anna said. She sat in the back seat with Wanda right next to her. "What are we doing first?"

"I don't know. Maybe we'll swim or take a hike. What do you want to do?"

"Everything!"

Rebekah looked over at Megan and chuckled. "You've created a monster."

"Good thing there are two of us. Maybe we'll be able to keep up."

"This is our first family trip," Rebekah announced. "And we planned this special weekend just for you, Miss Anna."

"Thank you. If we like this, does that mean we get to camp in a tent next time?"

"Let's try this first. Maybe Crystal and Kim can take you tent camping someday," Megan said.

"Now that's an idea," Rebekah agreed.

They sang songs and played a few car games along the way and eventually pulled into the campground. By the time they checked into their cabin there was still a little daylight left to explore the area.

"Let me build a fire in the fire pit and we can roast hot dogs and marshmallows," Megan said.

"We'll walk down to the shore and see how cold the water is. Okay, honey?" Rebekah said.

Their cabin backed up to the lake and it was a short walk to the water. They were surrounded by trees and they could hear the water lapping against the small strip of sand that was their beach. The air smelled of water and the outdoors.

"It's really beautiful here," Megan said when Rebekah and Anna walked back.

"We should be able to see the stars down by the water," Rebekah commented.

Megan got the fire going and after they ate hot dogs it was time to roast marshmallows.

"This is fun," Anna said as Megan handed her a stick with a marshmallow attached.

They dangled their sticks over the fire and watched the pillowy treats darken. The fire crackled and a soft breeze wafted through the trees.

"What does gay mean?" Anna asked as she stared into the fire.

Rebekah exchanged a look with Megan.

"It's another word for happy," Rebekah said. "But then some people turned it into a word that means when two girls love each other, like Megan and me, or two boys love each other."

"Is it a bad word?"

"No, but sometimes people say it and intend it as a bad word."

"Where did you hear it?" Megan asked.

"I heard someone say it at church. They said you and Mommy can't get married at church because you're gay."

"Some churches won't let two women or two men get married in their church," Megan said. "But Mommy and I are hoping that will change."

"Because you want to get married at church?"

"That's right."

"You could get married here. It's pretty."

Megan smiled at Rebekah. "It is, but we want to get married in the church."

"But they won't let you!" Anna said, beginning to sound upset.

"It's okay, Grandpa's church isn't the only church." Rebekah tried to soothe her. "There are churches that will let us get married in them."

"Which one?"

"Do you remember when we went to the church where you knew the songs?" Megan asked.

"Yes."

"We can get married in that church."

Anna nodded. "But you *are* getting married, right?"

"Yes we are," Rebekah said, reaching for Megan's hand.

"Someone at school asked me if you were gay," Anna said.

"What did you say?"

"I didn't say anything because I didn't know what they meant."

"You can tell them that yes we are gay because we are very happy," Megan said with a grin.

Anna chuckled. "Can I roast another marshmallow?"

Megan got up and put another marshmallow on her stick. "There you go."

"Sometimes people at school may tease you about me and Megan," Rebekah said. "If that happens I want you to tell us, okay?"

"Why will they tease me?"

"Because we're different from their family."

Anna sighed. "There are all kinds of families. I saw them on *Barbie* and *Luca* and other movies."

"That's right. We're one very happy family." Megan smiled at Rebekah.

"Do you have any other questions?"

"Nope." Anna shook her head. Then she suddenly yawned.

"I think it's time to check out those beds," Megan said.

"Not yet. I'm not tired."

"We have all day tomorrow to explore and swim and roast more marshmallows," Megan explained.

"Okay. I think Wanda is a little tired," Anna said. The dog had been sitting next to Anna and raised her head when she heard her name.

"Yeah, it would be really nice if you lay down with her."

After they put Anna and Wanda to bed, they went out to gaze at the stars. Megan spread a blanket out on the ground near the water and sprawled in the middle of it.

"Um, hello?" Rebekah said as she stared down at her.

"I've got a spot right here for you," Megan said, pointing to her shoulder and arm.

Rebekah smiled and cuddled next to her. "How about those questions?"

"I'm glad she asked. We need to check in with her from time to time."

"I know. Kids can ask a lot of questions and be so mean."

"That's another thing your summer project will do to help kids."

"I hope so, but I don't want to talk about that this weekend. This weekend is for us to spend time together as a family." She rolled over on top of Megan. "Right now, I want to spend time kissing this gorgeous woman who I'm going to marry."

Rebekah brought her lips to Megan's and kissed her softly.

"Mmm, I'm going to need more than kisses," Megan murmured. She ran her hand under Rebekah's shirt and up her back.

"Can you be quiet?" Rebekah slid her hand down Megan's shorts and inside her undies.

Megan gasped. "Baby!" She felt Rebekah's finger glide through her wetness.

"Oh, you do need more than kisses."

"That's what your kisses do to me," Megan said huskily.

"I'm not stopping. Look at me, babe."

Megan fixed her eyes on Rebekah's and felt two fingers slide inside her. She hissed as she inhaled and closed her eyes.

"Oh no. Look at me," Rebekah demanded. "Can you feel me, right here?"

Megan felt Rebekah's finger touch her most sensitive spot and she melted.

"Come on, babe. Come for me," Rebekah whispered against her lips. She pulled her fingers out and then pushed back in deeper and tenderly caressed that spot.

Megan tensed and held Rebekah tightly. She kept staring into Rebekah's eyes and she saw a flash of blue sparkle in them. Then she pressed her lips to Rebekah's and moaned her pleasure past Rebekah's lips, into her heart.

When she relaxed back against the blanket she looked up into Rebekah's pleased face. "You look awfully satisfied with yourself."

"You're the one that should be satisfied, aren't you?"

"Oh yeah," Megan said, trying to catch her breath. "That was intense."

Rebekah grinned. "Tomorrow it's my turn under the stars."

Megan pulled her down for another kiss and quickly flipped their positions. "Why wait until tomorrow? Let's see if you can be quiet."

38

"First week down, how did it go?" Megan asked as she hurried in from the garage to find Rebekah lying on the couch.

"Let's just say that I'm glad Anna is spending the night with my folks. There will be no shower shenanigans for us this Friday night. I'm tired."

Megan walked over, leaned down and gave Rebekah a soft kiss. Then she picked up Rebekah's feet, sat down, and held them in her lap. "Would a foot rub help?"

"I'll be your best friend," Rebekah replied.

"What?" Megan chuckled.

"I heard one of the little kids trying to sweet talk another kid out of their snack today. It was so cute. He said, 'I'll be your best friend.'"

"Did it work?"

"No."

"Well, lucky for you, I am your best friend." Megan began to rub Rebekah's foot.

"I don't know why it's so tiring. We only have the kids in

the mornings, but then I spend the afternoon getting things ready for the next day."

"It'll get easier. You're just figuring it all out right now."

"The big kids finished cleaning out a flower bed as one of our community projects today. I wish you could have seen how grateful the women that lived there were. They're sisters and approaching their nineties. They used to love to work in the yard, but can't keep up with all the weeding any longer. We took a team over to clean out the bed and the pride on those kids' faces when they finished was priceless."

"That sounds encouraging."

Rebekah nodded. "I noticed groups of kids playing together. It may not seem like much, but they come from such a variety of socioeconomic backgrounds, races, and schools. It made me think the program is working."

"It will work because you are an amazing leader and inspire everyone around you."

"You give me too much credit, babe. I have so many volunteers and good people helping. It's tiring, but so much fun."

"I'm so proud of you. Look at my wifey, changing our little corner of the world."

"I'm not your wife just yet."

"I'm getting used to saying it." Megan grinned.

Rebekah shook her head. "Wifey? Whatever. Come over here and kiss me and then feed me. In that order please."

Megan chuckled. "What do you want to eat?"

"Anything delivered."

* * *

Megan was right. As the days turned into weeks Rebekah had the summer program running smoothly and it was a success the first month. Expectations were high as it continued.

Rebekah, Megan, and Anna never missed a Sunday at church and more people began to greet them and they began to make friends. They were invited to a couples Sunday class and they began to attend that as well.

Before they knew it June had turned into July and it was time for their vacation to visit Megan's family.

"Are you apprehensive about leaving for a week?" Megan asked Rebekah.

"Nope. Kim has been there nearly every day and knows what to do. There are so many helpers from the different churches and teachers that have volunteered for various weeks during the summer. It'll be fine." Rebekah smiled happily. "I am so excited to meet your family! Aren't you, Anna?"

"I have cousins!" she exclaimed.

"And a Mimi and Poppie and an Aunt Trisha," Megan added. She held Anna's hand as they walked through the airport and could feel her excitement.

"Are you nervous to fly?"

"I'm excited!" She did a little skip step and grabbed Rebekah's hand while she walked between them.

"You get to sit by the window!" Megan grinned at Rebekah and thought how excited she was for her family to meet Rebekah and Anna.

Rebekah returned her smile and winked at her.

They boarded the plane and got settled in their seats. Megan reached for Rebekah's hand and intertwined their fingers. She looked from Anna to Rebekah and thought this must be what heaven is like. The two people she loved most were on either side of her, she held their hands, and they were off on a grand adventure.

"Tell me again what all we're going to do," Anna said.

"We're going to Disneyland, which I know you're excited about. And do you remember when we went camping and how beautiful the lake was?"

"Yes."

"We're going to this park where there are the most beautiful gigantic cliffs and the biggest trees you'll ever see!" Megan exclaimed.

"Really!"

"That's right."

"Remember, honey," Rebekah said, leaning forward to look into Anna's eyes. "We don't have to do something every day. I want to spend time with Mimi and Poppie and Trisha."

"Show me pictures of Nathan and Isabella again, Mama."

Megan took her phone out and showed it to Anna. "That's Nathan."

"He's twelve."

"That's right. This is Isabella."

"She's ten."

"They are going to love you and your accent," Megan said.

"My accent?"

"Just wait. You'll see what I mean. They'll sound funny when they talk."

"I don't sound funny." Anna shrugged and then turned to look out the window.

Rebekah chuckled. "This will be interesting." Then she furrowed her brow. "Do I sound funny?"

Megan laughed. "No. You sound like the sweet Georgia girl who melts me with her words. Sometimes when you say my name it sounds like honey dripping off your tongue."

Rebekah leaned over and whispered in Megan's ear. "I'll remember that tonight when I have you all to myself."

Butterflies fluttered in Megan's stomach as she felt a surge of warmth spread through her body. She turned her head and kissed Rebekah softly. "See what I mean? Your words." She huffed out a breath and Rebekah chuckled.

* * *

One night as the kids played in Megan's parents' backyard, the adults gathered around the patio table and shared a bottle of wine. Rebekah and Trisha had become fast friends, trading stories about Megan and their kids. Megan's parents, Curt and Lisa, welcomed Rebekah and Anna like they'd been part of the family for years.

"I think what you two are trying to do in your church is brave," Lisa said, "and I'm proud of you."

"It's amazing the differences in people in various regions of our country," Curt added. "I mean, in our church, we have a gay assistant pastor and no one blinked an eye. But in the south and through the Bible Belt of the country, you don't see gay clergy much, especially in the more rural areas."

"What exactly did you do to let the members know you're a gay couple?" Trisha asked. "I know you didn't announce it, but—"

"I'm sure you volunteer for more things that you normally wouldn't," Lisa interrupted.

"I feel like we signed up to do anything and everything. However, Meg did draw the line at teaching Sunday School." Rebekah chuckled and grinned at Megan.

"I can't believe you got my sister to volunteer for anything," Trisha said. "She didn't really like going to youth meetings or anything else but the church service."

"I understand why you didn't want to go to youth meetings; that's why I didn't force you," Lisa said. "Do you like volunteering now?"

Megan smiled at Rebekah then turned to her mom. "I do. I mainly help out with things that involve Anna. I'm not on any committees or anything like that, yet."

"She's an asset to the church," Rebekah said, looking at Megan with pride.

"Well, how's it going then? Are you opening minds?" Curt asked.

"We've made some friends," Megan said. "And gone to a couple of Sunday night family picnics."

"Oh my God, I would love to see that," Trisha gushed. "I'm so happy for you, Megan!"

Megan narrowed her eyes at her sister. "Are you kidding or do you mean it?"

"I mean it! I know, deep down, you have always wanted to do things with your family just like any other."

Megan's face lit up. "It's more awesome than I ever dreamed." She looked at Rebekah and beamed a smile just for her.

"What else did you want to show Rebekah and Anna before you have to go back?" Curt asked.

"I want to take Anna to the art museum. I'm telling you, the girl is gifted!" Megan exclaimed.

"I'd love to go with you," Lisa said. "You know, they have programs during the summer for kids. Anna could certainly come out and stay with us for a week and do one of them."

Rebekah's eyes widened. "She would love that."

"Let's look into it while we're there," Megan said.

* * *

The rest of the week flew by and Anna became fast friends with her new cousins.

"This has been the best week," Rebekah said as she put her arm through Megan's.

"The ocean has big waves!" Anna exclaimed.

They walked along the beach to the restaurant where Megan's parents were waiting.

"What have you liked best this week?" Megan asked Anna.

"I liked everything!" She skipped next to them. "But I really loved those paintings you took me to see."

"That's why we had to go see them again this morning," Rebekah commented.

"It was worth it," Megan said. "There's no telling what you'll paint when we get home."

"You know, Mimi wants you to come back next summer and take one of the art classes for kids," Rebekah said.

"Can I? I mean, may I?" Anna exclaimed.

"You'd have to come by yourself. Would you want to do that?" Megan asked.

"Yes. I can stay with Mimi and Poppie by myself just like I do at Grandma and Grandpa's. I'm not a baby."

"Excuse me," Megan sassed her.

Anna laughed and then yelled. "Look! There's Bella and Nathan. Can I go play in the water?"

"For a few minutes. Mimi and Poppie are waiting for us," Rebekah said. "There's Trisha." Rebekah waved. They ambled toward her and then Rebekah stopped.

"What's wrong?"

"I just realized something, babe. If the vote doesn't go the way we hope then why would we stay there? We could move out here. Anna could grow up with her cousins and there are churches here that want us."

"What about your parents? It's still your home."

"They could move here too. We don't have to stay in Georgia. I brought Anna there for help. We found you and now she's thriving. *We're* thriving. She would be fine out here. You stayed because you hoped I'd come back. I'm here with you now; we can move. This is your home."

Megan smiled. "My home is with you and Anna."

"It's an option, babe, and something to think about."

Megan leaned down and kissed her tenderly.

"Anna's right. You do kiss a lot," Trisha said as she walked up.

"I can't help it," Rebekah said. "Your sister is amazing."

Trisha chuckled. "If you say so."

"Very funny. You know it's true," Megan said, defending herself.

"I'm going to have to..." Trisha paused. "Agree with you, Rebekah."

Megan laughed.

"Did you see Mom the first few times she heard Anna call you Mama? I thought she was going to melt," Trisha commented as she waved at their parents on the deck.

"You should've seen me the first time," Megan replied.

"I'm really happy for you both. It's obvious you are good together. I wish it hadn't taken so long."

"Yeah, me too, but it happened when the time was right. All that matters is going forward, right, baby?"

"That's right."

"Look at them." Trisha said as she watched the new cousins play in the water. "You'd think they'd grown up together."

"Now they will." Megan smiled. "Let's go get them. I'm hungry!"

They enjoyed a wonderful lunch on the restaurant outdoor deck that overlooked the ocean.

"Let's all go back to the house and play games," Curt said.

"Can we go to the park by Mimi and Poppie's house?" Nathan asked. "I put my scooter in the car for Anna. There's a good place for me to skate."

"That sounds like fun. Let's go," Lisa said.

"Trisha, would it be okay if Anna rides with you? I want to show Rebekah something on the way home," Megan said.

"Of course. You were riding with us anyway. Weren't you?" Trisha reached down and tickled Anna.

Megan kneeled in front of Anna and looked her in the eye. "Is that okay with you?"

"Yes, Mama. I'll be fine with Aunt Trisha."

"Okay. We'll see you at the park later. I love you."

"Love you, too." Anna gave Megan a quick hug.

"Hey, don't forget me." Rebekah held her arms out.

Anna hugged her then ran to catch up with her cousins.

"She'll have fun," Megan said as she and Rebekah walked hand in hand to her mom's car.

Megan drove them away from the beach and to the center of town.

"I've never told you this, but I went to the First Christian Church until I was in high school."

"You did?"

"Yeah, I hadn't really thought about it until we drove past it earlier this week. See that building on the corner?"

"Yes. It's beautiful. It looks like a church."

"It's a private business now, some kind of healthcare agency. Anyway, it was a small church and there were only two other kids that went there. The church was dying, for lack of a better term. The members were old and my parents thought it would be better for us to be in a bigger church with a youth program. That's when we joined the Methodist Church."

Rebekah stared out the window at the church and waited for Megan to continue.

"My grandmother still went to church there and I was torn for a long time."

"What do you mean?"

"I hated leaving her, but she encouraged us to go. If you look right through there you can see my church." Megan pointed out the window.

"Oh yeah, I see it."

"When we first moved to the new church, I would go to Sunday School and then walk over and go to church with my grandmother."

"Oh babe, that's so sweet."

"I understand why your church is so important to you. My first church couldn't be saved, but I know why you want to change yours so desperately. I still have fond memories from my first church."

"It may be gone, but it lives on in you."

"The same way yours will always live in you, baby. No vote can take that away."

Rebekah reached over and took Megan's hand. "Thanks for sharing that with me."

"We'll be all right, no matter where we live and no matter how that vote goes."

"Because we have faith," Rebekah said as she raised her eyebrows.

Megan nodded. "Because we have faith and each other."

39

"What a wonderful summer," Rebekah said dreamily.

"School starts Monday. Are you ready?" Megan asked. She sat down next to Rebekah on the couch and handed her a glass of wine.

"My classroom is ready, but I'm not sure I am." Rebekah put her feet on the ottoman and leaned back. "I want to look back over the summer and enjoy it one more time."

"I am so proud of you. The summer program was such a success."

"It was a lot of work. We'll see if it paid off during the school year." Rebekah squeezed Megan's thigh. "I think my favorite part of the summer was meeting your family."

"They love you! I'm not surprised, but it will make it easier to talk them into coming here to visit."

"They didn't want to come visit you?"

"Oh they did, but the pull of another grandkid and a charming new daughter will be too much to resist."

Rebekah laughed. "I'm sorry we didn't get to go anywhere while Anna was with Ben's parents."

"It's okay. Maybe you can make it up to me since Anna's back to spending Friday nights with your parents." Megan leaned her head against Rebekah's.

"I know just how to do that. Do you hear it?" Rebekah put her hand to her ear.

Megan chuckled. "What?"

"That's the shower saying, 'It's Friday night fun time.' Hear it now?"

"Oh, *that's* what I'm hearing."

They looked at each other and laughed. When the doorbell rang, Megan furrowed her brow. "I'll get it."

She answered the door and could tell something was wrong. "Hey Daniel," she said cautiously.

"Hi Megan," he said with a forced smile.

"Is Anna okay?"

"Yes, she's fine. I wanted to talk to you and Rebekah."

"Hi Dad," Rebekah said when he walked into the room. "What's wrong? You look upset."

Daniel sat down in the chair across from Rebekah and put his hands on his knees.

"Can I get you a drink?" Megan asked.

He shook his head and Megan sat back down next to Rebekah.

"I want to prepare you." He sighed. "You both have worked so hard to show the congregation that your relationship is no different from most of theirs. You've given your time and the summer program you created was incredible, honey. I'm so proud of you."

"I feel a 'but' coming, Daddy."

Daniel nodded slowly. "I don't think the vote is going to go our way."

"We haven't even voted yet."

"I know." He nodded again. "I just came from a meeting

with the Pastor Parish Relations committee that oversees the church. I don't know how, but the majority is leaning towards the 'against' option."

Rebekah gave him a confused look. "Are you sure? I'm really surprised. I mean, we haven't asked people how they are going to vote, but everyone in our Sunday School class likes us." She looked at Megan. "Don't you think?"

"Yeah, I do. I don't know everyone in the congregation, but we've met a lot of them and worked with them on different projects."

"How could they know us and like us and not want to let us get married in the church?"

Rebekah shook her head in disbelief.

"Yeah, I could understand it if we didn't get along with everyone," Megan added.

"I think they do like you and might not have a problem with you two get married there, but they have a problem letting other gay couples get married in the church."

"I don't understand, Dad. That's the whole point. We are like most couples, gay or straight. Why would they have a problem letting anyone get married in the church?" Rebekah said, raising her voice.

"That's just it. They are going by the old doctrine where it says a marriage is between a man and a woman."

Rebekah reached for Megan's hand and shook her head. She stared out the window and Megan could see tears pooling in her eyes.

"Are you sure?" Megan asked.

Daniel nodded. "That's why I wanted to warn you. I've already told them that I will not go with them."

"Won't there be members that will want to go with you?" Rebekah asked.

"I think so. We'll find out how to deal with all that after the vote. I'm so sorry."

"Thanks for letting us know. I really thought they'd vote in favor," Megan said.

"If there's anything I've learned in all the years I've been a pastor, you never know about people. But Anna gives me hope."

"What?" Rebekah said, blinking back tears.

"Her generation, through programs like yours, will be more compassionate and accepting of others. It won't always be this way."

"I hope you're right, Daddy."

Daniel got up, hugged them both and left.

"I can't believe it," Rebekah said as she closed the front door.

Megan could see the tears in her eyes and held her arms open. Rebekah walked into them, put her head on Megan's shoulder and began to cry.

"Why can't they see we're people just like them?" Rebekah sniffled. "How can they be nice to our face and think we're something else behind our backs? They know what we're trying to do and yet they treat us this way."

Megan thought her heart might break. She was angry and hurt. They had opened their lives in an effort to open the minds of those church members who thought they were different. She took a deep breath and held Rebekah tighter. Those people had no idea what they were doing. All she wanted to do was take Rebekah's pain away.

Wanda whined at their feet.

Rebekah looked down and wiped the tears from her cheeks. "Oh, honey. Come on." She sat down on the couch and Wanda jumped up next to her.

Megan wiped her own tears and got them each a tissue.

Rebekah stroked Wanda's fur and smiled at the dog. "Wanda, we need some of your superpowers."

Megan chuckled. She put her arm around Rebekah. "We'll find our church or we'll make our own, baby."

Rebekah looked up at her and smiled. "That's a good idea."

"I'm so sorry they hurt you," Megan said.

"They hurt you, too." Rebekah leaned over and put her head on Megan's shoulder. "Don't give up on the church, Meg."

"What?"

"You quit going before, remember?"

"That was before you, Bekah. I will go where you go, remember?"

Rebekah turned toward her and put her hand on Megan's cheek and smiled. "God, I love you."

"I think God knows that." Megan smiled.

"We knew this might happen, but I really thought we'd bridged the gap."

Megan nodded. "We'll figure it out."

"I know."

* * *

Rebekah's eyes fluttered open. She felt Megan's arm around her middle and smiled.

Megan had tried to comfort her last night after her dad's visit. She knew Megan was just as upset as she was, but as usual Megan put Rebekah first.

Rebekah had slept off and on, but kept having pieces of a dream. Whenever she woke Megan had her arms around her or Rebekah was holding Megan. She finally realized what the dream was trying to tell her. It wasn't really a dream at all. It was more like picturing what the future could be.

She rolled over, faced Megan and couldn't stop the smile that formed on her face. Megan had helped her trust herself so many years ago. Their lives had changed in the last few months since she'd moved back home, but she had no doubts they would have found their way to one another somehow. Megan's faith was so strong it afforded Rebekah the opportunity to not only have hope, but do something to make that hope a reality.

She leaned a little closer and kissed Megan on the forehead.

Megan took a deep breath and mumbled, "I love you."

Her eyes opened and Rebekah was treated to those warm brown eyes full of love. "Good morning, love. I'm sorry things didn't work out the way we planned last night."

"Plans change," Megan said, her voice husky with sleep.

"No, those plans were postponed. You show me all day long that you love me in many ways, but the plans we had last night are important. I want to love your body with my body and it's important we do that."

Megan smiled. "We do, baby."

Rebekah eased on top of her. "Thank you for having enough faith for both of us."

"You know who I believe and I believe in us." Megan reached up and touched her lips to Rebekah.

"Your faith lets me hope and from something you said last night, my hope could be an answer for us."

"I'm listening."

Rebekah grinned and kissed her. "You always are. How about you let me cook you a scrumptious breakfast and I'll tell you all about it."

* * *

"Do you mind if we ride bikes?"

"I don't mind, but Anna will be mad if she finds out we rode without her."

Rebekah chuckled. "Believe me, Anna is having the time of her life with Mom right now. I'm sure they are cooking up some kind of delicious treat for her to bring home."

"I'm still not telling her."

"Are you afraid of our kid?"

Megan chuckled. "Don't act like you aren't."

They rode their bikes down the driveway and turned at the corner.

"I texted Dawn; she knows we're coming by," Rebekah said.

A few minutes later, they rested their bikes against Dawn's porch and Rebekah rang the doorbell.

"Good morning," Dawn said cheerily. "It's a beautiful day for a bike ride."

"I thought so, too." Rebekah grinned. "Thanks for letting us come by."

"I'm happy to see you both. Come in."

They followed Dawn into the living room and sat on the couch.

"Can I offer you coffee or tea?"

"No, Rebekah just made us an incredible breakfast," Megan bragged.

Rebekah smiled at Megan. "Thanks, babe. Dawn, I wanted to talk to you about the vote in our church."

"I figured as much."

"My dad is pretty sure it is not going our way."

Dawn nodded. "I'm not necessarily surprised, but I'm

really sorry. I thought your bravery and openness as a couple might open their eyes."

"We thought so, too," Megan said.

"My dad told them he wouldn't go with the majority. He doesn't know exactly what will happen to those that want to go with him, but the majority will get the church property and the building."

"I'm sure they have some kind of procedures already in place to make the separation less painful," Dawn said.

"When Dad told us, Megan commented that we would find our church or make our own." Rebekah took Megan's hand and smiled. "It got me thinking that maybe we'd do both."

Dawn furrowed her brow. "How so?"

"Well, what if we brought the members of the Methodist Church with us to your church?" Rebekah suggested.

Dawn's eyebrows raised. "That would give us quite a boost in membership."

"Do you think your congregation might want to be the new Methodist church? It comes with advantages," Rebekah said.

"That is an interesting proposition, Rebekah. We could grow our church and do so many things we've dreamed of, but haven't had the membership to do."

"I hope to continue the summer program and that goes where I go."

Dawn smiled. "I have so many things running through my head."

"Your church feels like the church the United Methodists envisioned," Megan said.

"I don't mean we would overtake or consume your church. It would be a blending of the two," Rebekah explained.

"I hear you. With that much growth, we would need more staff."

Rebekah smiled. "I know a guy that happens to be a wonderful preacher and could help with that."

"You don't think Daniel would want to take his parishioners and form the United Methodists?"

"I don't know. I haven't talked to him. Something made me think last night that he's at the point in his career that starting a new church may be more than he wants to take on."

Dawn nodded. "I get that. If we combined the two it would be a lot easier."

Rebekah and Megan sat back and smiled at Dawn, giving her the opportunity to absorb all they'd proposed.

"Let me think all this through and take it to my congregation. I have to say it's a great idea, though, and surely we can make it work."

Rebekah squeezed Megan's hand and gave her a hopeful look.

"If we make this happen, I have one request," Dawn said.

"What's that?"

"I want you two to be the first to get married in our new Methodist church."

Rebekah and Megan exchanged a delighted look.

"Then we'd better start planning our wedding," Megan said.

40

Anna looked up at Rebekah and Megan. "Are you ready?"

Rebekah looked into Megan's eyes. "I'm so ready."

Megan grinned. "I've never been this ready for anything in my life."

Anna held out her hands for Rebekah and Megan to each take one. "Then let's get married."

The music began to play and they walked down the aisle together, a family full of love and happiness.

Rebekah looked to her left and nodded at Mrs. Wiley. She'd told Rebekah she would be sitting on the aisle in clear view.

Megan looked to her right and could see Crystal and Kim sitting in the pew behind the one that held her parents, Trisha, Nathan, and Isabella.

The church was full of their new blended family and friends. There were friends they had made from their former Methodist church and new friends from what was known as the Community United Methodist Church.

Daniel was right, the church had voted against allowing gay marriage and gay clergy. There was, however, a large group that joined them at Dawn's Community Church. The new church was twice the size and offered a variety of services so the entire congregation could worship where and how they were most comfortable.

An early morning service offered more traditional music and ritual while a later morning service had more contemporary music. Between services, Sunday school classes were offered for the youth and adults. There were also adult and youth handbell groups along with a choir.

Daniel served as assistant pastor to Dawn and embraced his new lesser duties. Helen helped coordinate and form the United Methodist Women's organization.

Though they grieved the loss of the church as they knew it, the beginning of this new chapter in the life of the church was exciting, uplifting, and fruitful.

When they got to the end of the aisle, Rebekah and Megan bent down and each kissed Anna on the cheek. Anna clasped their hands together and Rebekah handed her the lily she was carrying and Megan handed her the orchid she had. Anna took the flowers and gave one to Lisa and one to Helen. Then she sat next to Helen and smiled at her moms.

Rebekah and Megan turned to face Daniel at the altar.

"It is with great joy that I welcome you to the first marriage ceremony performed in the Community United Methodist Church. And it's also with great pride that it happens to be my daughter and the woman that was meant for her."

Rebekah and Megan beamed at him.

"It was quite a struggle to get to this point and marriage can sometimes be the same. I want to encourage you to remember how you fought for this especially when times may be challenging. But also remember the joy you are feeling in this moment and how your efforts have been rewarded."

"If you'll face one another," Daniel instructed.

They turned to each other with such happiness on their faces.

"Rebekah, do you take Megan to be your lawfully wedded wife?"

"I do." Rebekah grinned and squeezed Megan's hands.

"Do you, Megan, take Rebekah to be your lawfully wedded wife?"

"I do." Tears pooled in her eyes.

"Anna, it's your turn." Daniel smiled at his granddaughter.

Anna came up and placed rings on each of their fingers. Then she handed Megan a chain with a ring dangling from it.

When they discussed how they wanted to do the ceremony, Anna had wanted a ring, too. As she explained it, they were getting married as a family. Megan had suggested that Rebekah take her wedding band from Ben and put it on a chain that Anna could wear as a necklace.

Megan fastened the chain around Anna's neck. She looked up at them with such joy that Megan felt tears sting her eyes once again.

"Ready," Rebekah whispered.

Anna nodded and together they said in unison, "With these rings we promise to love each other, listen to each other, keep our faith and always hope."

Anna grinned at them before sitting back down with Helen.

"Rebekah," Daniel prompted.

Rebekah took Megan's hand in hers once again and released a deep breath. "There are so many things I want to say to you, which I will later."

The crowd chuckled along with Megan.

"But for now, know that you gave me the courage to believe in myself and who I was inside when I was fearful to let anyone see. And on top of that you love me. This is what being blessed means. Our love is stronger than either of us imagined and it's everlasting."

"Megan," Daniel said.

Megan gazed into Rebekah's blue eyes and saw nothing but love. "We may be getting married today, but I've loved you for all time. I loved you from the moment I took a breath because I was made for you. Our love is endless and infinite."

"Colossians 3:14 says love is more important than anything else. It is what ties everything completely together," Daniel said. He looked at Rebekah and Megan and smiled. With a tremble in his voice he announced, "It is my utmost honor to proclaim you married. You may kiss."

Megan noticed tears in Daniel's eyes, but then she turned to Rebekah and the world stood still. She felt like this was where her life had been leading all these years. Rebekah was where her heart lived and would always be.

Rebekah held Megan's face in her hands and smiled. She brought their lips together in a firm kiss full of promise. When she pulled away she said, "We did it."

Megan pressed her lips to Rebekah's once again then said, "I had no doubts."

Laughter bubbled from Rebekah and Daniel presented them to the congregation.

Anna led them back up the aisle to the community room and the party began.

* * *

"Thank you for the best week of my life," Rebekah said. "I may not want to go home."

Megan chuckled. She sat next to Rebekah on a chaise lounge, gazing out over the water from their beachside cottage. "Have you thought about Dawn's offer to send you to seminary?"

"I'm on my honeymoon. All I've been able to think about is you." She reached for Megan's hand. "I can't believe that twelve years ago I didn't think I'd have a happy life, but here I am, right now, living the life I could only imagine." She got up and squeezed next to Megan in her chair. "It's because of your faith that I have this life."

"You're the one that did something about it though. Do you know how many gay people have left the church because they thought God didn't love them or that the church didn't accept them? You can change that. People who came before us made our life possible. You are the person who will make things possible for Anna's generation and our grandchildren's."

"Grandchildren!" Rebekah exclaimed, but she knew Megan was right.

"I couldn't believe I fell in love with a preacher's daughter all those years ago, but now, I'll gladly become a preacher's wife because you can reach more people that way. I know that church isn't for everyone, but there are people out there who want it and need it, but don't think they belong. You show them they do."

"But going back to school is huge," Rebekah said cautiously.

"It doesn't have to be. There is a part-time opening for a

youth pastor at our church. Why couldn't you do that and go to school?"

"We could do that?"

"Yes we could do that! I wouldn't have suggested it if we couldn't. You'd get to work side by side with your dad. All the kids already know you. Wouldn't it be amazing?"

"Work with my dad," Rebekah said softly. The idea of working alongside her dad had never occurred to her and now she couldn't understand why it hadn't. *What a dream that would be!*

As she rode a wave of various emotions, Rebekah looked at Megan, who was watching her with a soft smile. "But what about…" Rebekah didn't finish her thought.

"What about?" Megan prompted.

"What about a baby or babies?"

Megan grinned. "Wouldn't a part-time position be a great way to raise a family? Imagine how much extra time you could spend with Anna."

Rebekah stared at Megan. "You want me to spend more time with Anna, work part-time, go to school, and have babies?"

"You won't be raising Anna and having the babies all by yourself!"

Rebekah chuckled. "Oh I know that!"

"Is it too much? How did you see the next few years?"

"I think what you just described sounds close to perfect."

"Don't leave out all the lives you'll touch as a pastor."

"You really think I can make a difference?" Rebekah mused.

Megan nodded.

"It's all in who you believe, right?"

"That's right."

"With your faith...I know who I believe." Rebekah leaned in and gave Megan a warm kiss. "Let's go make a difference."

TWELVE YEARS LATER

"Look!" Rebekah quietly gasped. She had her arm linked through Megan's as they gazed at the painting. "You said she had a gift, but did you ever think she could do this?"

"I knew her art would touch people." Megan looked at Rebekah. "Just like her mom. You both know how to speak to people's hearts."

Rebekah smiled. "Her mama brought it out though, so it wasn't just me."

"There you are," Anna said. She put her arms around them both for a family hug.

"Do you have any idea how proud your moms are?" Rebekah said.

Anna chuckled. "My moms are always proud of me. Well, most of the time."

"That's true, but this is incredible, honey. Your own art show at twenty." Megan beamed.

"At my school. It's not quite as big as you're making it out to be."

"Oh please. These are amazing," Rebekah praised.

"Thank you. I think those summers at Mimi and Poppie's are beginning to pay off," Anna said.

"Art-wise maybe, but they always loved you coming by yourself so they could spoil you," Rebekah said, putting an arm around her and squeezing her tight.

"Oh how they spoiled you!" Megan exclaimed to Anna's delighted laughter.

"Anna?" A woman walked up to where they stood.

"Professor Blair, I'd like you to meet my parents." Anna introduced Rebekah and Megan to her art instructor.

"We are so happy Anna decided to share her talent with us." Professor Blair smiled. "She has bragged about both of you. As I understand, Megan, you are a counselor."

"That's right," Anna said. "She saved me years ago."

Megan smiled. "No, Anna."

"I don't care what you say. You did."

"And Rebekah, you are a minister in your family church?" Professor Blair asked.

"She's the lead pastor," Anna said. "I'm a preacher's kid just like you, Mom."

"It turned out okay for me," Rebekah said as she winked at Megan.

"She also loves to share stories from her family and superhero dog."

"Wanda does possess superpowers, but she misses Anna," Megan said.

"Thanks for saying that, Mama, but we all know she loves Mom the most. She always has."

"I don't know about that," Rebekah said with a smile.

"We like to say in our family," Anna began, "my mama shared her *faith* with my mom which gave her *hope* that they could have the life they dreamed of. Believe me, they made their dreams come true."

Megan and Rebekah laughed.

"And here they are now," Anna said. "Professor Blair, I'd like you to meet my sisters, Faith and Hope."

Anna's eight-year-old twin sisters walked up and grabbed Anna's hands.

"Is that painting with the two little girls really us?" Faith asked.

"It's really you. Can't you tell?"

"We can't see their faces," Hope said.

"Can you tell where it is?" Anna turned to her moms and asked, "Do you remember that day?"

"It looks like our tree at the park," Faith said.

"I remember that day," Rebekah said. "You girls weren't born yet."

"What?" Faith said, her face confused.

"Come on, let's show them," Megan said.

They walked over to the painting. In the foreground were two little girls with their backs to the observer. They were looking across a park to three people under a tree. It wasn't discernible what the people were doing, but Rebekah, Megan, and Anna knew.

"Can you see what the little girls are looking at?" Anna asked.

"Yes, they are looking at those people under the tree," Hope said.

"That was the day that Mama and Anna proposed to me," Rebekah said. She put her arm around Megan's waist and rested her head on Megan's shoulder. The memory was so clear in her mind that it felt like it was yesterday.

"That's the day our family began. You see," Anna explained to her sisters, "faith and hope lived in their hearts and they dreamed of you. So did I. You are our dream that came true."

The little girls stared at their big sister in awe.

"I love that story," Faith said.

"Me too," Hope echoed.

Megan turned to Rebekah and put her arms around her. They gazed into each other's eyes and smiled. In unison they murmured, "Amen."

ABOUT THE AUTHOR

Jamey is a small town Texas girl that grew up believing she could do anything. Her mother loved to read and romance novels were a favorite that she passed on to her daughter. When she found lesfic novels her world changed. She not only fell in love with the genre, but wanted to write her own stories. You can find her books on Amazon and on her website at jameymoodyauthor.com.

You can email her at jameymoodyauthor@gmail.com

As an independent publisher a review is greatly appreciated and I would be grateful if you could take the time to write just a few words.

On the next page is a list of my books with links that will take you to their page.

After that I've included the first three chapters of Where Secrets Are Safe, Book One in the Lovers Landing Series. Escape to the secret sapphic Hollywood getaway created by the famous movie star Krista Kyle. Shhh…it's a secret.

ALSO BY JAMEY MOODY

Live This Love

The Your Way Series:
* Finding Home
*Finding Family
*Finding Forever

The Lovers Landing Series
*Where Secrets Are Safe
*No More Secrets
*And The Truth Is ...
*Instead Of Happy

*It Takes A Miracle
One Little Yes
The Great Christmas Tree Mystery
Who I Believe

*Also available as an audiobook

CHAPTER 1

"Why am I here?"

A soft breeze rippled the water with just a hint of coolness, floating over pinkening cheeks.

"I hope you have on sunscreen."

"Sometimes the warmth of the sun on your face is worth the risk," she said, her eyes closed.

"Your adoring fans might not agree."

"That doesn't answer my question. Why have you summoned me home?"

"I didn't summon you home. This is when you usually visit."

"Okay, then why are we sitting at this rundown has-been of a lake resort, drinking beer?"

"We always come here. I can't believe you're speaking so harshly of the setting where many of our happy, coming-of-age memories were made."

"We did have fun, didn't we? We thought we were working a big-time summer job when really all we did was have fun and chase girls." Krista Kyle sighed, fondly remembering those summers over thirty years ago. Her best friend, Julia Lansing, sat next to her now just as she had so many years ago.

"You know it's for sale, right?"

"I did see the sign you pointed at on the way in, yes." Krista nodded with a smirk.

"What would you do with this place? If you could turn it into anything you wanted?" Julia quizzed.

Krista chuckled. "I'd make it a den of lesbian iniquity."

Julia laughed. "I can see it now," she said, sweeping her arm across the landscape. "The Lesbian Lagoon."

"How about the Sapphic Sound," suggested Krista.

"Oh, I know!" Julia exclaimed. "The Hidey Hole." She laughed raucously.

"I've got it. The Babe Bayou," Krista offered, laughing with her.

They sipped their beers, sharing a chuckle.

"If I'd had a place like this all those years ago then maybe I'd have a wife or partner today," Krista said wistfully.

"What? Really?"

"Yeah really. When I first went to Hollywood I had to be careful. I was afraid if the public found out I loved women then my career would be over."

"I'd say it all worked out. You were the favorite friend on the most popular sitcom all through your twenties and most of your thirties. And then in your forties, you became the mother everyone wanted. I think fifty looks good on you *and* me!" Julia stated boldly.

"We do make fifty look good," Krista said, reaching her beer over to clink with Julia's. "You remember Tara?"

"Of course I do. That is one beautiful woman with a spirit to match."

Krista smiled fondly at the compliment of her ex. "We might still be together if there had been someplace we could go to walk along and simply hold hands without someone jumping out, taking a picture, and selling it somewhere. She didn't care what others thought, but her career had already taken off so she didn't have to."

"Do you really think it would have mattered if someone had found out?"

"I do, Jules. It wouldn't be such a big deal now, but thirty years ago it was. Poor Tara hung in there with me for several years, but finally she'd had it."

"I thought she cheated on you!"

"She didn't really cheat. The last straw was when I wouldn't go to a party with her as her date. She was determined to go and went with a date anyway, but it wasn't me. And that, as they say, was that."

"I remember now," Julia said with a faraway look in her eyes. "I wanted to come out there and end her career as the beautiful detective in those spy movies."

Krista chuckled. "That's my Jules. Always defending her friend."

"Best friends since we were born!"

"Anyway, if we could have come here and been ourselves every now and then, maybe Tara would have waited until I was ready to come out."

"At least you were able to do it your way—unlike some people."

"That's true, it simply wasn't fast enough for Tara." Krista turned to Julia suddenly. "Did I tell you that right before I did my coming out interview the 'out reporter' contacted me?" she said, making air quotes with her fingers.

"Brooke what's-her-name?"

"Yeah, Brooke Bell. She said she'd heard some rumors

about me and several close friends of mine corroborated them."

"No way!"

"Yeah, that's what journalists like her do. They try to get you to out yourself. I called bullshit and told her she was late to the party, but not before I let her know what a terrible person she was for treating people that way."

"Good for you!"

"I do love this place," Krista said, sitting up and looking around. "How many cabins are here?"

"I think there are ten."

"Hmm, I wonder if those hiking trails are still maintained and what shape the beach is in," she said as much to herself as to Julia. She stood up and looked out to where the water met the sand. "It doesn't look too bad from here."

A smile crept onto Julia's face. "Are you going to buy it?"

Krista looked down at her, responding to her smile with a mischievous one of her own. "Maybe."

"Are there really that many closeted people out there looking for a place like this?"

"Well, not the way this place is right now, but maybe after I fix it up. To answer your question, yes—there are people that are very private about their sexuality and want to keep it that way. And not just in Hollywood."

"What do you mean?"

"You'd be surprised at the number of people that don't want their sexuality to come out because of their profession or their family."

"So this place could be where they come to live their secrets. Where their secrets are safe?"

"Exactly!"

"Hmm, and how do you propose to keep others from finding out what you're doing here?"

"Easy," Krista said. "The lake community watches out for one another. They don't care if a bunch of lesbians come here to have a good time as long as they're respectful, take care of the lake, and keep to themselves. You know that."

"That's true. There was that famous pop star that rented the Richardson's place to write songs and no one ever knew she was here. She shopped in town, hiked the trails, and no one said a word. I think she was here for six months!"

"What about when we were in college and came back to work that summer and George Clooney rented a house for a month? He had different people here every week. And no one said a word."

"Nope. Wait a minute," Julia said, turning to Krista. "You're really going to do this," she said as her face lit up.

"Isn't that why you asked me to come home?" Krista deadpanned.

"Well yeah, but I didn't think you'd do it," she said, laughing.

"Yes you did. When have I ever not done what you suggested?" Krista said, shaking her head.

"Well," Julia said, looking up. "There was that time..." she said trailing off.

"I know what you're going to say. I should have gone after Melanie and I didn't, but that was years ago. I'm sorry I didn't listen and I missed my chance to be with my first love. Since then I've listened to you."

"Young love; that was such a hard lesson."

They stared at one another, both thinking of the past. Krista smiled and clapped her hands. "Okay. Let's buy this rundown resort and make it our very own Hideaway Cove. Who has it listed?"

"Your old friend, Lauren Nichols. I bet if you offer to

spend the weekend with her she'd get you a better deal," said Julia.

"What? Lauren Nichols?"

"You know she's always had a thing for you, especially after you came out."

"I did not know that. We were friends in high school. Besides, she's married."

"That doesn't matter."

"It does to me!"

"Okay, okay," Julia said, raising her hands and holding them up toward Krista. "Just keep in mind she likes you."

Krista looked at her but didn't say anything.

"Hey, does this mean you're moving back here?" Julia said, clapping her hands.

"No, I'm not moving back. I mean, I'll be here more often, but I still have projects in LA."

"Then who's going to run it?"

A sly smile split Krista's face. "You are."

"Me!" Julia said, pointing to herself.

"Yes you. Who else is going to do it? Besides, you're not doing anything."

"I'm not doing anything because I've been an exceptional mother and raised my two girls to be independent and now finally, they're both in college. It's my time now!"

"And what does Heidi have to say about that?

"My wife knows how valuable my time is and how hard I've worked."

Krista gave her a skeptical look. "Oh does she?"

"She certainly does."

"Hmm," Krista said, getting her phone out. "Let me just give her a call." She wrinkled her nose.

Before the call connected a car pulled up next to the deck. Heidi got out of the car and waved.

"Look who's here. I can ask her in person," Krista said, standing up to greet her friend.

"Ask me what?' she said, pulling Krista into a hug. "I'm so glad to see you."

Krista smiled at Heidi. "You are even more beautiful than the last time I was here."

"You say that everytime you come home," Heidi said, leaning over and giving Julia a kiss.

"Because it's true!"

"It's because she has a wonderful wife that treats her like the queen she is," Julia said, winking at Heidi.

Heidi smiled down at her then looked at Krista. "Has she talked you into buying this place?"

"Only if she'll run it," Krista said, handing Heidi a beer.

"I can't think of anyone better," Heidi agreed.

"What!" Julia said, sitting up. "The girls have barely gone back to school. I have plans."

"Plans?" Krista looked at her in disbelief.

"Darling, I don't remember you sharing any plans," Heidi said.

"I most certainly did. I told you I wasn't doing a damn thing!"

"Oh." Heidi chuckled. "I do remember that."

"Be serious, Jules. When have you ever simply sat around? You're always doing something. And this," Krista said, spreading her arms wide, "this is our something."

Julia looked at her suspiciously. "Our something?"

"Yes. There's no way I'd attempt this if you weren't in it with me."

A grin grew on Julia's face. She looked at Heidi and then at Krista. "This really could be a lot of fun."

"Yeah it could." Krista grinned back at her.

"Then you'd better call your girlfriend and get her out here."

"Girlfriend?" Heidi asked.

"Lauren Nichols. You know she has the hots for Krissy."

Heidi nodded. "She does!"

"Not you, too! No she doesn't!" exclaimed Krista as she found the real estate listing in her phone and made the call. She asked for Lauren and waited, her foot tapping impatiently.

"Hi Lauren. This is Krista Kyle. I wanted to–" she began.

"Krista! How are you? It's been ages!" Lauren Nichols exclaimed. "How can I help you?"

Krista blinked a few times at Lauren's enthusiasm. "It has been ages," she agreed. "Actually, I'm out at the old Bailey place on the lake and wondered if you could show me around?"

"What! I'd love to! Let me see." Krista could hear papers rustling. "I can be there in thirty minutes. Would that work?"

"I'll be waiting." Krista grinned.

Julia and Heidi shook their heads in unison at her.

"See you soon," Lauren said, breathless.

Krista slipped her phone into her pocket and looked at her friends. "She'll be here in thirty minutes."

CHAPTER 2

"She sounded rather excited on the phone." Julia smirked.

Krista pursed her lips. "I'm sure she's excited to have a nibble on this place. I can't imagine she's had many offers."

"Right. I'm sure that's it," Julia said, taking a sip of her beer.

Krista reached for another beer and walked toward the beach. Memories flooded her mind. She could hear laughter and water splashing just like it was yesterday.

Julia walked up beside her. "Do you remember when those Italian women came and stayed for a week?"

"Of course I do. That was the first time we'd ever seen two women actually hold hands. We'd seen it on TV or in magazines, but not right in front of our eyes," Krista recalled.

"I didn't want to stare, but I couldn't keep my eyes off them."

"I know! Me too!" Krista exclaimed. "I think that was the

first time that I realized I could do that. That someday that could be me."

"Yeah. Before that it was like a dream."

"I couldn't wait to go to college. I just knew there had to be other girls like me there."

"I remember they were swimming and then ran back to their towels on the beach. They sat down and one leaned over and kissed the other. My heart nearly beat out of my chest! I felt like I was the one that had been kissed."

Krista laughed. "And then they saw us staring. My face was so red!"

"What did they do then?" Heidi asked, listening to the memory.

"They winked at us!" Julia chuckled.

"Yep and then we ran," Krista said.

"Ran?" asked Heidi.

"We didn't really run, but we hurried to the dock and busied ourselves with the boats," Krista explained.

"They were really nice and didn't seem bothered by our attention," said Julia.

Krista came back to the present and turned to Heidi. "I could use your legal skills to look all of this over."

"I'd be happy to, but what exactly do you plan to do with this place?"

"She's going to turn it into a lesbian brothel," Julia said with a straight face.

"Right," Heidi said, unconvinced.

"We're calling it the Hidey Hole," Krista said, just as serious.

Heidi looked from Julia to Krista and back. "I see that smile at the corner of your mouth." Julia and Krista laughed loudly. "You nearly had me," Heidi added, laughing with them.

Krista explained to Heidi what her vision for the place was.

After a few moments Heidi asked, "That all sounds great, but how are you going to screen who comes in? I mean, are you advertising it as gay-friendly or what?"

"I'm not advertising at all. It will be strictly word of mouth. Believe me, I know most of the closeted queers in LA. I'll look over the reservation list and if there's someone I don't know, my assistant can find out all about them."

"Your assistant?"

"Yeah, you remember Presley. She's incredible. That woman can find out anything about anyone, like the time you had a fight on the playground back in fifth grade. I don't know how she does it, but she's the master of background checks."

"Hmm," Heidi murmured in thought.

"What?" Krista asked.

"I'm just trying to picture how this is going to work."

"I'll tell a few friends that I've got this great exclusive, private place in Texas. Contact me if you're interested."

"Okay. Let's say five couples are scheduled for the first week in April. What do they do?"

"They fly to the Dallas Fort Worth Airport where we will pick them up. We drive them here, set them up in their cabins, and tell them about the activities available. They do whatever they want, respectfully. I mean, I can't have them fucking on the beach in broad daylight. That would be a bit much."

"Maybe not broad daylight, but I'm sure it's happened before and will again," Julia said. "That beach is kind of perfect in the moonlight."

A slow smile crept onto Krista's face. "Is there something you need to tell us?"

"No there is not," Julia scoffed. "But I will say this. Be ready, my love," she said, turning to Heidi and putting her hands on her hips. "We can sneak down to the beach one night. I know the owner." She pecked Heidi on the lips.

They were all laughing when they heard gravel crunching. Turning toward the deck they saw a car pull up next to Heidi's. Lauren Nichols got out and waved.

They walked up to meet her and she immediately smiled at Krista. "Krista Kyle, how do you get more beautiful?"

Krista smiled a bit timidly. Compliments like this unnerved her sometimes. She'd never considered herself beautiful. She had full, rich, mahogany brown hair that she took care of. Early on she knew it was a hereditary favor and she appreciated it. Her crystal clear blue eyes were also a gift of good genes she had thanked her grandmother for many times.

"Thank you, Lauren, but I could ask you the same question."

Lauren scoffed and looked down. "Now you're just being nice." She looked back up at Krista. "You were always so nice."

Krista smiled at her.

"It's nice to see you, Lauren," Julia said, speaking up.

Lauren looked over and smiled. "It's always nice to see you, Julia." Then she made eye contact with Heidi. "And you too, Heidi."

With the greetings out of the way Lauren turned back to Krista. "Since it's such a nice day for March, let's go look at the cabins by the lake first."

Krista walked next to Lauren as Julia and Heidi followed behind them.

"Do you have a realtor?" Lauren asked as they walked to the first cabin.

"No. Your sign was at the gate when we came in so I called you."

"What I mean is, if you're looking for a certain kind of property, I'd be happy to help."

"I'll keep that in mind, but I hope this one doesn't need too much updating."

"Are you looking to move back home?" Lauren asked, unable to keep the excitement from her voice.

"Not exactly. But I hope to spend more time here."

Lauren unlocked the door and walked in, holding the door for the others.

"This is one of the larger cabins and was updated a few years ago," Lauren said, walking into the middle of the room.

"Wow. This looks better than I thought it would," Julia said, walking to the door of the separate bedroom.

"Did you plan to open it as a resort, Krista?" Lauren asked.

Krista walked to the kitchenette and looked out the window. She could just see the deck and restaurant through the trees. "I'm not sure. It would be a fun place to bring a group of friends."

"Or big families could buy out the place for the week or weekend," suggested Julia.

"Are you looking for an investment? Because I have other properties that would be perfect for that," Lauren said.

Krista smiled at her. "Thanks, Lauren. You're not trying to steer me away from here, are you?"

"Not at all," Lauren answered quickly. "I simply want you to get the property that fits your needs."

"That's nice of you."

"She's doing her job," Julia pointed out.

"I am, but I'm also your friend and want what's best for you," Lauren declared.

"Thanks Lauren, I appreciate that."

"Come on, we have a lot to see," she said.

They walked out and looked at the rest of the cabins. Some were in better shape than others. Krista took a few notes and followed the group out on the dock.

"The Baileys reworked the dock two years ago," Lauren said.

There were several slips to tie boats in on one end. On the other end was a double deck for sunbathing on top and a diving board on the bottom. Between the dock and the shore was an area roped off for swimming.

"We sure would've had fun on this," Julia said, walking up the stairs to the top deck.

"We had fun on the old dock," said Krista.

"Oh that's right. I forgot that y'all worked here in the summers," said Lauren.

"We thought it was work at the time, but now all I remember is fun." Krista grinned.

"I don't remember hauling trash being fun," said Julia.

"Picking up trash on the beach sure was. I seem to recall you trying to pick up more than cans and bottles," Krista teased.

"Tell me more," Heidi said, chuckling.

"I did not! I wasn't brave enough then."

Krista laughed at her friend. "You sure wanted to though, didn't you?"

Julia laughed with her. "You did too."

"You both knew then?" asked Lauren.

Krista and Julia turned to her.

"I'm sorry! Was that offensive?" Lauren blushed.

"Not at all," Krista assured her. "Yes, I knew when I was in high school, but didn't think anyone else was like me."

"You knew I was!" exclaimed Julia.

Krista turned to her. "You were my best friend. I didn't want to kiss you!"

"Who did you want to kiss?" teased Heidi.

Krista looked out over the water back toward the beach. "You know, that pavilion area would be the perfect place for a firepit," she said, changing the subject.

"Okay then. I'll just have to get Julia to tell me your secrets later," said Heidi.

"Good luck with that," Krista said, winking. She noticed Lauren was engrossed in their conversation and hanging on each word. "Can we look at the restaurant now?"

"Sure," Lauren said, snapping back to attention.

As they walked up to the building Krista said, "I hope we didn't make you uncomfortable back there."

"Not at all. It's interesting to me. I can imagine it was difficult for you." She glanced over at Krista.

"It was hard for all of us at that age, wasn't it?"

"I guess you're right. Most of us were just trying to fit in."

"Or trying to find our people."

Lauren didn't say anything more and unlocked the door to the main building that also housed the restaurant.

She showed them the restaurant, kitchen, and bar area. They walked around taking it all in.

Finally Krista said, "Lauren, would you mind meeting me out here again this week? I'd like my cousin to come out and look around."

"Do you mean Brian? He does such good work. I recommend him whenever a client is looking for a contractor."

"I'd like him to give me his opinion if you wouldn't mind."

"I'd be happy to meet you out here. Let me know when and I'll be here," she said enthusiastically.

Krista wasn't sure if she did this for all her clients or if Julia and Heidi were right. Maybe Lauren Nichols had a little crush on her.

CHAPTER 3

The next day Krista drove through the entrance to Bailey's Camp on the Lake, as it was still known. She never was sure why they called it a camp unless many years ago when it first opened there were only campsites and no cabins. She parked down by the beach where two weathered adirondack chairs sat. She hoped they were still sturdy.

She got out and looked out over the sparkling water. A deep inhale followed by a slow exhale gently eased any tension in her body. There was something about this place that always calmed her. The idea of owning it had blossomed into a real possibility overnight. Turning this beautiful haven into a safe harbor for those that were afraid to be themselves in public for whatever reason had given her a new direction.

Krista's looks, talent, and a few lucky breaks had given her a profitable career. She was in a position now to pick and choose projects she wanted to be in. Realistically, she could never work again and still have more money than she could ever spend. But she wasn't ready to fade away just yet.

There were more roles now for gay men and women and they didn't automatically die or end with broken hearts as they had in the past.

She remembered how it felt to go to events and be expected to bring a man as a date. Later there would be an after party where she and Tara would meet. In the beginning it didn't bother her because she figured it was the price they had to pay. But when she and Tara ended their relationship, the hiding and secret keeping weighed her down to the point that she stopped taking dates to any of the award ceremonies or public appearances.

There had been a couple of relationships that lasted more than two years, but not much longer than that. She thought coming out would make these events bearable, and it had helped, but she simply hadn't found the woman to spend her life with yet. The notion that she could provide a place where those hiding could come and love one another openly made her heart happy.

The hum of a car grabbed her attention away from the water and her thoughts. She turned to see a pickup truck followed by a car making their way down to where she sat.

"Hey Krissy," her cousin Brian said, coming over to give her a hug.

"Hi Bri. Thanks for doing this."

"No problem."

Lauren joined them. "Hi Krista. Hi Brian."

"Lauren," Brian nodded.

"Thanks again for showing us around today, Lauren," Krista said.

"I'm happy to."

"Actually, would it be all right if I looked around on my own?" Brian asked.

Krista looked at him, her brow furrowed.

"It would be best for me to get an idea of what you've got here. Then we can sit down and you can ask questions and I can give you my assessment."

"That's fine with me," Krista said, relaxing. "I don't need to follow you around."

"I don't have to either. I'll give you the keys," Lauren offered.

She showed Brian the keys to the different buildings and he walked away.

"Care to join me?" Krista asked, pointing to the chairs. "They're sturdier than they look," she assured Lauren.

"Sure," Lauren said, sitting back in one of the chairs. "It's another beautiful day. You have calmed the March winds."

"I don't know about that." Krista chuckled.

"Do you have something in mind you want to do with this place? Because I can't see you coming back here to run a lake resort."

"You don't?" teased Krista. "That's why I'm going to recruit Julia to run it."

"Hmm, are you going to make it a place for the gay community?"

Krista eyed Lauren curiously. "Do you think that would be a problem?"

"No. You know how the lake folks are. As long as you take care of your business they aren't going to bother you."

"What about the town folks?"

"You're well respected in town, Krista. I don't see that being a problem either."

Krista nodded, appreciating Lauren's opinion since she lived and worked there. "Would you mind not saying anything just yet? I'm not exactly sure what I may run into legally. Heidi is going to look into that for me."

"Heidi is the best. I won't say a word. Besides, it's no one's business but yours."

"Thanks Lauren. I appreciate it. Hey, I meant to ask you yesterday. How's Marcus?"

"Marcus is fine," she said with a bit of disdain.

"Okay...?"

Lauren looked over at her. "I shouldn't have said it like that. He's fine, the kids are fine."

"I was about to ask about Emily and Justin."

"Emily will graduate this year and Justin's been living in Dallas for three years, working his way up the corporate ladder."

"You must be proud."

"I am. The kids are independent and know what they want."

"Why do you sound unhappy? I know you want them to excel."

"I do. It's just that since they are on their own, some things about my relationship with Marcus have been uncovered. Let me ask you," she said, looking at Krista. "Maybe I'm expecting too much, but the only things Marcus is passionate about are fishing and watching the Cowboys during football season. We have nothing in common except the kids."

"Oh. Well I'm not the best person to ask since I'm sitting here at fifty with a few relationships that lasted two years, but no more. However, I haven't given up hope of finding the woman to spend the rest of my life with. And I also plan to be passionate with and about this person until the day I die."

"Maybe I've watched too many Hallmark movies and read too many romance novels, but I believe there has to be more. Just because we're older doesn't mean we don't want to—you know," Lauren said.

Krista smiled. "Whatever do you mean?" she teased.

"You know what I mean," Lauren scoffed.

Krista chuckled. "Yeah, you mean have wild, passionate sex! I totally agree with you."

"But it's scary. I mean, do I throw away what I've known for over thirty years?"

"As I said, I'm not the one to ask. You should talk to Julia and Heidi. They are still crazy for one another. I hoped to have that someday. It's obviously taken me a little longer to find it. Have you thought about counseling?"

"I have. It's not like we aren't friends. There's simply not a spark there anymore. It's made me look at myself differently."

Krista gazed at Lauren kindly. "You have a lot of living left to do. We both do."

Lauren nodded and smiled back at her. They both heard Brian walk up before they saw him.

"Well, it isn't as bad as I thought," he said, sitting on the sand in front of them.

"Is that a good thing?" asked Krista.

He chuckled. "Yeah, it is. When were you hoping to open?"

"I'd like to by the middle of May."

Brian looked over at the cabins and then up to the restaurant. Krista could see the calculations running through his head.

"I think that's doable. We can sit down and prioritize, but I'm sure you'll be able to open in May. You may not be at full capacity, though."

"I don't plan to have all the cabins rented at the same

time. I think that would be too many people for what I want to do."

"Okay. Let me work up a plan and come see me tomorrow," he said, getting to his feet.

"Thanks Brian. I really appreciate it," Krista said, getting up and hugging him.

"Here you go," he said, handing Lauren the keys. "See you tomorrow."

Krista turned to Lauren. "Well, I want to talk to Heidi. Then I'll call you with an offer."

Lauren clapped. "That's wonderful! The best part is that you'll be home more."

"Thanks Lauren. That's kind of you, but we haven't settled on a price yet."

"We will. I'm sure of it."

They walked to their cars and before Krista got in she looked over the roof of her car at Lauren. "You deserve more, Lauren. I hope you find it."

Lauren smiled. "Thanks Krista. I hope to hear from you tomorrow?"

"You will. Bye," she said, a hint of her Texas accent slipping through.

* * *

"Lauren thought it was a good offer and felt sure the Baileys would agree," Krista said. She and Julia had met Heidi at her office and were waiting to hear back from Lauren.

"I thought it was fair to the Baileys and it's within your budget to renovate and open by May," agreed Heidi.

Julia eyed Krista. "You are staying to help with the renovation decisions, right?"

Krista chuckled. "What's the matter? You know you're the one with the design eye. You don't need me."

"Hell I don't! It's your secret hideaway."

"I'll be here the rest of the month. I have to go back in April for a guest spot and also to start promoting."

"I'm still not sure how you're going to do that, but that's your expertise. What am I supposed to say if someone around here asks for reservations?"

"Give them the Hidey Hole email address," Krista said, giggling.

Heidi shook her head. "Y'all have got to stop calling it that."

"Have we settled on a name?" asked Julia.

"I kind of like Lovers Landing. I hope that's what will be happening. Lovers come here to be together unapologetically and openly," said Krista.

"Do you think that would attract honeymooners?" Heidi asked.

"Any name we choose will have pros and cons," stated Julia. "Do you need to name it something neutral to protect those with secrets?"

"They'll know their secrets are safe or they wouldn't come here in the first place," Krista pointed out.

"Then I like Lovers Landing," said Julia.

"Me too," Heidi agreed.

Krista's ringtone interrupted the discussion. She looked at her screen and raised her eyebrows. "It's Lauren. Fingers crossed Lovers Landing is ours."

She connected the call. "Hi Lauren, I've got you on speaker."

"Have you ever owned your very own lake resort?" Lauren asked cheerily.

Krista smiled. "I'm trying to."

"Well, I heard this gorgeous Hollywood star is buying Bailey's Camp," she teased.

"Is that right?"

"It is if I can get her to agree to one concession," Lauren said.

"And what would that be?" Krista asked, her heart thumping in her chest.

"Your real estate agent gets a tour after you finish the renovations."

The smile on Krista's face lit the room. "My real estate agent is welcome anytime."

"Then let me be the first to congratulate you! Krista Kyle, you are the new owner of a lake resort," Lauren said, her voice rising in enthusiasm.

Julia and Heidi began to cheer and applaud as Krista released the breath she'd been holding.

"Thank you, Lauren!"

"It's my pleasure. I didn't have to do much, though; you gave them a fair offer. I'll get the inspection and title work started."

"Thank you so much, Lauren."

"You're very welcome. I'll be in touch."

Krista turned to Julia and said, "Here we go!"

They embraced and laughed a bit nervously.

"I remember nearly every day one of us would say, 'If I owned this place, I'd do this' and now you do!" Julia said, hugging Krista again.

"Actually, so do you," Krista said.

"What?"

"Jules, I couldn't do this without you. We're in this together. I'll put up the money, but you're the one that's going to be here running the day to day most of the time."

Julia stared at Krista for several moments. "Are you sure?"

"Of course I'm sure," Krista answered quickly. "Partner?" she said, holding out her hand to Julia.

"Partner." Julia grinned, shaking Krista's hand.

Now the real work began.

Printed in Great Britain
by Amazon